An open window

Amelia Patton is in hospital near the Welsh coast following a caravan gas explosion, when she hears that she is the residual legatee in her uncle's will. As she cannot attend the reading, her husband, ex-Detective Inspector Richard Patton, drives to the Midlands on her behalf. There he finds that the word 'residual' can be deceptive, and that the will is liable to provoke trouble. He is also intrigued by the coincidence of Walter's death being only two days after he signed his new will. The fall from a third-storey window and through his conservatory roof also appears to be suspicious.

But Walter Mann had become a virtual recluse, and had locked himself away in his rooms. When he was found, the doorkey was on its chain around his neck. Suicide? In which case – why?

Faced with enmity and suspicion, and strongly discouraged by the police, Richard explores a possible link between Mann's death and the earlier, equally suspicious, death of his son-in-law.

The deployment of the shares in the family business, a savage attack of reprisal, a drama of love and betrayal, all lead to a violent denouement, when at last Richard discovers the truth of the open window.

With his twenty-fifth crime novel, Roger Ormerod deploys elements of subtle elucidation he has not previously explored.

Also by Roger Ormerod

Time to kill
The silence of the night
Full fury
A spoonful of luger
Sealed with a loving kill
The colour of fear
A glimpse of death
Too late for the funeral
This murder come to mind
A dip into murder
The weight of evidence
The bright face of danger
The amnesia trap
Cart before the hearse
More dead than alive
Double take
One deathless hour
Face value
Seeing red
Dead ringer
Still life with pistol
A death to remember
An alibi too soon
The second jeopardy

AN OPEN WINDOW

Roger Ormerod

Constable London

First published in Great Britain 1988
by Constable & Company Limited
10 Orange Street, London WC2H 7EG
Copyright © by Roger Ormerod 1988
Reprinted 1988
Set in Linotron Palatino 10 pt by
Rowland Phototypesetting Limited
Bury St Edmunds, Suffolk
Printed in Great Britain by
St Edmundsbury Press Limited
Bury St Edmunds, Suffolk

British Library CIP data
Ormerod, Roger
An open window.
I. Title
823'.914[F]   PR6065.R688

ISBN 0 09 468230 5

My thanks go to Heather Rose, who, though she may not realise it, sparked off the subplot, which eventually took control.

R.O.

1

There was a foot on the back of my right hand, pressing my fingers into the soggy turf. I tried to lift my head. The foot went away, and a face was lowered, staring at me sideways. I tried to speak. All I managed to get out was a groan. 'You'll be all right, chum,' the face said. 'They've sent for an ambulance.'

'My . . .' I croaked. Oh dear Lord! 'My wife . . .'

The face went away. A more distant voice said: 'She must be dead. Got to be.' Another voice, gruff and choked, agreed. 'God, yes.'

I managed to raise my body, one hand still implanted, and draw up my knees. There was difficulty in breathing, and I realised my vision was bad, the images swathed in smoke. A breeze drew it aside and I could see the nearest caravan. Beneath its forward end, half tangled with the front manoeuvring wheel, there was a shape that was wearing Amelia's red and yellow anorak and her blue jeans. I whispered her name and began crawling towards it.

'Take it easy, old chap,' said the original voice. 'They're on their way.'

I continued to crawl.

She had her arm over her face. My eyesight was steadying, and I could detect that her right leg was at a strange angle. I touched her arm and she slowly lowered it, as though afraid of what she might see.

'Richard?'

''Lo, love.' Then my voice failed me.

'It's my leg,' she said simply, almost in apology. Her face crumpled.

'They're on their way.' But that was now evident, two sirens overlapping and interlocking as they raced closer.

7

She hadn't mentioned her left arm. Somehow she'd managed to get it up to her face to protect it from the blast. The sleeve was torn, hot flesh flaring through. The blast! It was only then that I remembered. I took her hand so that they wouldn't be able to sneak her away from me, and felt free to turn my head.

The caravan that had been on plot 13 was now no more than a ravaged frame, with smoking wreckage scattered around it. The woman who had to be dead was the one I'd last seen with her key in the door lock, a cold cigarette in her lips and her lighter in the other hand. Amelia had been moving towards the caravan to make a protest that I'd known would be unfounded. But she'd had no time to say one word. As the woman swung the door open and walked inside, the caravan had exploded, my last recollection, before the foot on my hand, being the flare of red behind the side window.

And now I could do no more than sit and wait, trying to force my brain into activity.

Right from the beginning I had felt we were making a mistake. Of course, some definite action had had to be taken. The tenancy on our cottage in Devon had expired, and though we might have renewed it I think both of us realised we simply had to find something permanent, of our own, where we could settle. Plant a tree or two and watch them grow – that sort of thing. And it was clear that using the cottage as a base for sorties in all directions, looking for a suitable property, was not working out. All it was doing was depleting our capital.

I can't remember who first mentioned the possibility of a caravan. The idea was that you took your home around with you, thus providing more freedom of movement. This was in March. With the summer ahead of us, it seemed to combine adventure with exploration, all with a hint of happy holiday capers in the background. There was an intuition of unperceived difficulties, but I ignored it, putting it down to a reluctance to part with my Triumph Stag, which had become part of my life-style. We went to look at caravans.

But the Stag would not do, the gentleman who sold the things assured me. With even the smallest of caravans, it would have a tendency to wag the car, when of course the objective was for the car to wag the caravan. Besides, if we were intending to spend some considerable time living in the caravan, we would need a large one.

These remarks should have warned me, but I was an innocent in these matters.

So . . . away with the Stag and in with the Volvo Estate. A gentleman's car with plenty of beef. Try wagging *that*, I thought, as we took it to pick up the fourteen-foot caravan we'd chosen. We drove away, and the caravan hung behind like a drooping tail. It followed exactly where the car went, and might not have been there.

Nobody had warned us.

We put our furniture into store, left a forwarding address with the Post Office, using our solicitor's name and address, and headed away towards Wales.

There are people who have years of experience with towed caravans, who disappear with them on every fine week-end in the summer, returning tanned and relaxed on Sunday evenings. I've met them on caravan sites. They stroll over to watch you backing in, and shout advice. 'Left hand down. Easy now. Right full lock.' They know it all. We knew nothing. I never reached the stage of relaxing. Tanned, yes, but relaxed no.

To start with, you have to avoid towns. A long car with a long caravan takes a lot of space. Which means you can't park. Try finding three empty meters in a row, or winding the whole thing up the curves of a multi-storey car park. It's just not feasible. So . . . where *do* you stop? You look for lay-bys, that's what you do. You pull in gingerly, and stop to make a cup of tea. It's no good expecting to spend the night there, though. Heavy traffic thunders past and shakes the whole set-up. So how on earth are you going to free yourself from the caravan in order to do your shopping, your laundry, take on drinking water, and all the other necessities? Don't tell me to try a friendly farmer and ask if you can use his field. He's too scared he'll never get rid of you.

Your only course is to find a licensed site that takes touring caravans. Suddenly you realise that you're not as fancy-free as you thought you were. You have become completely dependent on caravan sites.

Which seems all right at first. There's a booklet you can buy, listing all registered sites, so that a general route can be planned. But as the season wears on – and it *did* wear on – they become filled with jolly holidaymakers, and you have to track around from one to the other, searching for empty plots. One terrible evening we didn't find one until nearly midnight. Then I had to knock-up the site boss, and the harrowing business of backing into the slot had to be done in the dark. Suddenly the car was surrounded by experts in pyjamas and dressing gown, all waving torches and shouting: 'Left hand down, steady as you go. Full right lock.' And sundry other advice, all part of the fun.

It's the backing, you see. I knew the general idea. You steer the opposite way to where you want the caravan to go, then when it's doing that, you reverse the process and follow it with the car. Sounds easy. Just try it. As soon as the caravan begins turning, you lose touch with the back end and don't know where it's going. I never did get it right. Once I'd managed to force the caravan into its numbered plot, got it on its stays and level, and unhooked the car, all I wanted to do was stay there as long as possible.

That was where the first snag arose. We had decided that the best plan was to settle at one site and make forays with the unattached car to all the estate agents within reach. In this unfettered condition the Volvo felt like a greyhound. I drove it with the verve I'd used when handling the sporty Stag. So the caravan was becoming a liability, to my mind. I began to grow paranoiac about it, indulging in the odd furtive kick at its tyres. So I was all in favour of settling at any accommodating site that pleased us.

But there was a regulation. There always is. You couldn't stay longer than fourteen days without moving on. This was something to do with bye-laws which changed your status from touring to resident, with dire results to the site owner. So, at least every fortnight, we had to move on. We were getting nowhere, finding nothing that suited us, and we were already into August.

It was then that we discovered the second, and major, snag. All these holiday sites would close at the end of September. This meant that we would have to discover a site that truly was residential, the thought of which, for a whole winter, we found appalling. The caravan, which had seemed so large when we bought it, was shrinking daily and becoming claustrophobic. It also seemed to be taking on weight and bulk. Every time I hitched up and drove away, it was a proliferating hazard at my back. I had to force myself not to try to overtake anything faster than a farm tractor.

We had discovered a site, about four miles inland from Aberaeron. This one we liked. A farmer had converted a field, and had only twenty caravan plots. Not too crowded, yet large enough to justify a modern toilet block, with washing machines. Ideal. Twice we discovered that plot 13 was empty, and enjoyed our fourteen days there. So I made an arrangement with the farmer. He would try to keep plot 13 empty, being assisted in this by superstition, and we would leave him for a fortnight, then return. This arrangement began at the beginning of June, and had worked well for several return visits.

On a Friday at the end of August we were way north, exploring the Lleyn peninsular, so that it was a fair drive back to Aberaeron. By that time I was worried. There was something that needed doing to the carburettor and the Volvo wasn't pulling well, or the caravan was getting heavier. It was pouring with rain all the way south along the coast road, and we had just discovered this business about everything closing down in a month's time. We had found nothing in North Wales. Property was even tighter there than farther south. Or dearer.

So . . . arriving later than I'd have liked at our favourite site, tired and discouraged, I drove in through the gate without stopping to make our presence known, and discovered that there was a caravan already parked in plot 13. I stopped, well back.

There could have been other plots empty, but somehow this one had become ours. It had almost seemed that we were coming home. To Amelia, as weary and miserable as I was, it appeared to be an affront, and she was out of the Volvo before I was. The caravan occupying plot 13 was smaller than ours, and a young woman was just climbing out of a Ford Cortina. She hadn't, in the past few minutes, brought in the caravan, as it was settled with a possessive air on its jacking struts. Amelia moved as though to protest. I hurried after her. The young woman had a cigarette in her lips, and was reaching up with her key, a lighter in her left hand flicking uselessly in the flirty breeze.

I can still recall only that first flare of flame beyond the side window.

We waited. I cannot detail what was happening, nor how long we were there, because everything seemed distant and disconnected. I remember that it had stopped raining. I could see that our own outfit seemed reasonably undamaged, and I could hear Cindy barking in the Volvo. I worried a lot about Cindy, who was our small West Highland terrier, and a lot about Amelia, who had remained silent apart from answering when I first spoke to her. I also worried that I now had a great many worries to contend with, and that I seemed to be unable to marshal them in my mind for inspection.

Eventually they loaded Amelia into the ambulance and insisted I should go with them. I made feeble protests, confused about my priorities. The car . . . the caravan . . . Cindy . . . There was an assurance they'd be all right. I noticed that the sun had come out. It would, wouldn't it!

This was on a Friday. They insisted on keeping me under observation over the week-end, which allowed me to remain with Amelia. All I'd suffered was a blow on the side of the head from a passing portion of caravan. Amelia was much more badly injured: a severely burnt left arm and multiple fractures to the right leg. She would be immobile for at least a month, and in difficulties for quite a while afterwards. I was beginning to make frantic plans in my head.

On Sunday we had a visit from a young policeman. Or rather, I had – Amelia was not yet fit to talk to visitors. The dead young woman was named Nancy Rafton, he told me. She was twenty-five, and had been at the site for three days. She had been travelling alone. They were tracing her relatives through the registration of her car. I gave as much information as I could. He took it all down solemnly, and right at the end lifted his eyes and asked:

'So you can give no information about the enquiries she'd been making, sir?'

I must have looked blank.

'She'd been enquiring for your wife – Amelia Patton.'

I could only shake my head.

On the Monday, and with Amelia settled in her plaster and her bandages, I took a bus to Aberaeron, got a lift out to the caravan site, and found Cindy being walked by a little girl, both quite happy with the arrangement. Our caravan had been backed into plot 7, the car was parked beside it, and everything was locked. I stopped to answer anxious enquiries and to thank everybody for their concern over Amelia's health, then sought out the farmer, who had my keys.

Yes, he confirmed, Nancy Rafton had enquired for Amelia Patton, and she'd stayed only because we were expected back. No, she'd given no hint of her business. It was intriguing, but I could do nothing about it.

I drove to the hospital, leaving Cindy in good hands. We had plans to make. By the time Amelia would be discharged, the caravan sites would be closed. It was decided that I should begin a search around, using the car alone, for rentable properties, to tide us over the winter. This I did. Oh yes, I discovered, they were available, but furnished and at a prohibitive price. I began to lose hope.

On the Wednesday of the second week I returned to the hospital, spent a few minutes in the car park with my pipe, marshalling optimistic phrases in my mind and practising my smile, then went inside.

A man was sitting beside Amelia's bed.

He would have been in his thirties, and just the type of man most unsuited for hospital visits. His face was thin and dour, his mouth was like a trap, afraid to open too far in case anything encouraging escaped, and his general demeanour was that of exhaustion and misery. He was, it appeared, an enquiry agent working for a solicitor in Boreton-Upon-Severn. Another one! I caught Amelia's eye at that, but she made no comment. Was she, he wanted to know, the niece of Walter Mann? Yes, her mother had been Walter's sister. Age? Forty-one, said Amelia firmly. Even then, this man never faltered. Amelia, ill and in bed, managed to look very much younger than her age. I wondered whether she'd noticed his lack of reaction. Certainly her eyes brightened with amusement.

And so it went on. Where born? Father's name? Mother's full name . . .

'What *is* this about?' she asked at last.

He seemed surprised. At least, an eyebrow looked as though it might rise. 'Didn't you know? Then I'm sorry to have to tell you that your uncle Walter died on Saturday. I've been told to leave the solicitor's card, and get you to phone him. He'll want to see you, I expect.'

Very formal, he was, very correct. He got to his feet, nodded shortly, and left. There was a visiting card on the bed. Mantell & Carne, Solicitors, Boreton-Upon-Severn. Scribbled across it was: ask for Philip Carne.

'Better call him, I suppose,' I said.

'Now?'

It was four-thirty. 'Why not?'

I fetched the trolley with the pay phone and plugged it in,

found change, and dialled. When I'd reached Philip Carne, I handed the phone to Amelia.

For a minute I watched her nodding, listened to her saying 'yes' and 'no', and gained nothing. In the end she said: 'Will you have a word with my husband, please?'

I took it from her. His voice was young and brisk. Walter Mann, it seemed, had died only two days after making a new will, in which Amelia was named as residual beneficiary. Carne would have liked to see her, but in the circumstances, would I obtain a power of attorney, and take her place? And please bring along such documents as Amelia's birth certificate, marriage certificate, etc . . . etc. And when could he expect to see me?

His crisp efficiency overwhelmed me. I barely had time to say a word. I fed in more money and said: 'Just a sec'.'

Then I explained quickly to Amelia. She was the one at the end of the will who got what was left after the other beneficiaries and the capital gains people had taken theirs. 'I'd better go, I suppose, though you'd think he'd send a cheque or something. These things take months to finalise.'

She nodded, her eyes huge. 'I suppose you'll have to.' Solicitors and the law have always seemed rather awesome to her.

'Would Friday suit you?' I asked the phone. 'Around three.'

'Excellent.' He'd have been rubbing his hands if one of them hadn't held the phone. 'We must have a conference, and then I can read the will on Sunday.'

He hung up before I could query that. Did he expect me to hang around over the week-end? Certainly I didn't want to dash back and forth from Boreton to Aberaeron, a journey of around 150 miles, I guessed.

'How very annoying, Richard,' said Amelia. 'You'd think he'd have covered it with a letter.'

I tried to sound casual. 'They're like that.'

But not the ones I'd known. Will reading, for instance, with the family present, was a thing of the past. Letters, run off through the photocopier, including signature, were more the order of the present day, even for the major legatees. It was, indeed, annoying, so I dutifully frowned. But all the same, there was a touch of mystery in the background. I said nothing about that, and told her I would arrange about the power of attorney the following day.

I realised I'd forgotten to ask Philip Carne whether it was he who had sent Nancy Rafton with her enquiries. But of course . . . stupid of me . . . she had died a week before Amelia's uncle Walter's death. So how could the two enquiries be related?

2

Armed with my power of attorney and all the other documents, I set out alone for Boreton-Upon-Severn early on Friday morning. It turned out to be 152 miles, across country so without the dubious benefit of motorways, and took me four hours. Amelia was in good hands, Cindy was too, and the caravan was safe until the end of the month. I had time to relax, time for thought.

Amelia had not seen her uncle Walter for well over twenty years. All she could remember of him was a sad smile and untidy hair. She was aware that he'd started a small business, and she vaguely remembered that he had three children, Paul, Clare and Donald. For some reason she hadn't been able to rationalise, she thought of Walter as a lonely man. There had, she recalled, been trouble with the children after their mother had died. A sad and lonely man. Well, he was dead now, and he hadn't forgotten his niece.

Boreton is one of those towns that have grown up because of the river, and before it was decided to throw across a bridge. Early settlers had built along both banks, using locations best suited to their purposes; the water-mills where the water ran fierce, the woollen mills where it was more placid. On neither side had there been an urge to cross the river and say hello. Therefore, when a bridge became an absolute necessity, it could be sited only where the approaches were already dictated. The result is that you drive in from the west by a steep descent, made more gradual by a few vicious corners, to a short stretch of road following the river bank, turn right sharply on to the bridge, which you cross only to find a similar obstacle course the other side. Eventually, the town centre being on the east bank, you straighten out for a hundred yards or so of main street, only to be confronted by a timbered Tudor town hall arching across the street, with narrow driveways either side. Each is one-way, so you get no choice. You keep going, eyes searching for the magic P sign, so that you might stop and get out before you find yourself out in the country the other side of town. Only the most brave and the noblest would have towed a caravan through Boreton.

I found a car park. There was time for a quick snack, then I hunted out the office of Mantell & Carne. This was also on the east side, in a narrow street parallel to the river and above it, its door reached by a tight run of steps sideways against the wall, guarded by a black iron rail. Below, in half basements, were two tiny shops, one selling leather goods, the other woollens, both probably made locally. The leather smell persisted inside the offices. The receptionist wore one of the sweaters, which seemed to have shrunk badly. Mr Carne was expecting me, she told me. Would I go right in? I did.

The bay window of his office overlooked the river. His desk was located so as to present a placid view, if he so wished. He had one visitor's chair, an ancient swivel monstrosity with red leather-studded upholstery. There was no other furniture, apart from the books, files, boxes and dusted briefs scattered everywhere and lining the walls. He'd probably inherited it in this condition, and left it as it was for effect. Certainly, he was as young, brisk and efficient as he'd sounded, as tall as me but slimmer, pink and shining and clean. He was probably sufficiently meticulous as to be able to work in this clutter and know exactly where everything was.

'You brought the gubbins?' he asked, after we'd shaken hands. 'Good. Let's have a look.'

Then, while I took the swivel chair and marvelled how it accommodated itself to my bulk, he demonstrated his efficiency by carefully scrutinising every word of every item I'd brought with me.

'So,' he said, slapping his hand on them. 'Fine.' He flashed me a smile. 'Have to be dead sure, you realise, the way things are. Yes.'

I took out my pipe and moved it around in my fingers. 'I'm a little confused . . . a residual beneficiary . . . you under-stand . . .'

'Smoke if you like,' he told me. 'A good fugg. Nothing like it.' But he didn't, himself, offer to help it along. 'I'll be brief.'

I sighed. When they say that!

'Walter Mann,' he said, 'died nearly a week ago. Saturday. There had been a long-standing will, nothing out of the ordinary

16

about it, leaving his property and assets divided equally between his three children, Paul, Clare and Donald, plus one or two other bequests. But on the Tuesday prior to his death he called me in to draw up a new will. Against my advice. I want to make that clear. But he insisted. The new will, which was signed and witnessed on the Thursday, left ten thousand pounds each to his three children, ten thousand plus a few minor details to Mary Pinson, his housekeeper for many years – little change there – and the residue of his estate to his niece, Amelia, the daughter of his sister Jean. There, you see, I told you I'd be brief.'

He smiled again, then barked a short laugh at me. But I noticed that his eyes – clear blue – were keen and his gaze steady.

'Your man,' I said, 'did a quick job of tracing us.'

'Yes. A good chap.'

'And was it you who sent the other person, making similar enquiries a week before?'

He'd steepled his hands and was tapping his teeth with his thumb nails. 'It was not.' The tapping stopped. I could almost hear his brain working away. 'I understand . . . Walter and your wife were rather out-of-touch?'

'My wife hadn't seen her uncle for over twenty years.'

'There. You see. He'd naturally want to know she was alive, before mentioning her in his will. It was probably Walter who was making his own enquiries.'

I nodded. It seemed logical. 'Everything's happened at once.'

'Hasn't it!' he agreed.

'But tell me . . . you spoke as though Walter Mann changed his will in some way to the detriment of his children. But – ten thousand each – that's not to be sneezed at.'

'In this context it is, I can assure you.'

'Even so . . .' I didn't want to pursue that point at the moment. As an ex-CID inspector, I found my mind playing with the implications. 'Even so, if this was a virtual disinheriting, it was done on the Thursday. What you'd call a *fait accompli*. So surely, the children – Paul, Clare and Donald, was it? – would have known.'

'It was not part of my duties as a legal adviser—'

'But they did know?' I persisted.

'Don't try to bully me, Mr Patton,' he said gently. 'I know you've been a police officer, but not here. Not here.'

'Sorry. Got carried away.'

17

'Yes. A bit confused I'm sure. But I can see the way your mind's working, and I'm quite certain Walter would have let them know that he'd made a new will. He couldn't wait to tell them, in fact. Oh yes, he'd have pounced on his phone.' There was just a hint of distaste in his voice.

I took a few seconds to re-light my pipe. New will on the Thursday, died on Saturday. It was too. . . well . . . uncomfortable.

'And how *did* he die?' I asked, following the words with a casual puff of smoke.

'He fell from a third-floor open window at his home, through the conservatory roof.'

'Hmm!' I said.

'An obvious accident.'

'I'm sure it was.'

'As you'll see for yourself.'

'Shall I?'

'When you go round to the house.'

'Why should I do that?'

'Because it is now your property, your wife's rather, but yours as long as this power of attorney operates.'

I drew on my pipe. It was all coming at me too fast. 'But the words used were: residual beneficiary,' I ventured.

'Yes. All the word residual means is that once the other legacies are cleared and the duties are paid, the rest – the residue – is your wife's. *In toto*, as we say.'

I cleared my throat. 'Which would be? This residue of yours.'

'The house that I mentioned, in two acres, furniture and motor vehicles *in situ*, 51 per cent of the shares in Walter's factory, and his very interesting portfolio of investments.'

I had to grab at something solid. 'Factory?' Amelia had spoken of a small business.

'They make photographic equipment. Estimated capital value of around half a million. I have still to value the investments he had, and realise on part of the portfolio for legacies and death duties, but the balance should work out at between a hundred and a hundred and fifty thousand pounds. Less, of course, my fees.' I inclined my head. With a thin smile he went on. 'So you see, disinheriting isn't such an incorrect word for what Walter Mann did to his children. If you'll come over to the window, you can see the factory.'

18

Awkwardly, almost blindly, I moved to the window. He pointed it out, though you could hardly miss it. On a rise the other side of the river, and a little farther to the south, was a glittering array of glass, with a square column of concrete at one end. It dominated the town. Across the facade, in letters that must have been ten feet high, was the legend: MANN OPTICS.

I returned to my seat. There seemed nothing to say that wouldn't have sounded paltry.

'Such a complex estate,' he was saying, 'will naturally take some months to probate, but if there is anything . . . As executor, I can advance a certain amount of cash from Walter's private account, and the house – I see no reason why it should not be made available . . .'

I looked up. His keen eyes were watching me carefully. I said: 'Would there be room, in the drive for instance, to park our caravan?'

He laughed, then was at once intent. 'You're not serious?'

'Couldn't be more so. Just at this time, it's our home.'

'Oh dear,' he said. 'Oh dear me. Would I be correct in saying that your situation is difficult – your wife in hospital and your home a caravan? Towed, I presume.'

'It would be correct to say that.'

'Then I don't see why you shouldn't move into The Beeches at once. I'll just warn Mary Pinson.' He reached towards his phone.

'No,' I said sharply. Too sharply, judging by the lift of his eyebrows. But how could I explain to him what the past five months had done to me? After a life-time of work in the police force, which had trained me into a certain amount of self-confidence, I had felt it all draining away after only five months of fighting with a mere caravan. I was into my fifties, but only recently feeling it. That, I resented. With the culmination of Amelia's accident, I was undermined, and yes, in the background there had grown a muttering uncertainty. I no longer knew where I was heading. Now, fate had thrust this excess of fortune under my nose, and I couldn't help feeling that there was a catch somewhere, and it would turn out to be another facet of the trap. Relax enough, allow confidence to trickle back into my consciousness, and surely it would be snatched away. That would be a crippling blow, and I'd be lost.

I eased my way cautiously into it. 'There could be a protest. The will hasn't even been read. It could be opposed, sure to be.'

'Contested. No. A man's not allowed to disinherit his wife. *Jus relictae*. Children, yes. He can disinherit his children. On that score, there's no ground for contesting it.'

'Insanity,' I murmured. 'He couldn't have been completely right in his head.

'Now there . . .' He paused. His chair, too, was a swiveller. He swivelled it, a pencil dangling from his fingers and oscillating gently, illustrating the pendulum of my uncertainty. 'I tried to dissuade him, of course. I felt it was my duty. But he was adamant. He felt he had a valid reason for changing his will, and there could be no question that at that time he knew exactly what he was doing and understood it. On that score, he was sane. As to the validity of his reason . . . there could well be a psychiatric word for it.'

'There. See what I mean?'

'A persecution complex, manic perhaps. But there was no question of insanity. He knew what he was doing.'

'This reason of his . . .' I left it hanging.

'He believed his family were trying to kill him. Nonsense, of course. But he sincerely believed it. Given time, I was convinced he would have changed his mind, and we'd have had a fresh think about the will.'

'But he wasn't given time.'

'Accidents are unpredictable. That is the legal definition.'

'Was that the inquest verdict?'

'We haven't had it yet. It's to be on Monday. Morning. On Sunday afternoon, I shall acquaint his family with the contents of his will.'

'Which you're certain their father will already have told them?'

'Exactly. I can see no grounds for it to be contested.'

He seemed a bit complacent about that. I was still cautious. 'But there'll certainly be opposition – unpleasantness – disappointment?'

He shrugged. 'Not disappointment; they already know. But the rest . . . A man makes a will, and then dies. It happens. We can't change anything.'

'You'll read it . . .' I gestured around his office. '. . . here?'

'At the house, I thought.'

'Ah! Then it's obvious I'd better do nothing about anything until then.'

He smiled. I'd let him off the hook. 'Perhaps you're right. But at least, you ought to go and look at The Beeches. As a former policeman, you'll be interested in the scene of the – er – of Walter's death.'

He had managed to give me a hint that he, too, wasn't happy about Walter's death, and at the same time had achieved another objective, agreeable to both of us: I was to look, but not to stay.

I levered myself to my feet. I would have to get away from the dry and soulless dust of the law, and think. I would have to phone Amelia . . . or perhaps not. On that point I was undecided.

'I'll keep in touch,' I said.

'You must certainly do that.'

'The address?' I asked. 'The Beeches.'

'Of course.' It seemed to surprise him. This was the first sign he'd given that he wasn't completely in control of the situation, even well ahead of my thoughts and wishes. For a second his mind had not been on the matter in hand. He was, indeed, uncertain.

He drew me a map. The house was on this, the east side of the river, about two miles upstream. I thanked him and left, standing for a few moments at the top of the steps as I collected my thoughts.

I allowed it all to trickle back.

The air seemed different, the afternoon sun more kind. The light had changed, softer and warmer. My own weight was less, my steps lighter as I ran down to the cobbled street. My mind was suddenly clear. I reached to the future, and with relaxed anticipation.

For half an hour I walked the town, exploring the main shopping area. The narrow side streets, which were almost completely pedestrian only, were quaint and precipitous, using steps to accommodate the steep inclines. The town had grown on the high banks of the river each side. There seemed to be nowhere you could walk on the level for more than a few yards, and always there were inviting corners, alluring dead ends, and forever surprising discoveries of enchanting shops. Amelia would love it. She would take it to her heart, if this became her town. Here, the motor vehicle would never become dominant. They'd either have to drive on through, or park on the outskirts. The town would survive. Amelia would like that thought. If this should become our town.

21

It was not until I reached the car and sat inside, strangely unwilling to drive away, that I faced the source of my uneasiness and analysed it. Philip Carne hadn't voiced it, but I was sure it had been in his mind. Walter Mann had made a new will, because he felt his life was in danger. Whether or not this was valid was not relevant – he had believed it. Carne had not been too concerned at the time, because he thought Walter would change his mind – and this new will – given time. He hadn't been given time. Two days, that was all he'd been given. The coincidence hit me between the eyes. If a man lets it be known he is going to disinherit his close relatives, he stands in mortal danger until he has done it. That danger would have been removed as soon as he made the new will known, as Carne had seemed sure he would. But had he? And was the fall necessarily an accident? Carne had realised this uncertainty. As a solicitor probably specialising in the civil side of the law, he would be reluctant even to think of the word: murder. But it had sat there between us in his office, almost shouting itself aloud.

It seemed that a visit to The Beeches was necessary, as Carne had hinted, though I'd have preferred to keep my head down until after the will was read.

But, for my own peace of mind if for no other reason, it would be comforting to prove that Walter's death had been an accident, as Carne described it. This I set out to do.

3

The road from Boreton turned away from the river a mile north of the town, then a little farther on there was a left turn, back towards the water, signposted: Knightsford. It was a narrow lane, so that the ford could never have been significant. The collection of buildings alongside the river confirmed this, the water here being narrow and swift, but shallow enough for the shingle bottom to be visible. The lane headed straight to it, and stopped. On the opposite side of the river there was a similar approach, so perhaps it was still fordable. On a horse, maybe, knights in armour clanking across on their way to Worcester. But now, no knights, and the four tiny cottages seemed deserted, though I saw a lace curtain here and there. A lane to my right was signposted: The Beeches. Its surface was rough shale and gravel. This was the approach drive. Each side there were high hedges, encroaching closely, as though resenting this narrow slice through the stretch of pastureland.

The hedge to the left fell away abruptly, and I was aware that I was now on the actual drive. Beyond a group of beeches, the house waited. The drive swept across its front, and curved away around the far corner, out of sight. I drew up in front of the house, got out, and absorbed it.

Due to a bend in the river, the rear faced directly south, and later I came to realise that this must have been the reason for its location. The front certainly wasn't inspiring, but all the care and attention was at the rear. Visible to me now was a plain, almost square building, three storeys high, with an insignificant porch, rather dim because it faced north, and two sets of plain windows each side. These rooms would be forever dark and depressing, I thought. A wistaria, planted at the east corner, had been allowed to grow rampant, and had spread itself halfway across the front, where it met with, and embattled, an ivy from the west corner, between them managing further to obscure any light trying to penetrate the windows. But it was a large house. Room for better things. I was not discouraged, and walked on round the side.

Here the drive terminated in a wide stretch of gravel fronting three wooden garages, all their doors shut. A high hedge at their end marked the boundary of the property. There was a gap between the garages and the side of the house, so I walked on through to the rear.

Here the house came into its own. It became alive. The day had turned dull, but as though to welcome me the clouds now drew aside and the sun shone on my right cheek. The ground fell away steeply to the river, which was thrusting itself round the bend below, the sun caught in it, almost blinding with its sparkles and flashes. The slope had been terraced, not evenly, but with a cunning plan, allowing a winding progress gently down through flowered and shrubbed gardens, at this time of year a blaze of colour. Along the back of the house there was a wide terrace, which curtsied aside to skirt a large conservatory, some twenty feet by fifteen, which thrust itself out from the house.

It was, presumably, through the roof of this that Walter Mann had fallen to his death. I walked towards it, and saw that it was wooden framed, and glazed to within three feet of the ground. It had an outside door. I tried it, and it was unlocked. I walked inside.

There was shelving all round the sides, lined with pots of flowering plants. Some of them looked exotic. Large containers on the floor sprouted vines and sub-tropical plants, and amongst it all were scattered white-painted metal chairs and two round tables. I believed I spotted orchids, to my unspecialised eye. If that were so, then the large hole in the arched roof, close to the house, was doing no good at all.

The broken glass was still there, scattered on the floor. Part of the wooden frame lay to one side. It was possible to detect where Walter had fallen and lain, as the glass had followed after him. Put your fist through a window, and it's not the passage of your flesh that causes the wounds. The bruise, perhaps, but not the cuts. Those come from the rest of the glass that showers on to you. So it had been with Walter. The hole in the roof was larger than a human being. Most of the glass had fallen on and around him. I could have almost traced his outline.

Looking upwards through the gap I could see the two windows, one above the other, vertically above me. It looked a long way down from the top one.

I went outside, closed the door, and turned. A woman was standing outside an open door towards the far end of the house, a boxer dog beside her. As the dog had only a stump I could see nothing wagging, so I wasn't sure of my welcome. The same with the woman. She was small and thin, with a sour face and a wide, expressive mouth. At that time it expressed disapproval. Her arms were folded across what would have been her bosom, had she possessed one, and her head was nodding in tiny jerks, in an I-told-you-so gesture, congratulating herself about something.

'I'm sorry,' I said. 'I should have rung a bell or something. My name's Richard Patton.'

'Mr Carne said to expect you.' Her voice was younger than her appearance, but any warmth was firmly held in reserve. 'The residual legatee.' She said those words with a wry and contemptuous twist to her lips, though whether aimed at the ponderous legal phrasing or the expected value of 'residual' I couldn't tell. It might even have been aimed at me, as the 'legatee' part of it.

But my impression of the situation was that Mary Pinson, as

24

this clearly was, although knowing there was a new will, could not know the exact contents of it. It meant I had to be careful, so that I had to find some reasonable explanation of my presence. As a residual legatee, or representing one, I must have appeared in indecent haste to view the goodies.

'I'm Mary Pinson,' she said. 'Miss. You'd better come in. I've got the kettle on.' She made a beckoning jerk with her head. 'Sheba won't hurt you. Providing you don't attack me, of course.' Then she gave a short snap of laughter, dismissing the possibility. It was like cracking a nut.

Yet Sheba was eyeing me with uncertainty, her face as bleakly unwelcoming as Mary Pinson's. Her jowls vibrated gently, and a quiet growl throbbed past them.

'You're sure?'

'Not really,' she admitted. 'She was Mr Mann's dog. Raise a hand to *him*, and she'd have had it off at the wrist. Mind you, I have wondered . . . try it, shall we? You raise your hand—'

'Thank you, no. I'll take it as read. Good dog,' I said.

Sheba glared at me, and trotted in so close to my heels that I feared for my ankles.

Facing the doorway was a flight of wooden stairs, uncarpeted. No doubt, in Victorian times, there would have been a squad of servants. Perhaps the cottages at Knightsford had supplied them. Now there was Mary Pinson. She turned right, through a door into her kitchen. It was *her* kitchen, you could tell that by her possessive gesture of welcome.

She was dressed, for a woman of her age – I guessed the 60s – rather younger than one would expect, rather more smartly too, in green slacks and a Fair Isle jumper, with the points of a jade shirt showing at the neck. No apron. Her method of making tea involved a lot of noise, the banging of the kettle on the stove, the rattle of the lid on the pottery pot, the clatter of cups on saucers. I guessed that this in no way indicated her mood. Noise, to her, was equated with meaningful performance.

She looked round and caught my eye on her.

'You're wondering,' she stated, 'why I'm showing no signs of mourning, the funeral being yesterday. I didn't go to that. Not welcome – but that wouldn't have stopped me.'

'I'm sure it wouldn't.'

'St Stephen's. They cremated him. He put that in his will.'

'Ah!'

25

'But I've no time for all this outward show. They go with their black veils, and weep. They have to be seen weeping. Not me. If I want to weep, it's my affair. I can remember Walter without a black arm-band to remind me. I remember him in here.' She prodded her hard chest. In spite of her rejection of outward display, her voice was unsteady.

'Help yourself to sugar,' she said, banging down the sugar bowl. It was steady enough now.

I sat at the plain wood table, and helped myself. 'You were with him for long?'

'Thirty years. I'll be sorry to leave.'

'You're leaving?' I asked, surprised because I'd assumed otherwise.

She was now seated opposite to me, her hands completely round her cup and saucer, hugging them to her. 'I'd not be staying with that Clare Tolchard. She wouldn't have it, anyway. We never got on. She's made it plain, how things stand. Been round here and made it very clear . . . I wouldn't be wanted. That was after she'd been from top to bottom of the place, checking I hadn't sold anything.' She said that in a flat voice. 'But of course, it was always going to be hers. The others wouldn't want it – Paul and Donald. They were all born here, but she was the only one who really loved the place.'

Oh dear, I thought.

Her eyes wandered away from me, her gaze now from the window, to the woods on the rise beyond the river. 'It's only to be expected,' she murmured.

And yet, I thought, Walter's daughter, Clare, must surely have known. Wouldn't Walter have told all three that he'd changed his will?'

'It'll be the cars,' she said suddenly, swinging her eyes back to me. There was a brisk triumph in this statement. She'd solved the meaning of 'residual'.

'Cars?'

'Mr Mann's Granada, and that sports thing of his he's always made such a fuss of, though how he expected to drive it at his age, and him locking himself away for the past two months in his room, I'll never know.' She took a breath, and I managed to get in:

'What sports thing?' I'd noted she'd slipped and called him Walter, but he was now back to Mr Mann.

'Oh, something he reproduced – no, restored, that was it. A

26

funny name for a car, if you ask me. Something with horns on. Deer or the like.'

'Stag?' I whispered.

'That was it.'

'Triumph Stag?'

'I said that.'

I was silent. How fate bounces you about! I only hoped that fate wasn't dangling it, only to snatch it away again. Eventually: 'No, it wasn't the cars.' I'd thought of a valid reason for my presence. 'Mr Carne suggested that I ought to come and look at the situation, the inquest being on Monday. I'm an ex-police officer, and it seems necessary to make certain it *was* an accident.'

'Of *course* it was!'

'The coincidence,' I suggested gently.

'Ridiculous.'

'Would you show me? The room. The one you say he's been locking himself away in for the past two months. Please.'

Her eyes were like shiny, dark pebbles, holding mine. 'You're up to something.'

I nodded. 'And I can't tell you what.'

I'd offended her. 'You'd better go, before I set the dog on you.'

Sheba's head was on my knee, and I was fondling her ear. I said: 'But *you're* not sure, are you? Wouldn't you like an expert opinion?'

'Some expert, you.'

'The police were here?'

'You can guess. Here for hours. That was after I got back, of course. It was me found him. Saturday, it was. Usually, Saturdays, I go out and do the shopping and the like. Sort of pop in and see my sister, in town.'

'You mean Boreton?'

'It's all the town we've got. That's where they came from, the police. You can't get past it. Accident they said, and accident it was.'

I nodded. Of course it was, I had to hope. 'It's for the inquest to decide.'

'Oh . . . them!'

'But all the same, you don't mind if I have a look at the room?'

She stood up, her face set suddenly in firm rejection. It was all very well to indulge in idle chatter, but behind it she had been realising that she was the present custodian.

27

'And have Clare carping and griping? Oh no. The house'll surely be hers, and she won't want any old Tom, Dick or Harry prowling round. No, Mr Patton. I'm sorry, but I can't allow that . . . whatever Mr Carne says.'

My luck had run out. Before the will was read I could hardly tell her the truth. The way things were looking, I felt that the truth was best left for Philip Carne to reveal.

There were a few moments of silence, and in the interval I heard a car drawing up on the gravel, followed by the clack of hard heels on the terrace surface outside. Mary Pinson's eyes met mine as I rose to my feet. She nodded, lips pursed.

'And she'll tell you the same. It's Clare herself.'

I turned to the door as Walter Mann's daughter swept in with a flurry of anger. 'Whose damn car's that in the drive?' She saw me and stopped. We stood looking at each other.

Walter's second child would have been about thirty, and would perhaps have been a very good looking woman ten or so years before. Maybe a little sturdy, perhaps now wearing too much make-up, but unlike Mary Pinson, Clare was showing evidence of mourning. Her skirt was pleated and black, the jacket was grey, over a blue blouse. Her handbag was black and her shoes were black. But strangely none of these accessories seemed new; her mourning was worn with an air of acceptance, of confidence. Her face, too, was shadowed with a suffering that had been there much longer than a week. The lines round her mouth and the wrinkles in her neck had taken time to mature. As had the sharpness of her tongue.

'I take it that's your car,' she said to me, her eyes assessing me and not pleased with what they saw. 'You've got no business here, so you'd better go.'

Although she had not enquired about what my business might have been, I would have complied, but she took it too far, her anger spilling over on to Mary Pinson. To tell you the truth, I was anxious to get out of there. It was all right with Mary Pinson to be flinging round words like 'residual legatee', because she could hardly have failed to know that Walter had drawn a new will. Philip Carne had said her position was unchanged in it. But I couldn't declare any personal interest in it to Clare, who was showing every sign of being ignorant of any new will. My position would have been embarrassing at the least.

But Clare now turned her bitter tongue on Mary Pinson. 'You

28

had no right to let him past the step, Mary. Anyway, I'm surprised you're still here yourself.'

'The will's to be read on Sunday, Clare.'

'I hardly think it will affect your position.'

The corners of Mary Pinson's tight mouth twitched. It occurred to me that she could have known rather more than she had revealed. 'I'm prepared to wait and see.'

Clare, angry, turned away from her, and faced me. 'Are *you* still here?'

'He's from the police,' said Mary, her voice so gentle it barely stirred the air. But it had been a subtle attack, disturbing Clare's peace of mind with no more than a suggestion of doubt.

I was caught. I couldn't deny it, and dared not admit it. I stared at Clare, impassive and I hoped expressionless.

'He wishes to see the room,' Mary continued placidly. 'Your father's room. I can't think why.'

She had been speaking to Clare's back, as Clare hadn't taken her eyes from me. They were a matching grey to her jacket, mourning eyes, tragic eyes. Her lips were quivering, and for one moment I thought we were in for a display of the tears Mary had scorned. But if so, they'd not have been from grief. All I could detect in her face was despair, and a desperate weariness.

'I can't stand any more of this!' she cried abruptly. 'I just can't!'

Then she pushed past me and through the doorway, and I heard the clatter of her heels in close to a run along the terrace.

Mary put the back of one hand against her lips and thumped the table with her other fist. 'Oh damn!' she said bitterly. 'Why do I let her do it?'

'What does she do?' I was casual, filling my pipe, going for a peep at the gardens from her window.

I could hear that she'd begun clearing up the cups. 'I came here when she was born,' she said quietly. 'Came to look after her really, but when Donald came, their mother died.' Her voice was equally dead. It had happened; it had to be lived with. 'From then on, it was me running the house. Virtually. Walter wanted it like that. Didn't want the trouble. Three children. Paul – he was five, and Clare was two, then along came Donald, and I had him from a baby. But as Clare grew up she resented me. It was *her* home, and she tried to make that very clear. In her immature way. I'm not to be bossed, Mr Patton, you can take that as you like. Clare tried it, and she failed. That's how she is. She has to be able to

29

order people around. Dominate. And she can't always do it. It makes her furious, as you saw. That husband of hers, Aleric Tolchard . . . she tried it with him, but it was due to fail from the first moment. Anybody could have seen that, but she was blind, blind.'

Her voice had drifted into a chatty tone. I felt free to turn around. 'A forceful type,' I guessed, 'this Tolchard?'

'Too high and mighty for anybody around here, him and his high-faluting degree. He only had to stare her down, and she flopped. Just flopped.'

I'd noticed the past tense. 'He doesn't now?'

'Poor Clare,' she said softly, her eyes on her hands, which were resting on the edge of the table. 'Two funerals in three months. But does she come to me? No. Only to throw out her orders.'

'He died, three months ago?'

'He fell down an iron staircase at the factory. She's barely out of mourning for that one,' she murmured.

I could understand now why she found Clare's attitude annoying. Clare had not come to Mary for sympathy and advice.

'You realise what you've done?' I asked her.

'Upset her again.'

'No, not that. But you've made it impossible, now, to refuse to show me the room.'

'Yes.' She lifted her face, a hint of humour in her eyes. 'Haven't I!'

So there and then, before she changed her mind, she took me up the wooden staircase to a landing, which ran right across the house. Perhaps it gave her time to control her emotions.

'Further along is the main staircase,' she explained, her voice now casual. 'Down to the hall.' She had produced a key from her pocket.

'That, too, was an accident?' I asked, taking the key from her fingers because I wanted to feel the action of the lock.

She knew what I was talking about: Aleric Tolchard's death. I was trying the key in the lock, feeling the smooth movement of the wards, while she decided how to answer.

When she spoke, it was an indirect answer, though her meaning was clear. 'It was just after that when Walter had that lock fitted and came to live up here. For over two months he's locked himself away.'

The lock was new. The key, though small, was sufficiently

complex to indicate it was virtually un-pickable. It was a safe deadlock. I opened the door.

'What you're saying,' I told her, 'is that Walter didn't think Tolchard's death was an accident.'

She made a clicking noise with her tongue. 'Shall we say that it was an accident that Walter thought had been intended for himself.' Her voice was daintily precise. 'He thought,' she amplified, 'that one of his children was trying to kill him.'

4

I continued to walk into the room, partly to keep my back to her. They kept on flinging themselves at me, these coincidences. Another death. Another accident. There had been a gap of three months between Aleric Tolchard's death and Walter's, but during the whole of that period Walter had feared for his life. It would be extraordinary if his death, when it came, had also been accidental.

'Which one?' I said, for something to fill the gap. 'Which one of his children had Walter got in mind? Paul? Clare? Donald?'

'I'm sure I don't know,' she said distantly. My remark had not been in good taste.

The room was wide and lofty. They built their ceilings high in those days. It had three matching sash windows evenly spaced across the facing wall, overlooking the conservatory and the gardens. To the left was a bathroom, its appointments modern. It had no door into the hall. I went into the room on the right. His bedroom. The bed was an old iron-framed monster with brass knobs and a king-sized mattress. There was a hint of puritanical frugality in the room. He'd used it to sleep in, during which time his eyes would be shut. It therefore needed to possess no aesthetic appeal, and had none. It did have, however, firm bolts, top and bottom, to the door that would have opened into the hall. The bolts were stiff – I tried them – and must have been shot home a great number of years before, and not since touched. Since his wife's death? That seemed possible.

So I had to consider a suite of rooms with only one usable door, and that possessing a new and efficient deadlock.

I returned to that room and examined it in more detail.

He had clearly used it as a living room and office. There was a good-quality carpet on the floor, and heavy drapes at the three windows. Central heating radiators between the windows looked starkly modern against the Victorian woodwork and fittings. His desk was dark and solid and old, yet held the modern necessities of two differently coloured phones, a desk lamp, and a semi-portable manual typewriter. The four-drawer filing cabinet was in matching dark wood. All the surfaces were tidy. There was no indication that anyone had been through his papers, so perhaps Philip Carne would have to do that later – or had done it and left a neatness behind him that wasn't reflected in his office.

If so, he had missed the white plastic carrier bag on the floor beneath the central window.

Walter had a round table with a stuffed armchair beside it, a standard lamp carefully positioned just behind. On the table surface were a spectacle case and a pair of glasses, beside them was a bulky book, the title of which was: The World of 3-D. To me this meant stereo. The author was J. G. Ferwerda. I flicked a page or two. It did not deal with stereo sound, but with stereo photography.

Behind me, Mary Pinson said: 'I fetched that book for him from the library, that Saturday morning. He'd had it on order, and it was in. I'll have to take it back, I suppose.' Sadness flooded her eyes as I turned to face her.

'That day,' I prompted. 'The Saturday he died, you mean?'

She was so long in answering that I began to think she was not going to do so. Then I understood why she had been reluctant to bring me here; it saddened and upset her to be in Walter's room. She seemed to shake her shoulders, then she said: 'I was confused. It was a . . . bad day. I brought it up here and put it beside his glasses, just as though he was still alive. I'll have to take it back,' she repeated. She looked round in confusion, as though he might appear from either of the side doors at any moment. I would have liked to ask her to leave me alone in the room, but I needed her. There could be questions.

I went over to examine the central one of the windows. The frames were hooked together with the usual swivel latch, which I swung aside. The lower frame went up very smoothly. He'd probably used it often. At its full height, there was room for me to lean out freely. The sill was level with a point a foot above my knees. I looked down. Directly below was the conservatory, with its hole in the roof exactly in line with my body, should I have wished to lean just a little too far. Or should Mary Pinson have wished to come up behind me and help me on my way.

I withdrew my head, and turned. She was within a yard of me.

'The window,' she said, 'was wide open when I got back, just the same as it was when I saw him last.'

'Oh?' I said. 'He liked it wide open, did he?'

'No. Not really. That was what struck me as strange. It was quite cool that day, with a brisk wind. I remember that particularly, because it was blowing the bag around.' Her lips twitched. Something was amusing her.

'I don't understand.'

'The plastic bag,' she explained, pointing to it, on the floor beneath the window. 'Now *that's* a good indication of what he was like.'

She spoke as though I had to become fully conversant with Walter's habits. I prompted her. 'What *was* he like? Tell me.'

'He was kind and considerate . . . and vague. Always thinking of something else. That could be irritating at times. I know – though I've never been there – but I know that if he was asked to make a decision at the factory in, say, a week's time, he was absolutely hopeless. Hivvering and hovering around, you wouldn't believe, and just incapable of making his mind up. But ask him for a snap decision, and he'd come right out with it. Take shopping days . . . now there's a good example. I'd come up here to see if there was anything he wanted, and there'd be ten minutes of trying to decide, and in the end: "No, I don't think so, Mary," he'd say. And by the time I'd got down and got my clothes on he'd have thought of half a dozen things. And d'you think I could get past the conservatory! Never once, I do believe. Of course, from the back door to my Mini in the garage I had to come past here, beneath that window, and it'd be: "Oh, I've just thought, Mary . . ." Then a whole list of things.'

'Which involved the plastic bag?'

'Things for me to take. Like a library book or two, or his shoes to be mended. All last-second thoughts. He'd put them in that bag and lower them to me.'

I looked again. There was a length of string fastened to the handles of the bag.

'Rather like the maiden, locked in a tower, hauling up her food in a basket,' I observed.

'Oh, it wasn't like that! I brought him all his meals on a tray . . . Oh, I see. It was a joke. You shouldn't look so solemn when you say things like that, Mr Patton.'

I grinned at her. Her mood was now completely gone. 'But I was thinking serious thoughts, I assure you. This was why you had the key, I take it? His meals . . .'

'But no,' she corrected me sharply. 'I would come up and call out: "It's Mary." And he'd let me in. With a tray or the cleaner, or to make his bed and keep him tidy. I never used the key, not once, but he made me promise to keep it with me – always. I remember, the man came to fit the lock and gave Walter two keys. I had one, as I say, to keep for emergencies. If something happened, I'd need to get in.'

'Something?'

'An accident, so that he couldn't get to the door. A stroke. A heart attack.'

'So there was medical history . . .'

'Oh, you will *not* understand! I was just giving you examples.'

'Sometimes I'm a bit slow,' I admitted. 'So you had the key, and you kept it with you all the time.'

'Certainly.'

'Under your pillow at night?'

'Now you're doing it again.'

'Now I'm being serious. Don't you realise, Mary, that it could be very important! The whole point is that this door, which was in effect the only one, was locked. It matters about the keys.'

She looked disturbed. I had diverted her into thinking this was no more than an interesting interlude, and now I'd told her it was not. She walked past me and slammed the window shut with a show of vigour, then spoke with her back to me, her hands supporting her on the sill. Her voice was quiet.

'Walter was serious about the key, so I did as he asked. Nobody could ever have touched my key, and I had it with me when I left to go shopping, that Saturday morning. He had his own, and he used to lock the door behind me the moment I left. His own key . . . he wore it. Wore it on a gold chain round his neck, hanging inside his shirt like a medallion. He locked the door after me . . . that last time. I heard him do it. He wouldn't have opened it, except to me, or to Kenneth Leyton. Walter was very meticulous.'

She turned to face me, half seated now on the sill. 'So you see, Mr Patton, whatever strange ideas you might have that Walter's death wasn't an accident, no one could have entered this room unless they were invited in.'

Standing there, the sun sideways from behind her and caught in her hair, her face half-shadowed and softened, I could see she had probably been a very beautiful young woman. She had been speaking with a strange and mature authority, completely unlike anything one would expect from a housekeeper. There was no servitude in her tone. I could imagine that Clare's immature resentment would have bounced impotently from that placidly remote personality.

'You're saying,' I said quietly, 'that the ones he wouldn't invite in here would be his sons, Paul and Donald, and his daughter Clare?'

Her shoulders moved in a discreet shrug. 'Why else the lock?'

'But . . . you mentioned someone called Kenneth Leyton.'

'His friend. His dear friend. He could trust Kenneth. They virtually built up the factory between them. *He* was always welcome, always here. That last fortnight, he was here most days . . . evenings. Keeping Walter in touch with what was going on at the factory. To talk about Kenneth . . .'

'Then we'll forget him,' I said gently, determined not to. 'Which would leave only yourself, Mary.' She thrust herself from the window sill. 'If we're to assume he'd admit no one else . . .' I lifted my eyebrows at her.

'I take it this is another of your jokes.'

'I get these flippant moods.'

'If you've seen enough . . .' She lifted her head and stared around the room. 'If you've gone far enough . . .'

'There's the window, you see.'

She turned at the door. 'I don't know what you're saying.'

I gestured towards it. 'The window that was open. He opened it as you were leaving, and it was still open when you returned.'

'He *fell* out of it. How could he have shut it after . . .' She bit her lip.

'You spoke of a sharp wind. He wouldn't, surely, have left it open for long.'

'Perhaps it stuck.' Her voice was now flatly dismissive. She'd lost sympathy with my eccentricities.

I shook my head. 'It moves very easily.'

She made her impatient little ticking noise again. 'You're not very bright, are you? But I never thought of policemen as bright. I explained. He threw up the window and called down, asking me to pick up a book they'd got for him at the library. *That* book.' Pointing to the table. 'But of course I'd need his library ticket, one of those plastic computer things they use now. So he couldn't just throw it down, because it might've landed on top of the conservatory. Am I getting too complicated for you, Mr Patton?'

I shook my head. She was very graphic.

'So he put it in his plastic bag and lowered it to me. But because it was blowing all over the place, he put a book in with it that he'd decided could be returned, and lowered it like that. Though he had to do his pendulum thing. The conservatory's quite wide. He'd swing the bag from side to side until he'd got it going, then let out the string. So I got his library ticket and book, and he hauled it in. Must have done, because he . . . because . . . oh dear Lord!' She put her hand to her face.

'What is it?'

She sank into the easy chair. After a minute she looked up. Now the light wasn't kind. 'I've thought – assumed – that *that* was the time he fell out. Pulling the bag up again. I'd collected his post, you see, from the hall, and put it all in the bag, to give it a bit of weight. But it wasn't much, all told. Oh, I should have waited, but I just hurried away. He'd made me late. The bag was blowing around. I assumed, later, when I was thinking how it could've happened, that it'd got caught in the guttering, and when he was trying to get it free . . . I thought he'd leaned too far out. But . . .'

'But?' I prompted, my fingers on her shoulder, feeling the shaking and trying to still it.

'But the bag was *here*, where it is now. It's *me* who's stupid!' she declared violently. 'He *did* manage to pull it up, so it wasn't then that he fell out.'

I gave her a few moments, walking away from her and stuffing my pipe. Too firmly, it wouldn't draw. I looked out of the window. A young woman was walking in the garden. At last I said:

'There's also the point that if he'd fallen then, only a minute or so after you'd left, you'd have heard it. I can tell you, it would've made an almighty crash.'

When I turned round she was watching me with large, terrified eyes. 'You're right, of course. Oh, poor, dear Walter.'

'So we have to assume he closed it at that time, having brought in his bag. There'd have been no reason to leave it open then, so he'd close it. And he opened it again later.' I glanced at her. 'Or somebody else did.'

'No . . . please . . .'

'Somebody he *did* allow in, despite what you say.'

She came to me and put a hand on my arm. 'You're intending to say this at the inquest?'

'Of course not. It's only conjecture.'

She nodded. 'Because if you did, I'd have to give evidence against you myself.'

I smiled down at her. 'That won't be necessary. What evidence, for instance?'

'The door was locked. I had to open it for the policeman who came. If Walter did admit anybody, he would have locked the door behind them at once. It was habit. So how d'you explain the fact that Walter still had his key when they went to him? It was still on its chain round his neck.'

'Ah,' I said. 'Yes,' I said.

She patted my arm. Clever boy, you're seeing sense at last. 'So we'll go down and I'll make another pot of tea.'

'Good idea.'

I noticed that she carefully locked the door behind us.

So there we had it, the classical situation of the locked room. Walter had locked himself in. No key was available to anyone who had plans to push him from his open window, and the door was still locked when he was found, his own key still on its chain round his neck. So how could it have been anything but an accident? Suicide, perhaps? No, I couldn't accept that.

But of course, it's obvious how it could have been done. You'll have seen it before I did. But you wouldn't have said anything to Mary Pinson, seeing how upset she was already. If you'd observed her carefully, of course, because it wasn't obvious, she who controlled her emotional responses so proudly. In her own domain, that square and rather drab kitchen, not particularly relieved by the array of modern equipment, she was soon bustling and crashing around. I watched her quietly, trying to get my pipe going.

It seemed clear to me, in spite of Mary's certainty, that Walter must have admitted one of the people he suspected of trying to kill him. But these people, if Walter was to make any sense at all

37

out of changing his will, must surely have been told he'd changed it, so that it had then been too late to do any good by killing him. Think about it, and you could see that this might have been the reason he would feel safe in admitting them. But one of them at least, Clare, had shown indications that she did not know of a new will.

This problem I felt to be more difficult to solve than the question of the locked room.

I wondered who was the young lady I'd seen in the garden.

'I noticed,' I observed, 'that you call him Walter.' I'd noticed other indications, too.

We were going to get cake with our tea this time, a cake she'd cooked herself. She waved the knife under my nose.

'Lacking in imagination, too,' she said severely. 'Can't you *see* the position I was in when their mother died? Just try to understand the effect it had on the two elder ones, Kathleen dying like that. There'd been so little time, you see, for her to use any influence on Paul and Clare, even if she'd had any to use. What she *had* done, between you and me, hadn't been for the best. Clare, you see, had had all the attention, with Paul, who was never a happy lad, getting more and more sullen. Then – Kathleen was gone. Walter, at that time, was almost completely absorbed . . . no, obsessed would be closer to it . . . obsessed with this business of his. Struggling to get it going. It must have been a strain, but he tried. Give him credit for that. Tried to find some time with the children.'

She was quite determined to be as fair as she could. I nodded. I now had my slice of cake. Caraway seed. Years since I'd had any of that. I nodded, mouth full.

'But he was always so exhausted, and he felt the loss of Kathleen so terribly. Virtually, I brought the children up myself, a nanny as well as a housekeeper. All right, say I failed if you like. But you haven't met the two boys yet. Perhaps Kathleen would have made a better job of it, but I was having to contend with three children growing up without a mother. I tried to take her place. But how could I do that?'

She was being more open with me than I had any right to expect. Perhaps she needed my sympathy; she obviously felt her failure strongly. No, I decided, what she felt strongly was that any failure might be attributed to her, when she had had to carry an unfair burden alone.

I said: 'Walter expected too much from you.' It was an exploratory remark.

She moved a hand in a tiny, dismissive gesture. 'It's not that. Walter had hardly noticed Clare when Kathleen was alive, but in no time at all, after her death, Clare became his favourite. That was only natural . . . I suppose. He saw in her the wife he'd lost. There was nothing he could refuse her. And Paul watched it happening. I could see him resenting it. How do you deal with jealousy? I don't know. Perhaps it's built-in with some people. It'd been there from the time of Clare's birth. Up to then he'd had the full attention of both parents. But to Kathleen, Clare was no more than a pretty doll she could play with and dress and coo over. Paul looked to his father. He loved him, Mr Patton. Loved and admired. But Walter didn't see that. Even so young, Paul would have loved to be taken down to that shed – that's all the business was, at first – and just left to watch and help. But Walter didn't see that.'

'So that when his wife died . . .'

'Paul was right out of it, with very little attention from his father. The only one Walter noticed was Clare.'

'And Donald?'

'There was nothing left for poor Donald. How could I give him a mother's affection? I tried. It seemed to confuse him. I do believe he's never really known where he stands in this world. Spends all his time hunting around for some sort of security. Never finds it, of course. It's not the sort of thing you can find, hiding round a corner. The point about security is that it's there. Poor Donald. Every time I see him – which isn't often – he seems more down-at-heel and more hopeless. He still . . .' She stopped.

I looked up from my cup. She was stirring, stirring, her eyes vacant.

'Yes?' I asked.

'Still calls me mother. I never did break him of that.'

'Did you try?' I smiled.

She shook her head, lower lip caught in her teeth. 'Not very hard.'

It seemed likely I'd be meeting them all on Sunday, in this house. 'I'll be seeing them.'

'Yes,' she agreed. 'When Mr Carne reads the will.'

I considered that quietly, and we sat in amicable silence. It was strange that we had reached this relationship.

'I don't think you've been completely honest with me, Mary.' I said that with a smile, indicating I wasn't taking it seriously.

'I don't understand—'

'You know exactly who I am and what I'm here for. You know the contents of Walter's new will.'

Her lips tight, she nodded.

'Not in detail, perhaps,' I suggested.

Another nod. She wasn't going to give me any help.

'But you knew a new will was being made, and he would surely have given you some idea of its contents . . .' I left that hanging, waiting for her response.

She spoke, at last, with reluctance. 'I didn't agree with what he was doing. He knew I disapproved of this silly business of locking himself in his room. Of *course* nobody was out to kill him. Whyever would they?' She paused. I wasn't going to say anything about that. 'But he was determined. Said he would show them they wouldn't gain by it. His death, he meant. He gave me the shudders. And he said there was a niece somewhere he was trying to trace. Give her a pleasant surprise, he said. But he didn't tell me any details. He simply said there'd be no change in it as far as I was concerned.'

'Which was?'

'I'm not telling you *that*.'

'I shall hear on Sunday.'

'Then wait, like everybody else.'

Fair enough. I was being just as close with my own information. 'Let me guess that it would be a sum of money and no roof over your head. Am I right?'

'That's all I expected.'

'After all these years? After bringing up his family, looking after his home and his welfare! Damn it, you were virtually his wife.'

She gave me a thin smile. 'You put it exactly. For the past twenty years I've lived with him as his wife.'

'Then don't you see . . .' In my agitation, my anger at the way she'd been used, I got to my feet and looked for something to throw. But you can't do that in other people's kitchens. Unless it was now Amelia's and mine! I turned back to face her. 'Why didn't you get married, for heaven's sake? You were already only a couple of signatures away from it.'

'And have to face the hatred of all three?' she asked placidly.

'Oh, you can be sure, over the years they've known I slept in his bed, and all I ever got from them was hints and taunts that I was looking after myself—'

'As you should have been.'

'No. I was doing a job and I was paid for it. If I was giving Walter comfort, he was giving me love. Don't try to soil it for me, Mr Patton. Please don't make it into something sordid.'

'That was not . . .' But how could I get through to her? Marriage, she was implying, might have ruined their relationship? No – she thought I was blaming her for enjoying the relationship without the blessing. 'Very well, Mary,' I said, breathing out gently. 'We'll leave that for now. But you witnessed his signature on his new will, knowing that if he died you'd be homeless.'

'So you see,' she said sourly, 'I would hardly have killed him.'

'You know I was not being serious—'

'But you don't expect me to have *my* little joke?'

'Ah!' I said. I grinned at her. 'Your point.'

'And of course, I didn't witness it. Mr Carne wouldn't allow that, because I was a beneficiary.'

'However minor!'

'Now, now.'

'So who did?'

'He brought his articled clerk along, and Mr Leyton was the other witness.'

'This is the Kenneth Leyton you mentioned, Walter's life-long friend? There was nothing for him, then? Not even a painting and the grandfather clock?'

'Now you're being facetious.'

'I'm becoming a little annoyed at the behaviour of your wonderful Walter.'

'Then don't be. Kenneth and I knew it was only a phase. Give Walter time, and he'd realise he was being foolish, thinking somebody was going to . . .' She stopped.

'But somebody did, didn't they?'

'No they didn't. It was an accident. Nobody could have done such a thing.'

I was shaking my head. 'I can show you how it could have been done. But that hardly matters now. He didn't get time to change his new will . . . so, I take it, Kenneth Leyton lost something.'

'If you must know, they argued for hours over that new will.

41

Kenneth wanted to put a stop to it. In protest, he said he wanted no part of it, and Walter could cut him right out, if he liked. And Walter took him at his word.'

Very soon, I realised, I was going to be surrounded by a lot of angry people. There was, perhaps, some comfort to be extracted from Amelia's injury; it was keeping her out of it.

'What, exactly, was cut out? Do you know?'

'Not for certain, but I always understood that he'd have got ten per cent of the company shares.'

This was a company of a capital value of half a million, Carne had said. Not a fortune to some people, but a lot to others. Perhaps Kenneth Leyton would have treasured those ten shares.

'There's going to be high jinks on Sunday,' I said ruefully.

'I thought I ought to tell you the background. Kind of to prepare you. Now you run along and have a look at that car. Oh, don't look like that. I saw the expression in your eyes. And you never know, that could be *all* he's left you.'

'My wife, in practice.'

'Same thing. Isn't it?'

And, you know, I was surprised to realise I'd assumed this. But perhaps Amelia, as a wealthy woman, would cast her eyes elsewhere. I wasn't much of a catch, my only expertise being an ability to back a caravan all over the place.

'You'll have to ask my wife about that.'

'Mr Carne told me she's in hospital.'

'When she hears what's going on around here, I'll have difficulty keeping her there. I'll see you on Sunday, Mary.'

She was on her feet. 'But . . . you can stay here.'

'That wouldn't be a good idea, would it?' I asked, smiling.

She was nodding, her eyes huge with contained amusement. 'Perhaps not,' she agreed.

I left abruptly, because there was a strong desire to remain with Mary Pinson and get to know more about her. But there were things to be done, such as the drive back to Aberaeron and a conference to be held with Amelia. Yet already it was too late for that. They'd hardly welcome me in their wards at ten o'clock at night.

So I went to look at the Stag.

5

It may seem strange that a man of my age should have a fixation for a sports car called the Triumph Stag. But it's unique, a car built for a specific market, which turned out to be quite limited. Why limited? Well . . . you design a sports car, open, with a folding hood. You realise that the weather in this country will probably provide, in an average year, seventeen suitable days for driving with the hood down. So you design it to take a removable hard-top, converting it into a neat little closed coupé. But the snag is: when the top is removed, where to put it? The thing's quite bulky, and will need storage room. This is an important point if the price you're aiming for does not include people who would naturally possess large garages. Add to this the fact that it was available with six or eight different engines, and you're on to something unique, even though the uniqueness possibly lies in the fact that the designers were trying to get it right. I've heard it called the Triumph Snag. With affection. Mind you, these cars are getting a bit elderly now. All the same, you see them around, long after the small saloons of that era have dissolved into rust. They're preserved, you see, nurtured and revered by their owners.

I'd had mine from a pup, and parting from it had been painful. The Volvo's a nice drive, but the Stag's an experience.

I opened the first garage door. A Mini. Mary Pinson's, no doubt. The middle door, a Ford Granada, two years old. The third . . . and there it was.

I'd looked after mine carefully. This one had been restored to perfection, and made mine seem a wreck. It squatted there, gleaming, a low, purposeful shape. I didn't know whether Walter had been an engineer, or someone else had done it for him, but it had clearly been a labour of love. I sighed, standing back from it, noting it had the twin exhaust stacks of the 3½-litre Rover engine. Mine had had the straight six two-litre.

A voice said behind me: 'A beauty, isn't she?'

I turned. It was the young woman from the garden. I'd seen her at a distance with her corn-coloured hair caught in the sun. Close-to, it seemed untidy, held down by a red ribbon above her forehead and fastened at the nape of her neck, the ends flying all over the place. She would have been twenty, perhaps. You can't be sure these days, with those ubiquitous blue jeans, and a short man's shirt dangling its tail behind. There was a leather jacket over it, reaching her waist. Her blue eyes – where had I seen such blue eyes before? – were sparkling, her elfin face seeming too small for them. Small, pert nose, pointed chin, a smile a mile wide. She stood with her slim legs apart, her hands on her lips.

'You're Mr Patton,' she informed me, jutting her lower lip and blowing hair out of her eyes. 'Philip said I'd probably find you here.'

So that was where I'd met the blue eyes. 'And you are?'

'Heather Carne, Philip's sister.'

'You felt you had to meet me?'

She grinned. Her cheeks rose to it and her tiny white teeth peeped through. 'He said you're a policeman.'

'I was. What else did he tell you?'

'That you're too old for me.'

'The cheeky devil! It seems to me he told you too much.'

She cocked her head, almost in challenge. 'He mentioned you're married.'

'Ah! Warning you.' I considered her warily. I had already decided it would be prudent to keep very silent about the will and its contents until it was read. 'I hope he hasn't been completely unethical. A solicitor's supposed to keep secrets.'

'I can keep a secret.'

'If he's trusted you with any, you ought to be careful what you say.'

Then she laughed. It would have disarmed anybody. If I'd been her age it would have completely unmanned me. Or the opposite.

'I'm at his office,' she explained. 'I've finished my degree, and I'm working out my articles with my brother. I know,' she told me in a conspiratorial whisper, 'everything.'

I scratched my neck with the stem of my pipe. 'Shall we walk down to the cars?' I was assuming she had one there, and I was playing for time.

'Mine's a motorbike,' she said. 'But I don't mind walking to it.'

I closed the garage doors and we strolled away together to the front of the house. The sun had now gone round far enough to slant a ray or two on the facade, so that it looked less gloomy. Her motorcycle was propped in front of my Volvo, a 500 cc Honda twin, her crash-hat on its seat. Her long legs matched my stride, though her head came barely above my shoulder. I'd decided I already had enough information for one day, and hoped she wasn't going to offer more.

'The idea was,' she said, 'to give you enough time to see how things stand, then ask you to help us.'

'You and your brother?' What was she talking about?

'Me and Chad. We're sort of engaged, though all that's a bit archaic now. He wants to get married, but I don't see why. Anyway, whatever it is, we can't do it if he's in prison, can we?'

I was determined to be flippant. This young lady seemed set to involve me with something. 'No, they won't let you do it in prison.'

'You!' she cried, stopping and turning to me, and remarkably with a blush on her cheeks. 'If you're not going to take me seriously . . .'

'Perhaps that's exactly what I'm doing. I'm seriously advising you not to involve me . . . in whatever it is.'

'But you *are* involved.'

'I'm completely unreliable.'

'You just won't listen!'

'I heard the word prison. That implies law-breaking, and I'm no longer a policeman.'

'Philip warned me,' she told me fiercely. 'He said all you could think about was what you were going to get out of it.'

I lowered my head, tapping out my pipe on my heel, the other hand reaching for my pouch. When I looked up, she was pulling a face. Pugging, we used to call it, like a naughty child. 'I don't believe he'd say that,' I told her quietly.

'Of *course* he didn't,' she said firmly, as though it was my fault. 'It was me being bitchy. Chad says I ought to grow up. Don't you think I'm grown up, Mr Patton?'

'Physically, without question.'

'You will *not* be serious!' she complained.

'I'm being patient. If this Chad person, whom you don't intend to marry, is in danger of going to prison, then he needs a good solicitor—'

'He's got one. My brother.'

45

'Very well. If there are enquiries to be made, then he needs a private investigator, a professional. Solicitors usually have their own contacts.'

'But we can't afford a *real* one!' she burst out.

I had to laugh at that. The blood ran from her face and her mouth went tiny. No trace of lipstick or any other make-up, I noticed. Then the colour flooded back, and she laughed. 'Didn't that sound dreadful?' she asked, and I had to agree it had.

'This Chad,' I asked. 'What's he done?'

'It's what he hasn't done. And it's Chad Leyton.'

'Leyton? I know that name. Kenneth, I think.'

'He's the office manager at the factory. Kenneth Leyton. Chad works in the research lab. Ken's his father.'

'Still works there?'

'They adjourned the summary hearing, and he's out on bail. My brother persuaded the magistrate he wouldn't abscond, and that he'd keep an eye on him. He meant I would, of course.'

'Yes. I get the point.'

The sun was slanting orange light on the right side of her face, casting hollows beneath her cheeks, cutting purple shadows into her hair.

'This crime,' I ventured cautiously, afraid to hear. 'Of what is he accused?'

She seemed to relax. Even her ears were less tense. 'You've heard of Aleric Tolchard, Clare's husband?'

'Oh no!' I whispered.

'He fell down an iron staircase at the factory, and broke his neck. That's what Chad's accused of. Pushing him.'

If he was out on bail on a murder charge, there must have been something not satisfactory about the evidence. That much was encouraging. I concentrated on my pipe and finally managed to light it. 'And?'

'He didn't do it. Mr Mann . . .' She nodded towards the house. '. . . was certain he hadn't done it.'

That was not surprising, considering that Walter had been convinced the death should have been his, and that the culprit was one of his family. 'Don't tell me.'

'He put up the bail.'

'Break it gently.'

'A hundred thousand. Which of course would come out of the estate, if Chad *does* abscond.'

46

'I'm ahead of you.'

'But I've managed to persuade him not to, seeing that we've got an expert on hand.'

'Me?'

'I've promised to bring you to dinner.'

How could I refuse? I was being offered a fee of one hundred thousand pounds, which would rightly be Amelia's.

'You know something?' I said.

'What?'

'When you're qualified – *if* you're ever fully qualified – you'll be a whizz in court.'

She smiled. For one terrible moment I thought she was going to kiss me. 'Thank you, kind sir. Just follow me.' Then she spoiled it. 'I'll drive as slow as I can.'

'Just one promise?' I asked. She nodded. 'You'll let me use the phone when I get there.'

She nodded, satisfied. 'I knew you'd want to call your wife.'

She fastened on her helmet, and became an alien creature. I went to the car. She swept round and waited, engine throbbing. I admit to a sigh when I fastened the seat belt. It was for my lost youth.

If that was her version of slow, I should not have liked to be around when she was in a hurry. From time to time I lost her, but all I had to do was look for a helmet with a bit of red ribbon flying at the back. I felt she was teasing me, and wished I'd been behind the wheel of the Stag, so that when we arrived I drew to a halt nonchalantly, climbed out, and said: 'That the best you could do?'

We had turned away from the river before we reached Boreton, driven past the entrance to a safari park, and very nearly reached a village, judging by the lights ahead. But she'd signalled, then turned in at the entrance without gates in a low, confining wall, and swept up a short drive. The bungalow, in the declining sunlight, looked old and weathered, complacent in its security. The porch was on the near corner, and the front door was open as soon as her engine had died. She swept off her helmet, and the ribbon with her other hand. A wash of blonde hair flowed free.

'You can hear the lions from here,' she told me. 'On a still night.'

I wondered how many still nights she'd spent there. 'Really?'

'Aren't you coming in?' called a voice from the hall.

We advanced towards it, Heather urging me to the front. This

47

had to be Kenneth Leyton, Walter's lifelong friend, though I saw that this could not be the literal truth, as Walter would have been in his sixties, and Leyton must have been eight or ten years younger. Or had worn well. He stuck out his hand.

'So here you are. Heather said she'd bring you.'

No, he hadn't worn well, I realised, as he backed beneath the hall light. His hand was dry, and showed traces of arthritis. His clothes hung too loosely, his shoulders were rounded. But he was an accountant, wasn't he, living bowed over a desk. And bowed down by his responsibilities, perhaps. Fully erect, with his shoulders back, he would have been a powerful man. He had been handsome, and might still seem so in better circumstances. Better? I asked myself. This was his home, where a man might be expected to relax. Yet his eyes were tired and worried, deep-set, the flesh loose on the strong bones of his face. I reminded myself that he would be under strain, his son having been accused of murder.

'I didn't get a chance to refuse,' I told him, and now it seemed that the wrinkles at the corners of his eyes owed something to humour, though it would be a quiet humour, gentle, I thought. 'You'll be Kenneth Leyton. Miss Pinson has spoken of you.'

'Kindly, I hope.' But he said that with a shade of anxiety. 'Come along through, Mr Patton. This is very good of you, at such short notice.' He looked beyond me at Heather as she closed the front door. 'You'll want to tidy up a bit, Heather, I'm sure. Your hair, dear.'

'My hair will do very well, and I don't intend to miss a word.'

The corners of his mouth moved, and he glanced quickly at me. These two, I guessed, maintained a constant war of words, as might be expected of a father with his son's young woman, but each taking secret delight in it. 'My son's in the kitchen,' he told me.

But he wasn't, entirely. A door at the end of the hall opened, and appetising smells wafted around me. A younger version of Kenneth, taller, his slimness that of fitness, stood in the doorway, wearing an apron. 'Be with you. I daren't leave this.'

Heather hesitated, caught Kenneth's eye, and called out: 'I'll come and help.'

It was mutually understood that Leyton would want a prior word with me alone. He led me into the front room, putting on the lights, and gestured vaguely. I had a choice of either of the ancient and battered armchairs, one each side of the fireplace. The evenings were becoming cool, and he had a small log fire going. Gas and electric fires throw out heat; a real fire projects comfort. It was a square room, the furniture having crept into its own arrangement with time. No one had rushed round to prepare for my visit, and deprived it of its humanity. I sank into one of the chairs. The springs creaked, but took my weight.

'Would you care for a sherry?'

I said I would. We sat with glasses in our hands, a round, low table between us. I waited. He seemed uncertain how to get going.

'I wanted you to see Walter's house, and speak to Mary first,' he said at last. 'It's just a stroke of luck that you happen to be an ex-policeman.' He put down his glass and was massaging his fingers. I'd given him no clue as to my attitude, and he was finding it difficult to lead himself in.

'That matters, does it, that I'm ex-police? Heather told me something – relating to your son, and about Aleric Tolchard. But you're speaking now about Walter Mann's house.'

He considered me for a moment, then nodded.

'About Walter's death, in fact,' I amplified.

Now he was eager with his advance. 'The local police, not understanding the background, they were only too anxious to see Walter's death as an accident. But you, an outsider, I thought you might . . . well . . . have other ideas.'

I needed time. I wanted to stall. 'D'you mind if I smoke?'

'Heavens no. An ashtray? Hold on a sec'.' I'd flurried him. He wanted no interruptions, and scurried across the room in a frantic search. I filled my pipe. Everybody wanted to get me involved, but I'd come here to listen to young Chad's difficulties. All right. Don't tell me. At any time that day I could have turned away from it. It's this damned curiosity of mine.

As he sat down again, I said: 'You ought to be quite clear on one point, Mr Leyton. I'm here on my wife's behalf, as a residual legatee.' I wasn't sure how much he knew, as he'd been very close in Walter's confidence. 'Theoretically, all I need to do is hang around until the will's read, then go away again. My interest in this is purely selfish. An inheritance, and the legal necessities involved.'

I said this as coolly as I could, wondering how easily he might be discouraged. He treated it as a challenge.

'If you hadn't been personally interested you wouldn't have come to see us, whatever Heather said.'

'She bullied me.'

'You don't look like a man who's easily influenced, Mr Patton. She can't even bully me.' He said this seriously, as though she often tried. But nevertheless I was getting the impression that Leyton, frail and vulnerable as he might seem, had a reserved indestructibility about him. He would bend to force, but not break, would simply continue in his own quiet way, certain it was right and true.

'What brought me here was a reference to your son,' I told him. 'But now you're talking about the death of your friend, Walter.'

'Don't you think they're connected?'

'I don't know enough to form an opinion. You got me here, so you tell me.'

'Ah! I see. You want to get down to business. That's obvious.'

'I'm a guest here, Mr Leyton. I just wanted to make it clear that you're talking in conundrums. Aleric Tolchard, who was Clare's husband, fell down a staircase at the factory and broke his neck. Until Heather told me so, I had no idea the police thought it was murder. Now you're saying this death's linked with Walter's—'

'Obviously it was. Immediately after that, Walter locked himself away. He thought Tolchard's death had been aimed at himself.' Almost Mary's words.

'It's only what he thought. Are you saying Walter was there at the factory at that time?'

'Walter always liked to be last out. That dates back to the very beginning. Tolchard . . . has anybody told you about him?'

'Only that he existed.'

'Then I'll sketch him in for you.' He leaned forward. As he spoke, from time to time his knuckles rapped the table for emphasis, his arthritis forgotten. 'He came to us, to the firm, ten years ago, and married Clare soon afterwards. Walter wanted a research manager who knew optics. That's what we do, you know. Optics as related to photography. Walter had dreams . . .' He smiled, a wistful, fond smile. 'Anyway, Tolchard came, and he wasn't quite what we needed, even though he'd got his doctorate with a thesis on optics and camera lenses. It was just that he didn't fit. Not to my mind. We've always been a friendly sort of business, no pressure, no fuss. Tolchard was all push and authority, one of your dark and intense types. He completely

50

dominated Clare, and was all set to do the same at the factory. If Walter would've let him.'

'They had disputes?'

His hand flapped a negative. 'I gave you the wrong impression. Tolchard was boss of research and development, but he tried to spread his influence. Walter had to be firm. Tolchard even put his nose into my department – accounts and production control.'

'And Walter intervened?'

He compressed his lips. 'I did. I told him, when I put a foot in *his* department, then he could do so in mine.'

I could just see it, but suppressed a smile. 'So he was a nuisance?'

'Mainly on the board. Walter told me about it. You'll have to understand that I was with Walter from the beginning. He was eight years older than me, and started the business in a shed more than thirty years ago. We had four employees, and I came in as wages clerk, straight from school. I had to do a night school course to keep up.'

His version of evening classes. He was eyeing me aslant, almost ashamed of the admission.

'And it grew from there?'

'We started off making mounts and frames for photographs. Now it's anything related to photography. But as time went on, Walter formed a private limited company. A hundred shares. On my twenty-first birthday he gave me ten shares. It was a bit of a joke, really, but that was when the company was incorporated, and he said there had to be a second shareholder. "All I can give you, Ken," he said. They were worth next to nothing then.'

'And now?'

He grimaced, and changed it to a smile. 'Paul would give me twenty-five thousand for them. But no. They're for Chad and Heather, when they get married.'

'Heather says she doesn't want marriage.'

'Heather says all sorts of things. But I was saying . . . as the years went on, and Walter's children grew up, he gave all three thirteen shares each, so that finally he was left with his majority of fifty-one. It was still his company. Then along came Tolchard. Clare gave him a legal authority to vote her shares, so he had a seat on the board.'

'Along with Walter, Paul and Donald? And you?'

51

'I never wanted that. Administration's not for me. Damn it all, Mr Patton, it's been all I can do to keep on top of my own job. It's grown. It gets more and more complicated. All computers and print-outs now. You'd never believe it! We feed in the parts lists and the order quantities, and out it pops, a bit of paper with details of how to load each machine and operative. We talk to a set of damned screens. It's . . . it's immoral, that's what it is. At one time, I'd put up the wages packets, and if there was a query I could explain the figures, and if I'd made a mistake I could put it right. Now the computer prints out the pay slips. Get a query, and I have to punch in the clock number and type something like: why increased social security contribution? And the screen prints it out: because it's changed. I tell the man that, and he says: *how* has it changed? I punch that in, and up it comes on the screen: tell him to bugger off. Well . . . I mean . . .'

I refused to smile. He had been leading round to something, and found himself unable to face it. I didn't press him. 'You were saying – board meetings.'

'Tolchard was always pressing for more money for development, to chase up his grand schemes. Chad can tell you about that, because he was Tolchard's senior research assistant. And Tolchard, as I said, was always trying to ease his way into other sections. Paul had row after row with him, for trespassing on the shop floor.'

'Paul, I take it, is works manager?'

'Exactly. Good guess. So . . . on that Thursday evening, late, Walter was waiting to do his final rounds, and Chad, as usual, was stuck in some research work or other, and Tolchard hadn't gone home. He reckoned it was *his* job to lock up the research section, which is kind of separate from the rest. Walter reckoned it was his.'

'Now wait a minute,' I cut in. 'You're not going to tell me that Walter shoved him down a staircase . . .'

'What nonsense! Walter believed that whoever did it – *if* anybody did – they'd mistaken Tolchard for himself. It was dark where it happened. It was Walter who could have been expected to do the rounds, and he came running down the stairs from his office. I heard him doing that, when he wouldn't have had time to get *up* there. If you get what I mean.'

'I've registered the fact that *you* were there. You didn't mention that.'

52

'Oh – didn't I? Sorry. I was stuck there late, as usual, struggling with the wages.'

'Walter hadn't chased you off home?'

'He didn't include me in that.'

Walter, it seemed to me, had been well aware that the job was getting on top of his friend Kenneth, and had given him a free hand to fight it on his own.

'But you seem certain of the time of Tolchard's death?'

'Oh yes,' he said brightly. 'I heard it, you see. The scream. Distant, but that floor was quiet. I went running and, as I told the police, I heard Walter clattering down from his office and saw Chad running from the research lab . . .'

Running *from*, I thought. But didn't say. 'What's your point?'

'Somebody else must have been in the building. Must have.'

'Would that be possible?'

He smiled again. When he did that you'd believe every word he said. 'We're not on high-security work, you know. The research block has special locks, but the rest . . .' He shrugged. 'More sherry? No? I expect they're waiting for us in there.'

But his physical attitude indicated no hurry to move. He sat back, limp and resigned, as though he'd said all he dared, and now cringed from my expected questions. So I complied.

'Did your son have a special motive for killing Tolchard?'

'There were terrible rows. He'll tell you.'

'All the same . . . rows hardly justify murder.'

'The police seem to believe they do. There's the possible promotion, too.'

'All right. But earlier on you were suggesting that Walter's death is linked with Tolchard's.'

'How could it be otherwise?'

'Walter's was an accident. Why couldn't Tolchard's have been an accident? A simple slip on the top step . . . something like that.'

'Walter's was not an accident.'

'He'd locked himself away.'

'But you'd know about such things.' He'd stated it as a fact, but he was exploring my potential, his forehead creased with anxiety.

I shook my head. What was he trying to get across to me? 'It's got all the indications of an accidental fall from his window through the conservatory roof.' He said nothing. 'In any event, who would stand to gain? Except my wife and myself, and we

53

were in Wales at the time. He'd changed his will. Everybody else stood to lose by his death.'

'So it would seem.'

'Well . . . wouldn't they? Hasn't Heather told you about the provisions of the new will?' It was a gentle trap.

'Heather will say nothing.'

Good girl. 'But you knew?'

'Walter and I had long arguments, up there in his room. I didn't like what he was doing, not at all. Disinheriting his family . . .'

'And disinheriting you, too?'

He inclined his head. 'I insisted on that. Otherwise – consider my situation. I'd be accused of using my influence.'

'As you were.'

'But *for* them, though. Even so, I could foresee a great deal of unpleasantness. So I insisted. Threw it at him. Shouted at him. I can see his face now. We'd never raised our voices to each other before. But he did it – excluded me. I knew that, when I was asked to witness it. He smiled at me when I took up the pen.'

He shook himself, dragging his mind from the memory.

'But the original will included you?'

He nodded soberly. 'To the sum of twenty-five thousand pounds.' So Mary Pinson had been wrong about that.

'And it was you who had the job of telling the family they'd been cut out of his will?' I knew otherwise, and waited for his confirmation.

'He told me he'd do that. Couldn't wait. By phone, he said.'

'And yet, he was still locking himself away. Afterwards.'

'Ah, but you see, he'd expected anger and dismay. Or I assume he had. Sometimes he could be quite close. But there wasn't any trouble. None I heard about. Nobody went rushing round to the house. So I assume *that* made him suspicious. It would, wouldn't it!'

'Nevertheless, if he told them, then his death, if not accidental, couldn't have been related to money . . . to the will. They, at least, would know they could gain nothing.'

He seemed surprised at that. It was a point he hadn't considered, which I found strange. 'Well of course. I do believe you're right.'

'Yet you still consider the two deaths are connected?'

'I'm certain of it.'

54

I considered him seriously for a moment, then looked down at my pipe. Up again when I had my thoughts organised.

'Mr Leyton,' I said, 'you have just gone to some lengths to explain to me that your friend Walter Mann thought his life was in danger, and that his money and his control of his factory were the reason. No . . . let me say this. You believe that Aleric Tolchard's death was in fact an attempt on Walter's life. You've told me that Walter took measures to protect himself, by locking himself away and changing his will. You're certain he informed his family about that change. And yet you come to me for help for your *son*.'

He stirred uncomfortably. 'I don't see . . .'

'Because you haven't thought this through. If, as you say, Walter would have wasted no time in telling his family about the new will, then none of these would have any reason to kill him, even if that room had been easily accessible. But you still believe that Walter's death and Tolchard's death are linked. You *do* say that?'

'I believe they are.' But his voice was uncertain. I'd shaken him.

'Then we'd have to look for someone who *didn't* benefit from Walter's original will. Someone who didn't kill Tolchard by mistake, but simply because he was Tolchard. Someone who might have gained access to Walter's room because he would not be suspected of offering any danger. Perhaps someone whom Walter had realised was the murderer of Tolchard.'

'You're not to say . . . no, I won't have it.'

'Damn it all, you've brought me here to *prove* your son killed Tolchard.'

He slapped his hands on the arms of his chair, and seemed about to fly at me, but Heather put her head round the door.

'Are you two going to be at it all night? It's a good job it's something that'll keep.' She meant the dinner, but the remark was apposite.

I glanced at my watch. 'Oh hell,' I said. 'If it'll keep – d'you mind if I use your phone? Five minutes,' I pleaded.

Leyton appeared not to understand what I was saying. He stood and stared at me, his mouth moving. Heather looked from one to the other of us, sudden concern darkening her eyes. She took his arm.

'Come along, Ken. It's your favourite.'

They left me alone in the room. The phone was on a table by the window. I had to look up the dialling code for Aberaeron.

But of course, I'd been talking nonsense. Hadn't I? Yet I'd been searching around in my mind for someone whom Walter would have admitted to his locked room. He would probably have done this for Chad Leyton.

I reached Amelia after a short wait. But I was more than five minutes.

6

'Can you speak?' I asked. 'No nurses fussing round?'

'Where are you, Richard?'

'How are you feeling?'

'My arm's very painful, and they've got my leg in traction. Otherwise, I couldn't be better. When shall I see you?'

'I'm stuck here,' I told her. 'At Boreton. It's a wee bit complicated.'

'There shouldn't have been any difficulty over a bit of a legacy.'

'It's rather more than a bit. Not just a piece of silver and grandad's watch.'

She clicked her tongue. If I'd been there, a silent frown would have covered it. On the phone it had to be aural. 'If it's no more than a couple of thousand pounds, Richard, we might just afford that place at Abersoch. I like that.'

'It's all rather complex.'

'Isn't it strange! Whenever you go near anything, without me to look after you, it becomes complicated.'

I didn't want to become involved with explaining all the ramifications over the phone. I'd have been talking for hours. There was also the fact that I wanted to be watching her face as I did so. So I temporised. I told her that the manner of her uncle's death was in question, and that another person's was far from straightforward, my brain racing as I spoke, trying to find some way of putting it and remain unspecific. This is a difficult thing to do without provoking further questions. I was almost in despair when she eventually sighed and said:

'So when shall I see you?'

'Hopefully, tomorrow morning. I'll have to be back here on Sunday, though.'

'Don't hurry,' she advised me. 'Give yourself time to clear up all the details.'

We hung up. I'd need a bit longer than she'd imagined. I went out into the hall, and there was Heather, waiting for me.

'It's only beef stew,' she told me, as though we were sharing a secret. 'It could wait.'

'I'm sorry to have kept you.'

'It doesn't matter. Come and meet Chad.'

They were intending to eat in the room opposite the living room, the two men quietly talking as they waited. Standing together, they were obviously father and son, each wearing the same expression of controlled tension as they spoke of any subject than the one uppermost in their minds.

Chad Leyton greeted me with reserve. He'd heard my verdict on the facts, and had obviously decided that it hadn't been a good idea to bring me there. But nothing was said about it. We sat down to dinner. Throughout it, Heather chattered away blithely, tossing the conversation from father to son, retrieving it, leaving me openings if I cared to use them. Still not one word was said about the business on hand. Kenneth Leyton fielded his share of the chit-chat with a wry smile and a dry wit. Chad gesticulated, laughed, was entertaining, and his eyes, when they met mine, were saturated with misery.

Over the port, I shattered the mood. Yes, we finished with port, but the lady had no intention of retiring. I said:

'There must be something more than I've been told. The motive is weak. The means – a push – would be available to anybody, and so would the opportunity, apparently. The police wouldn't make a charge on so little. The magistrate would have had to be persuaded there was a case to answer. I'm told he adjourned the hearing, but he certainly didn't dismiss the charge. So . . . what about giving me some facts.'

The two men glanced at each other. I beamed at Heather, who looked down at her glass. Leyton said: 'You led me to believe you think Chad is guilty.'

'That is not so. I simply tried to show you that pushing the facts around can only lead to a complete absurdity. Would you care to tell me, Chad? What case did the police present?'

'Heather's better at that sort of thing, and she was in court.'

'Assisting her brother, no doubt. So hers would be the case for the defence. You would have been interrogated by the police. Let's hear the case for the prosecution.'

Heather pouted at me, and Chad gave her a tentative smile. Leyton merely nodded, and kept his eyes on me. Suspiciously.

Chad spoke in a matter-of-fact voice, clearly attempting to take a dispassionate view, but he was serious, not flippant, as one might be when displaying the strength of the enemy. His words were carefully chosen.

'Motive. Dad's told me what he said to you, but that's only a part of it. Tolchard had this rather grand idea . . . do you know about photography, Mr Patton?'

'Very little of the technique.'

'Then I won't go into detail. Perhaps I'll get a chance to show you in the lab. But the company . . . it's made its name with photographic accessories, slide mounts and projectors and screens, developing equipment and special enlargers for colour prints, flash guns, that sort of thing. We've never ventured into actual cameras. I mean to say . . . the Japs have got it all. To compete in that field, you'd need millions of capital. But there's one tiny corner that's hardly been explored. There's been only one stereo camera made anywhere since the fifties.'

'That's the Nimslo,' put in Leyton softly.

'Now dad! It's renticular. It's not the same. Have you seen stereo, Mr Patton? Possibly you saw one of the films they made. No? Well, basically the idea is that you see the picture as it actually was in front of the camera, not just as a flat surface, but in depth, one thing behind the other. The snag's always been that you've had to look at it on a screen, with special glasses, or with a hand viewer to your eyes. And you really needed a special camera. So it never really caught on in a mass way. Tolchard had this idea. If there was some way that a simple print – a pair, in this case – could be picked up and looked at, like an ordinary photograph, but be seen in three dimensions . . .'

There was nothing dispassionate about him now. His face was flushed – possibly the port, though – and his eyes shone, his gestures became eager. And this enthusiasm was, strangely, for Tolchard.

'Say what you like about him,' he said, 'Tolchard was a visionary. A genius, I suppose, all enthusiasms. He saw this – wanted to manufacture a simple camera to take the pairs of negatives . . . . but I'll show you all that. You must come to the lab.

58

The trouble was, he had some idea of a table viewer with back projection on a special glass screen, and I wanted to work on my idea, which was a polarising coating to the actual prints . . . I'll show you,' he repeated.

'I'm sure you will.'

'And mine worked! I spent nearly a year in that lab, working late every evening.'

'Every one!' said Heather in a sepulchral voice.

'*Nearly* every evening,' he qualified. 'And I finally got something that worked.'

'Tolchard wasn't pleased?'

'He was pleased enough. I mean, we hadn't lost any time on *his* ideas, and *they* weren't working. But he was delighted when mine did.'

'A realist,' I suggested.

'A cheat!' said Leyton harshly.

'Let me tell it, dad,' said Chad without emphasis. 'What my father means is that when I spoke about applying for a patent on the process, Tolchard said it belonged to the firm. He said it was in my contract.'

'And was it?'

'We'd find it difficult to dispute,' said Heather. 'Chad worked in his own time, but with lab equipment. There's a very technical legal wording.'

'Tolchard said if I filed for the patent, he'd sue me for breach of contract and claim the patent for the company,' Chad said, his eyes hot.

'But surely,' I protested, 'it would be for Walter to say.'

'You'd think that. But there was something about it in Tolchard's contract,' Heather put in again. 'He had the overall control of his section. It would be difficult to dispute in court—'

'You didn't try!' Chad said warmly.

'It didn't reach the courts, Chad,' she pointed out. I thought she was showing less spirit now than she had to me, her voice was so even and quiet. But she had her reward. She knew how to handle him. Chad gave her a smile, all the anger flowing from his face.

'I rely on her,' he told me.

'But I take it . . .' I glanced round the table. '. . . you weren't prepared to wait for a protracted legal operation and court battles?'

'He told me he could dismiss me, whatever Walter said.'

'And what *did* Walter say?'

Leyton senior rapped the table. 'You know Walter.' I shook my head. He went on: 'Would never make a decision if it could be put off. He thought it would all sort itself out.' He looked hurt. Walter should have done more for him, and for Chad.

'Was he against this scheme?' I asked. 'It would take a lot of money to set this up, the camera and the rest.'

'He was all for it.' Chad was eager. 'Paul was against it, good old no-risk Paul. But Walter wanted more work done on it, more figures. You know what managing directors are like.'

'It was his money, after all.' There was a silence. I'd broken the sequence of narrative. 'And it didn't sort itself out?'

'Tolchard asked me to resign,' said Chad hollowly.

'And I suppose you said something silly, in front of witnesses.'

'I told him I'd see him dead first.'

Leyton looked down at his empty glass, then reached for the decanter. Heather made an impatient sound. I sighed.

'So much for motive,' I said. 'But you know, the prosecution doesn't have to prove motive. It's useful, but it's not a central point of their case.'

Leyton lifted his eyes. 'You're forgetting, we've got our own legal expert.'

'So I was.' I grinned at her. She grimaced. 'What about means? What's special about you, Chad? Are you a better pusher-down-stairs than anybody else?'

It didn't get a smile. Chad said: 'I was working late, on a design for a possible camera. It'd only need to be simple, you see, because the depth of field—'

'Never mind that,' I interrupted.

'Yes. Of course. I was working with a drawing board, using a round ruler. You roll 'em, and all your lines are parallel. It was a bit late, and I'd got absorbed. Then I heard Heather's bike in the car park. She pipped her horn. It's where you can't see from the lab, so I ran out and up those iron stairs, and along the corridor to the left, where she could see me from the end window. I'd grabbed up a couple of the round rulers, to hold up as an X, telling her I'd be down in ten minutes.'

'Which you did? Held 'em up?'

'I saw him do it,' she said.

'Don't tell me.' I held up my hand. 'The medical evidence was that the impact that killed him—'

'The edge of the bottom iron stair,' said Leyton emptily. 'His forehead.'

'All right. So there was perhaps evidence of another blow—'

'The back of his neck.'

'Do be quiet, dad,' said Chad.

'Which,' I plugged on, 'could well have been made by a round ruler.'

'They're rather heavy,' Chad told me. 'Ebony.'

'And of course, when your father said you were running towards him, it was from along the corridor at the head of the stairs, at the *head* of the stairs, not from the lab, at the foot of them?'

Chad nodded solemnly. I stared at Leyton. 'But you said you told the police he was coming from the lab. As you did me.'

He inclined his head. His smile was rueful. 'That was what I said at first.'

'But you . . .' I turned to Heather. 'You told them you'd seen him at the upper window.'

She bit her lip. 'I thought it would help. At the time.'

'And I had to change my story,' Leyton admitted.

'Lovely!' I said. 'I can see now why the police think they've got a case. Motive, means and opportunity, all in one neat little package. And a few lies thrown in for good measure.'

There was an uneasy silence. I felt that in some way I'd let them down, but I couldn't understand what they expected from me. They would have gone over and over it, hunting for a way out. Now they asked me. Was I to snap my fingers and say: 'Well, it's obvious.' Because it wasn't. Nothing was obvious.

Heather was turning her glass in her fingers. She spoke in a stubborn, repressed voice. 'Our defence would be—'

'To hell with your defence,' I said, more angrily than I'd intended. Then I softened it. 'Let's hope he never gets sent for trial.'

'There's something you can do?' Leyton's voice was pitifully eager.

'Not that I can see. I'm not even sure that I ought to get involved. But there's one small point you ought to consider.' Oh, those eyes, fastened on me so expectantly! 'Your father and I were discussing the possibility that Walter Mann's death and

61

Tolchard's were linked,' I said to Chad, who nodded encouragingly. 'It got to the point where I told him you could have done both.' I said that casually. He would have interrupted, but Heather grabbed his arm. 'That was by using the theory that both deaths were motivated from Tolchard's, for which you're the favourite at the moment. But reverse that, and see what you get. If Walter was correct, and Tolchard died in mistake for himself, then you've got to look for somebody who was intent on killing Walter. You get the point? You, Chad, wouldn't have wished that.'

While they were silently considering that, heads together and whispering, I blew through my pipe and began to fill it. I was aware that my pronouncement had not promoted delight. The silence was almost of embarrassment, even disappointment. In the end it was Leyton who spoke for them, in response to eye signals from the other two.

'But we know Walter couldn't have been killed. So it puts a stopper on that idea. How could anybody have got out of that room and locked the door after them? You surely know he had the only available key.'

'There's a way. I'd have thought it was obvious. The point is, *did* Walter have any reason, apart from Tolchard's death, to believe his life was in danger?'

Leyton seemed to think my dismissal of his remarks was a little short, perhaps condescending. But I was tired. It had been a long day, and I wanted to get on the road. He seemed about to protest angrily, but again Chad restrained him.

'You mean before Tolchard's death?'

I spread my hands. 'That seemed to be the final straw for Walter.'

'He nearly had an accident with his car, six months ago. The wheel nuts were loose on one of his front wheels.'

'Anything else?'

'He was almost jostled under a bus,' Heather remembered.

I couldn't recall seeing any buses going through Boreton. 'Where?'

'Birmingham.'

I shook my head. 'Anything else?'

'The river,' she said. 'Don't you remember, Chad? He went fishing. Waded into the Severn, and his thigh boots filled with water. That can be fatal.'

62

'A leak,' protested Chad. 'Anybody can get a leak.'

'In both boots?' she demanded.

'How long ago?' I asked.

'Over a year.'

'Hmm!'

But there could have been other incidents that none of them knew about. Walter, perhaps, had been justified in believing somebody wanted him dead. I slapped my hands on the table.

'Well . . . I really must go. Thank you for the meal. It's been an interesting evening.'

'Is that all you've got to say – hmm?' asked Leyton.

'I'm afraid so. I've got a hundred and fifty miles to drive, and I'm very tired. You really must excuse me.'

'I'll see you out.' Heather was on her feet. 'You clear the table, Chad.' She obviously wanted the final word. I said my good-nights, and she and I went out into the clear, cool night.

She spoke to me as a legal expert, smoothing the emotion from the situation. 'It's bad, isn't it?'

I agreed that it was.

'But you'll think about it?'

'I'll try not to, but I don't suppose I'll succeed.'

'They expect too much.'

'I know how it is. I'll see you on Sunday.'

'Will you?'

'You'll surely be with your brother for the reading of the will.'

'I didn't intend—'

'The reactions could be important.'

She squeezed my arm. 'You've already done some thinking,' she accused me.

I slid into the car. 'Good night. Try to stop them from worrying.'

I like driving across country at night. This time I drove as though the devil was chasing me, the devil of my thoughts. At speed, I needed all my concentration for the road, and the thoughts were shut away.

At a little after midnight I drifted the Volvo on to the caravan site, engine ticking over. Everything was dark and silent. I backed in so gently it wouldn't have disturbed a mouse. I didn't even slam the car door, and paused only to turn on the tap of the gas bottle on the front frame of the caravan.

When I opened the door I paused for a second. I'd need my

lighter for the mantle. I flicked it into flame. Nothing happened. We were no longer in plot 13, though. And anyway, it was too late to blow us up.

7

They had moved Amelia to another bed, next to the end window overlooking the car park, so that I could see her waving as soon as I got out of the car.

Saturday. A relaxing day for hospitals, when nobody seems to mind how long you stay. They'll even find you a cup of tea. I nodded around to the other five women in the ward, all fracture cases, rescued a chair from the side, sat beside Amelia's bed, and said: 'It's me again.'

'You are,' she told me, 'permitted to kiss me.'

I got to my feet and kissed her. 'The way I feel, I was afraid I'd break something else.' I grinned at her. 'How're you feeling?'

'Frustrated.' She pouted.

'I can understand that.'

'And all ears. I notice you haven't brought me any grapes. Not a single one.'

'Later. I'll be back this afternoon.'

'So come on, tell me everything.'

She is remarkably resilient, I've come to appreciate, and now seemed cheerful, though it can't be comfortable with your leg hoisted up in the air. Her arm, though, was clearly the more painful, bandaged and padded in an exaggerated way. She admitted that the painkillers made her drowsy. She was at that time bright and attentive, so I had to guess she'd taken nothing that morning. She didn't tell me, but I could see the pain behind her eyes.

I told her everything. This I managed without too many interruptions, covering first the family relationships and the background to Walter's death, and including the side issue of Tolchard's. This took a long while. I felt in need of my pipe, but couldn't smoke it there.

She said gently: 'Why are you teasing me, Richard? Why tell me all this before you get to the details about the will?'

'It's so that you'll understand. Your uncle changed his will two days before he died. He told his friend, Kenneth Leyton, that he was deliberately disinheriting his family. It was carefully planned. His solicitor wasn't happy about it, but said Walter knew exactly what he was doing. Briefly, each of his children, Paul, Clare and Donald, gets ten thousand pounds, there's a small something or other for Mary Pinson – and the rest is yours.'

Her eyes were huge, her lower lip tucked in her teeth. She nodded.

'There'll be the house and all the furniture in it, and two cars.'

She made a sound in her throat.

'There'll be the balance of his personal investments, when all the dues are cleared. Say a hundred thousand, give or take,' I said casually.

She whimpered.

'And you'll have the controlling interest in a going concern with an estimated capital value of something like half a million pounds.'

'It's ridiculous,' she said quietly, gasping it out. 'Why're you saying this?'

'Because it's true.'

'I don't believe it. There's a catch somewhere. You didn't listen . . .' She stopped on a groan of pain, having moved her left arm in agitation.

'I listened very carefully,' I assured her. 'That's it, more or less as it stands. When you're mobile again, you can walk into that factory and take charge.'

'Such nonsense! It'll be disputed,' she decided.

'Or you could sell your shares, I suppose, though I don't know much about that sort of thing. It's a private limited company.'

'Will you please slow down, and talk sense, Richard. Of *course* it'll be disputed. They couldn't let it go.'

'I'm told by the solicitor that there're no grounds.'

'Insanity, Richard. Poor uncle Walter must have gone crazy, locking himself in his room like that. It's wicked!' she declared, clamping her jaw together angrily.

'What is?'

'Leading us on like this. They'll contest the will – that's the word, contest it – on the grounds of insanity.'

Though I didn't dare to get it going, I took out my pipe and fondled it. She was discussing theory. To her it was a quantity of words signifying nothing concrete, which could be expunged by one touch on the correct button of fate's computer. But I had seen what was involved. The situation was a concrete reality to me. The difficulty was that Amelia has never, I believe, seen life itself with any clear vision. She'd seen it through a rosy screen of her own delightful but naïve personality. She believed that life could be fair, that there was a pattern involved that automatically included a quality called fairness. It was, therefore, not fair that this teasing possibility should be dangled before her, only to be withdrawn, as withdrawn it must be, because it was just as unfair that she should be offered it only at the expense of the others' loss. Even though they might deserve to lose it.

But I am more pragmatic. I'm prepared to face the iniquities, and therefore equally prepared to warm to the smiles of fate when they come along. Besides, Amelia deserved it.

I knew, though, that I'd have to work hard to convince her.

'Insanity in law,' I said solemnly, 'which is what we're talking about, is a rather strange thing. It varies. In murder, to plead insanity you have to show that you were in such a mental state as not to know the nature of the crime. That's the phrase. It's a very difficult thing to prove, because it's hardly sane, in any event, to kill somebody, but if you do, you clearly know you're taking a life.'

'I don't need a lecture, Richard.'

'I've got plenty of time. Now, take wills. To challenge one on insanity grounds, you'd have to show that the chap didn't know what he was doing. But your uncle knew *exactly* what he was doing. He was disinheriting his family. He *did* know the nature of his actions. The inversion of the murder business, sort of.'

'You're very plausible, Richard.'

'It's a right and proper thing that a person's wishes should be complied with,' I said with dignity.

'My, my! You're annoyed, I can see.'

I rubbed my face, in case it'd got a scowl on it. 'I was hoping to see you pleased and happy.'

'I'm happy to know he remembered me at all.'

'He went to the trouble of tracing you, to make sure you're alive. He wanted you to have it, my dear.'

'He traced us?'

'The young lady who died in the explosion – Nancy Rafton –

had been making enquiries for you. It was why she was waiting there, in plot 13, to see you in the flesh.'

'Oh! Yes, I see.' The fingers of her right hand were plucking at the edge of the neatly folded sheet, her eyes watching them. 'But poor uncle Walter, however you weave your legal phrases, couldn't have been right in the head. He'd got a fixation. He thought his family was trying to kill him. One of them, anyway.'

I inclined my head. 'Possibly with good reason. It doesn't mean he was crazy.'

She looked up, shaking her head. 'But of course, I can't accept this. It wouldn't be right.'

I spoke with a neutral tone. 'I'm not sure you can refuse a legacy.'

'You must enquire about it, Richard. There's always something for everything, in the law.'

'You'd probably have to make a deed of gift, or something like that. Giving it all back.' I cleared my throat. 'Or nearly all.'

She nodded, sat back, and smiled. 'There you are then. Simple.'

Simple? I nearly laughed, which would have been a mistake. It would have sounded too full of despair, even for a hospital ward full of fractures.

'All right,' I said. 'You say it wouldn't be right to accept it, but would it be right to hand over a share to the person who killed your uncle? It'd be a complete reversal of what he intended. By law . . .'

'Not some more of your laws!'

'This is criminal law. You're not supposed to benefit from a crime. A murderer can't inherit from the person he's killed. You wouldn't want to go against that, would you?'

She sighed. 'I suppose you're right. That *would* be a bad thing.' You'd have thought she'd just decided to accept a great disappointment, and smile through it. 'But of course.' She brightened. 'Uncle Walter *wasn't* killed, so that's all right. If I thought he was . . .' She shrugged, forgetting, and winced with pain.

I sighed too, but from relief. 'I can't see that it could have been an accident.'

'But of course . . .'

'The window was open, you see. As soon as Mary Pinson had left, and he'd pulled up his bag with the post in, he'd have shut it. He couldn't have died at *that* time, or she'd have heard. So he must have opened it again later. Why? Just so that he could have an accident out of it?'

'Perhaps somebody came and shouted to him from below.'

'All right. Say they did. He wouldn't need to lean out to shout back.'

She waved her good arm. 'So tell me.'

'Somebody else must have opened it, in order to push him through. Perhaps he was knocked out first.'

'Ha!' she said in contempt. 'Somebody he allowed in? When he was keeping people out!'

I got up and went to look out of the window. My Volvo looked very tiny from there. I'd left the door open, I saw, in my eagerness to get to her. Perhaps I should have taken my time, preparing myself. After all, I ought to have expected her reaction. When I turned round, she was watching me with amusement. My move. It was like a chess game for high stakes.

'He'd changed his will,' I reminded her. 'He had no more reason to be afraid that somebody was after him.'

'But he was still locking his door. So he still wouldn't open it.'

'Suppose he did, to somebody he believed to be safe. Will or not, somebody he had no reason to fear.'

'Suppose away. But do sit down, Richard, please. It's more comfortable for me.'

'Sorry.'

As I walked back round the bed, she went on: 'He'd surely lock the door, after letting this person in.'

'Yes. I'd say that.'

'And this person subsequently pushed him from the window?'

'That's how I see it.'

'But Richard, you're forgetting the key. The door was found locked, and he had the key on him. You're not suggesting this mythical murderer climbed out?'

'It's not that sort of thing. No mountaineers amongst the suspects.'

'Then it could not have been done.' She nodded, satisfied.

We were then interrupted by a nurse, who'd come to take temperatures and things and make marks on the chart. Have you ever noticed how trim and efficient, and utterly feminine, the women nurses look in their uniforms? And don't they know it! It will be a great loss for humanity if the feminists manage to neutralise them into drab, sloppy white trousers and jackets.

'Richard,' Amelia was saying, 'you know it had to be an accident.'

'The key?' I dismissed it with a gesture. 'The locked door means nothing. If Walter was knocked out, the key would have simply been taken from round his neck before he was pushed from the window, then replaced down in the conservatory. Simple. The thing was on a chain round his neck.'

She considered this, took a drink of her orange juice, and considered it some more. At last, having given me enough time to revise my theory, she asked: 'But haven't you forgotten something, Richard?'

'Have I?'

'The dog, Richard. Sheba.'

'Oh Lord!'

'Exactly. The way Mary Pinson spoke, Sheba must have been Walter's dog. She said Sheba would have your hand off if you raised it to Walter. So surely Sheba would spend a lot of time with him in that room, and surely, when Mary went out, she'd leave the dog with Walter. And with Sheba there, what then? A murderer would have to have the key in his hand before he'd dare to push Walter through the window, and how could he get hold of it without some sort of violence? With Sheba there? Really, Richard!'

The way I see it, sitting in that bed, almost lying and with your leg up high, the blood runs from it to your head, and gives your brain a boost. Mind you, Amelia's pretty smart at any time. It's just that she'd seen it at once, and it'd never occurred to me. Annoying.

'Don't you think, Richard, that you ought to find out where Sheba was that morning?'

'I shall certainly have to do that.'

'Because if she was in there with my uncle, you'll have to accept it as a locked room situation. Isn't that what the police call it?'

'They don't call it anything, my love, they simply break the door down.'

'But it would mean he couldn't have been killed.'

I simply looked at her.

'And I don't feel I could accept anything from this will unless he was.'

'I suppose not.'

'And by his family,' she specified.

She was adding conditions by the second. 'Will one of them do, or must it be all three?'

She laughed. Heads turned in the ward. Amelia, of them all, had the least to laugh about. 'Don't look so glum, Richard.'

But I hadn't told her about the Stag. I tried to grin, but my face was stiff.

'Look on the bright side,' she told me severely. 'With uncle Walter's death virtually proved to be an accident, it's reasonable to assume this Aleric Tolchard's death wasn't meant as an attempt on Walter's life.'

But the window was open, I told myself. I had to cling to the fact of the open window.

'So that Mr Tolchard's death,' she went on placidly, 'was probably quite unrelated to the will and all that. And you can see what that means.' In case I couldn't, she spelled it out. 'It means that your young friends, Chad Leyton and Heather Carne, are in deep trouble. Unless you can find any new motives, and all the other stuff you're always digging for. So . . . if you need my advice . . .'

She waited. Could she possibly imagine that I did not? I nodded, trying to look attentive when my mind was racing.

'Then you'd better forget all about uncle Walter's death, and concentrate on Mr Tolchard's. I know that's really what you want to do. It's been obvious all the time.'

I licked my lips and cleared my throat, and said: 'If you're quite decided to reject your inheritance, then all I've got to do is hear the will read, and come away. All the rest could follow later. I'd have no further business in Boreton.'

She tilted her head, pursed her lips, and her eyes glinted with humour. And love. I ached, then, to take her in my arms.

'I want you here, Richard,' she said softly. 'I need you – it's a lot to handle on my own. But I don't want you here with a vacant mind, most of it back at Boreton, and sulking because there's a problem that's beaten you.'

'You know I don't sulk.'

'You brood. You go vague. You walk into trees and things.'

I grinned. 'I never.'

'So you go back there, and clear it all up for those two young people, and as quickly as you can.'

I got to my feet. 'Is it all right if I just *think* about Walter?'

She smiled, lifting her head and pursing her lips. I kissed her gently, so as to cause no pain. Just try holding back in those circumstances. Her eyes were moist when I turned away.

With a last wave to the window, I drove back to the caravan site. There were plans to be made, but I couldn't make up my mind what plans. Did I, for instance, leave the caravan there, and dash wildly backwards and forwards with an unfettered Volvo? Or did I tow the caravan to Boreton, as a useful place to lay my head? But the only parking available at Boreton would be the drive at The Beeches, when I could just as easily accept Mary Pinson's suggestion of using one of the available rooms. Yet, if I was to assume that Amelia was not to take up her inheritance, I theoretically had no moral right to use the house. Nor the drive, come to think of it. Add to this the fact that to take the caravan there would carry the implication that I'd moved my centre of residence to Boreton, and I had to consider the emotional effect this would have on Amelia. It would verge on desertion.

No, the caravan would have to be left at Aberaeron, and my forays to Boreton would have to be made with this in mind. It was a question of priorities, and there was no doubt what those were: Amelia's welfare and peace of mind.

So that settled the question of shopping. I didn't need to do any; I could eat anywhere and not live from the caravan.

I had time to enquire about Cindy's welfare. On that Saturday morning the site was busy, with people leaving and people arriving. The friends who'd offered to take care of Cindy weren't due to go until the following week-end, so no decisions had to be taken immediately. I discovered the little girl walking Cindy on her lead.

Cindy knew me. She licked all available surfaces of flesh, but clearly life with the little girl was pleasurable. She had not, as I'd have expected, treated the tiny dog as a baby, wheeling her round in a pram and cooing over her in her arms. She was copying the grown-ups by treating her with dignity. She did, however, her parents told me, allow Cindy to share her bed. They were happy to allow the situation to continue.

That off my mind, I cleaned the caravan, had a meal, and returned to the hospital for a long, afternoon stay, accompanied by grapes. Plural. We chatted a little about Boreton, me filling in details I'd missed, but Amelia had had to resort to her painkillers and was dozy.

When the house physician came round, and the dressing had

to be changed, I left. Amelia plainly didn't want me there to witness her distress.

Evening at the site. The sun was declining. A man in jeans and a blouson was sitting on the front frame of our caravan, smoking a cigarette. He stood and watched as I backed the Volvo into the space available, then approached as I shut the door.

'Detective-Inspector Melrose,' he said, producing his warrant card. 'Can I have a word with you, Mr Patton?'

I didn't look at his warrant. No need. He was definitely a policeman. Inspector, though! He couldn't have been more than thirty. But they shoot up the scale these days, starting with a law degree. He was casual and bland, but his mouth was determined, and his chin jutted with a challenge he would need to control if he wanted to get to the top. There was no trace of a Welsh accent.

'Better come inside, and I'll brew some tea.'

I paused to turn on the propane gas bottle, then opened up.

8

He sat on the bench seat behind the folding table and watched me, tapping a cigarette pack on the table surface.

'You always do that?' he asked.

For a moment I thought he was querying my tea-making technique. I glanced round.

'Turn on the tap outside,' he explained.

Busying myself with cups and sugar, and putting out the milk, fresh from the farmer's Jerseys that morning, I said: 'It's habit. A safety measure you get used to. Always turn off at the mains, sort of.'

'So you have to use mantles.' He waved, utilising the end of the gesture to prod a cigarette between his lips.

I now saw where we were heading, and gave him the information he wanted.

'A lot of the sites have standpipes for water and outlets for electricity these days. You just connect up, and pay as you use. That's fine for the people who come and settle for the whole of their holidays, but if you move around there're places that don't have the outlets. Like here. So you'll find most caravans carry gas bottles and gas cookers, and of course gas mantles, unless you're going to run your battery down. It becomes routine to turn off the tap on the gas bottles every time you leave your caravan. Safety, you see.'

The kettle was singing. I had time to light my pipe. He was not actually smiling, but the wrinkles round his eyes were deeper.

'I know you're an ex-copper, Mr Patton.' At my raised eyebrows, he went on: 'Yes, I checked. My rank, you were. So we talk, and I don't have to draw it out, word by word. All right with you?'

I didn't ask why he'd found it necessary to check on me. I nodded. 'But you'll need to ask. I don't know what's on your mind.'

'Plot 13.'

'That much I guessed.'

'That day, you came back late.'

'We'd been way up north, Abersoch way.'

'And the young woman, Nancy Rafton, was already occupying plot 13?'

'She was.'

'Which you'd come to consider as virtually yours?'

'Not quite like that. But it's superstition, you see. We'd go away and return after a fortnight, and usually it'd be empty. The farmer said he'd try to wangle that, but he couldn't enforce it.'

I got up to pour boiling water in the pot, and sat down again to give it five minutes.

'Your wife isn't superstitious?'

He hadn't asked about me. On Fridays I walk between the joints of paving slabs, if there's an 'r' in the month. 'Amelia,' I said, 'will cross the road in order to walk under a ladder. She's very superstitious. She thought plot 13 was lucky.'

'But it wasn't, was it?'

'Perhaps she'll change.'

He rattled the spoon in his saucer. I got up to pour the tea. He continued placidly. 'This time there was the other caravan in plot 13. You parked your outfit a little distance back, and you both got out to look. Miss Rafton had apparently just driven in, but the caravan had been there . . .'

'I could tell that. It'd got a settled look.'

'Been there for three days. She got out of her car and went to the door . . .'

73

'Flicking her lighter.'

'Yes. But did *she* go to her gas bottle first and turn it on, as you did?'

I screwed up my eyes, concentrating on the visual memory. Tea slopped in my saucer. 'No,' I decided. 'Straight from her car to the caravan door.'

He was spooning in sugar, concentrating on it. 'So that *she* couldn't have been an experienced caravanner – as you are?'

'True,' I admitted modestly.

'She probably always left it turned on.'

'Conceivably.'

'Mr Patton . . .' Now his eyes, clear grey I saw, were on me above the rim of his cup. 'I've been making a few enquiries. She was away all that day. She'd previously been asking around for your wife.'

'I was told that.'

'And she worked for an enquiry agency. Possibly she'd decided to report back, personally, to the client.'

Whom I now knew to have been Walter, but I said nothing.

'Then returned, perhaps, for a bit of a holiday herself. I'm only guessing,' he admitted, almost with shame. He was a man who had to have facts, not conjectures. 'But in any event, I have a witness who was up with a sick child, and who can say that Miss Rafton was awake very early that morning, because she saw a light in her caravan. That would be a mantle, Mr Patton. There is another witness who will say that Miss Rafton drove away just after sun-up. Have you anything to say to that?'

I thought about it. The question was: did I have anything I wanted to say? I looked at him. He seemed a tough and inflexible character, but at that moment his thin, firm mouth moved towards a smile, before he tamed it.

'I'm asking,' he said, 'because I need your help. My super would tell me I shouldn't involve civilians, as you are now. I would tell *you* that I'll use whatever and whoever might help me. So – on those terms – what do you have to say?'

This is a well-used trap for the unwary. I'm trusting you, so you can trust me. But he knew I wasn't one of the unwary, so perhaps *he* knew that I could trust him, and that I'd realise that. I said carefully:

'A person, perhaps an amateur with caravans, might wake in

the dark and light the mantle, but leave when the sun's up, and not notice it was still on, and leave it going.'

'Just as I thought. So if somebody came along and turned it off at the bottle, casual-like, then on again, the mantle would go out but the gas would go on feeding in slowly, turning the caravan into a potential bomb.'

'A child,' I ventured. 'Not understanding.'

'I've tried it with yours. The gas control taps are a bit too stiff for children.'

'So you reckon you've got a murder enquiry on your hands?'

'Rather more than that.' He sounded self-satisfied about it. 'Plot 13, you see. It could well be expected that your caravan would be occupying that slot. If she'd reported back to the client, quite specifically: she's at plot 13, so and so and so . . . You get my point? I believe that caravan explosion was intended for your wife, and that someone, who didn't know her by sight, mistook Miss Rafton for her.'

You will have realised that I'd already thought of that, but had tried not to allow it to intrude in the forefront of my mind. The idea made my flesh crawl, now that it'd been prodded into life.

'I wouldn't want to think that,' I murmured.

'But I have to. Don't you realise? I've got to consider whether it's necessary to put a guard on her.'

'You don't need to take it—'

'With you dashing off for days on end, the moment your wife's in hospital . . .' His nostrils quivered with distaste. '*Somebody* ought to keep an eye on her.'

I sighed. If there was anything I didn't want, it was this possibility being brought to Amelia's attention. To have my own vague conjecture confirmed in this way also intruded into the arrangement I'd made with her. How could Walter's death have been anything but murder, if the explosion had been intended for Amelia? I had to stall him off. Of course, a punch on the nose is useful for this sort of thing, but the truth's less energetic.

'It's complicated,' I said, 'but I don't have to go into detail. It's true that my wife might have been a target. It's one of these will situations. Her uncle has died, just a week after the explosion. She inherits a great deal. If she'd died in the explosion, her inheritance would've been returned to the estate, and shared out, and the status would have been quo-ed.'

His eyes were bright, and he was leaning forward eagerly. 'Go on.'

I shrugged. 'As my wife didn't die, she's already inherited. If she died now, I'd inherit from her. So you see, whatever motive there was for killing her *then*, it's gone now. You needn't trouble your head about protection.'

Did I think I was going to get away with that? Not a bit of it. His rather expressionless face came alive with interest, and he was impelled to his feet. You can't do this in caravans; he got his thighs caught under the table. He slumped down again.

'So that's where you've been!'

I nodded. 'Legal details.'

'Legal details, my ass. You've been poking around.' He thrust a finger towards my nose. Another snag with caravans, there's no retreat from thrust fingers.

'One can't,' I said with dignity, 'help asking questions.'

'And this place, where the uncle died?'

'Boreton-Upon-Severn,' I told him reluctantly.

'Anywhere near Bridgnorth?'

'They're both on the Severn, some miles apart.'

'Then *that's* where I'll find my murderer.' He thumped the table with enthusiasm. 'Miss Rafton's agency's in Bridgnorth.'

If there was anything I didn't want, it was police intervention. They already had one murder investigation on their hands at Boreton, into which I hoped to make my own discreet intervention, but it wouldn't be easy to link two murders 150 miles apart. Yes it would. Tolchard's death had provoked Walter into changing his will, which had conceivably led to the explosion, possibly – no, probably – intended for Amelia.

'It's a bit out of your territory,' I said, to discourage him.

'You don't know my super. He'll get me a dispensation.'

'*They* won't like that.'

'My super will. He'll love to see the back of me for a while. When are you going there again?'

Did he expect to cadge a lift? 'Tomorrow morning,' I said bleakly. 'Reading of the will. Inquest on Monday,' I added. 'Morning,' I said, rubbing it in, knowing he'd never be able to make it.

'Inquest?' He blinked.

'I told you. My wife has already inherited. Her uncle died.' I couldn't help taunting him with an extra titbit. 'He died two days after changing his will in her favour.'

'Did he now!'

'An accident. A pure accident.'

'Another accident? Oh brother!' He glanced at his watch. 'I'll be off. Might just catch the super at home. Get him out of bed if I have to. I could still get to the inquest.'

'I'm sure they'll welcome you with open arms,' I assured him.

He'd mastered the trick now, and slid sideways along the bench seat. He thrust out his hand. 'You've been very helpful, Mr Patton. We'll meet again.'

Not if I could help it. I think I smiled, but it was becoming dark in the caravan. I watched him from the window, a flitting shadow, and tried to light the mantle, but my hand wasn't steady and I broke it, so I had to set fire to a new one. Yes, I was upset. He'd out-thought me all the way through.

In the morning there was time for an early visit, but I said nothing to Amelia about Inspector Melrose and the thoughts he'd provoked. I tried to be cheerful, and promised to phone, or be back, the following evening. She told me not to forget to ask about the dog. I didn't tell her that dog or not I was going to have to prove her uncle had been murdered.

I got away from there at ten o'clock. Or rather, I walked out to the hospital car park at ten o'clock, but Melrose was waiting by the Volvo, trying to hide his delight behind a cigarette. It was a small barrier for such a grand delight.

'I've got it!' he burst out. 'On liaison. Full support from the local lot.'

I was clearly expected to be pleased. 'Smashing,' I said.

'I'll make it for the inquest. See you there, shall I?'

'I hadn't thought of attending.'

'Then I'll see you around. Look after yourself.' He slapped me on the shoulder as though we were long-established friends, and opened my car door for me.

I got in, my face fixed, raising my hand. The fool was waving when I glanced in the rear-view mirror.

I'd done nothing, absolutely nothing, to inspire his obvious friendship. But a professional policeman, especially in the CID, can find it a lonely and friendless existence. Perhaps he saw me as the only innocent creature in a world crawling with predators.

Satisfied with this rationalisation, but not with the possible complications, I drove fast for Boreton, and straight to The Beeches. I was now becoming familiar with the route, so that there was a corner of my mind available for thought. This was not necessarily an advantage. I should have used it to assess the current situation, but there was a vague and tenuous trend to my thoughts, more an assembly of mood than an arrangement of fact. Surprisingly, there was a distinct reluctance to be returning at all.

This I recognised in its contrast with my mood on the previous journey in the other direction. Then there had been eagerness, to get to Amelia, and afterwards to return. There had been something specific to return to, a security, a home, a new start. Now all this was melting into the mist. I should have anticipated Amelia's reaction, and planned how best to handle it, to persuade her. Now I drove fast to The Beeches, with specific instructions from her on how best to justify shading her from the warm glance of fate.

There would be no sun that day. I had watched the clouds mounting ahead of me as I drove eastward. The day of the reading. I could see no possibility of anything but stress and anger ahead. At one-thirty I parked in the drive, behind a BMW 320. The reading was to be at two.

I walked round to the rear, which already had impressed its lure on me. Three men were erecting tubular scaffolding over the conservatory, preparatory to starting the necessary repairs. Clare was standing a little way back, watching them with a proprietorial interest. She was dressed not as a visitor to a formal occasion, but casually in a tweed skirt and a light jumper, a black silk scarf at her neck. She gave the impression of one who had come intending to stay.

'And look for any cracked panes. Every one to be replaced – you hear? It's to be exactly as it was.'

She cupped one elbow in her other palm, poising a cigarette in front of her face, and nodded, though whether in emphasis or acknowledgement of my presence I couldn't tell. The men continued as though they hadn't heard. I could have told her they would not be the team who did the glazing work, but I didn't trouble. I edged past, but I'd guessed she had noticed me from the first moment. Very little would escape Clare.

'I had to see Carne about this,' she said into the air, though it must have been intended for me. 'He had to authorise it. Such officious twaddle! There's a snack in the dining room, if you're hungry.'

I realised I was. I said thank you and went into the kitchen.

Mary Pinson smiled, the brightest bit of the day so far. There might have been a snack around, but in the kitchen there was a meal.

'So there you are,' she said. 'You're cutting it fine. I've done you a bit of sirloin, and there's lemon meringue pie to follow.' She eyed me with calculation, as though detecting a depleted pound from my regular 225. 'You'd better have it here.'

I grinned at her. 'Wheel it on.'

She was the type who likes to watch others eating heartily. I was aware of her attention. She allowed me to work my way into it before she spoke again.

'Mrs Patton – how is she?'

'As they say, as well as can be expected. She won't be mobile for some time, though. Her name's Amelia, by the way.'

As I spoke, I realised I was assuming that Mary Pinson might at some time need to know that. To welcome Amelia. I put my head down and continued to clear the plate, pushing it aside in time to receive the pie, and asked: 'The dog. Sheba. I don't see her around.'

'Donald's taken her for a walk.'

Ah . . . Donald! I hadn't given much thought to Donald, who hadn't been mentioned in connection with the factory.

'He came by bus,' she went on, her voice even, 'and walked from Boreton.'

'And he still had enough energy to take Sheba for a walk?'

'Clare came, you see. I think he prefers Sheba's company. Would you like coffee?'

'Love it. White, with sugar, if you don't mind. I was going to ask you, Mary. About Sheba. That day, the day Walter died . . . where was Sheba? Did you leave her down here, in the kitchen?'

I managed to say this casually, though so much depended on her answer. It did not deceive her; I saw her mouth twitch.

'You won't leave it alone, will you! I *told* you – it had to be an accident. But I didn't tell you about Sheba. I kept that in reserve, to see if you'd persist. And you *are* persisting.' She shook her head, sad for me and my delusions. 'Sheba was Walter's dog. She spent most of her time up there with him in his room. Of course she was there that day, when I left. And there she was when I

79

came back, her head out of that open window and howling. It was how I knew that Walter had fallen. Knew at once. Poor Sheba!'

She placed my coffee on the table before me, her head close to mine, suddenly speaking softly. 'So we'll have no more silly talk about murders, shall we? Unless you're going to say . . .' She drew back, her face distorted by an abrupt, girlish giggle. '. . . that Sheba pushed him from the window.'

I thrust my chair back and got to my feet. 'It would explain Sheba's distress,' I pointed out.

Which had now disappeared completely. She burst into the kitchen, the smell of food tormenting her and the excitement of company distracting her from it.

Standing behind her in the doorway was Donald.

Donald – the youngest of the three children. He'd have been about twenty-eight, old enough to have grown away from the rejection gesture of untidy disorder, as adopted by youth, and yet still carrying it with him. Tall and slim, even thin, with the tattered hair Amelia recalled as belonging to his father, riotous above a wide forehead and a long face, clean and shaven. The anorak, in the pockets of which his hands were buried, had suffered the constant wear of a vast number of days, and possibly nights. His slacks were baggy and dirty, his suede shoes scuffed. The pallor of his face seemed to indicate illness, but his eyes suggested strain.

'If those are your men outside,' he said to me, his voice tight, 'you ought to keep an eye on them. They'll smash the place down with their damned scaffolding.'

And that, it appeared, was all he had for me. He looked away. His smile at Mary softened his expression.

It was to me she spoke. 'I've let him have the room he's always used, when he's here.'

It was a hint to him, a warning. His eyes were at once cautious. I wondered how much she'd already told him. He spoke as though I was no longer there.

'There's otters under the bank, higher up. Sheba went wild, but they swam rings round her.'

I was aware of a wet nose in my hand. A boxer's face is flat, so you don't get just the nose, it's the whole face. 'She's soaking,' I told him.

'She's got her own towel,' Mary said. 'You'll want to wash your hands. I'll show you.'

She wanted to get me out of there, and away from Donald's surly attitude. I glanced at him. He was unsure of his position, the poor manners masking his embarrassment. In any encounter he would always react in the wrong way, self-consciousness crippling him. Yet there was intelligence in his eyes, and an awareness. His sensitivity was over-active.

I followed Mary through a door in the rear of the kitchen, along a short corridor, and thus into the hall. It was the first time I'd been to the front of the house, to view its faded splendour. The trend was towards marble and dark oak, to ponderous hat-stands and gloomy oak chests, black with an eternity of dust polished into the grain. The stairs ran up from one side of it, wide, curving towards the landing, the deep carpeting firmly trapped with brass stair-rods, each one polished to perfection.

'Up to the landing, and the first door on the right,' she told me. 'I've put you a clean towel.'

I found myself in a reception bathroom for guests, complete with facilities that were very old, yet apparently little used. Everything worked. The tablet of soap was fresh. She had prepared for me, yet had not been certain whether or not I was simply a guest.

It was unfortunate that my return down the stairs coincided with the new arrival, Paul obviously. He was talking forcefully with Clare, who'd gone round to the front to meet him. Mary Pinson was standing at the open door. I marched down like the lord of the manor.

'It's quite out of the question,' Paul was saying. 'I'm seeing the shop steward tomorrow. Really, Clare, my life's been a misery . . .'

He saw me, and stopped dead in the middle of the hall. Behind him, almost hidden by his bulk and subdued by his forceful character, followed a thin and sallow woman in full mourning, her face set in stubborn patience.

'Who's this?' asked Paul.

It had been an effort not to pause, myself. I continued down to face him. Perhaps I smiled. I left it to him to make the first move towards extending his hand. He didn't make one.

'Richard Patton,' I said. Nothing else. Let him guess.

He frowned. There was puzzlement in his eyes, and a sudden confusion. He blustered his way out of it. 'Guests? At this time! Really . . . Clare . . .'

His air of injured authority had melted away. It was something he exercised with those who would accept it, and who understood his necessity for it. He was, after all, works manager, and in this role must have been using authority every minute of his working days. But did he merely toss it around, instead of exercising it? Now that I came to consider him more carefully, I saw that for all his bulk – as tall as Donald but much thicker about the neck, wider in the shoulders, even sporting a small pot – he seemed to shrink within himself. There was a flabbiness to the flesh round his jaw, and a looseness to his mouth. The movements of his head suggested uncertainty. He was a man aware of his inadequacy, using bluster to hide it, unaware that in this way he drew attention to it.

Mary, with pursed lips, was shaking her head. He scrambled for it, managing to say: 'For the will, is it? Well . . . I suppose . . .'

Donald rescued him, coming in from the kitchen. 'Paul,' he said. 'How are you? And Evelyn. You haven't changed, Evelyn.' There was a hint of irony there.

Paul nodded. Not a smile, I noticed. There was even disapproval, which might well have been meant for Donald's clothes, for such a formal and important occasion. But it was deeper than that. His words indicated so.

'They managed to locate you, then?'

Donald shrugged. 'You know I always kept in touch with dad.'

'You'd need to, of course. But no word for us . . .'

'Would there have been any point?' Donald demanded, bitterness carving sharp edges to it. Then he walked past his brother to his sister-in-law, took her shoulders in his hands, and leaned forward to kiss her on the cheek. 'As lovely as ever, Evelyn. Why don't you leave him and come to live with me?'

It was only then, walking past to get out into the air, that I realised this woman must have been about Donald's age. The beaten resignation had fooled me. When she put her hand to Donald's cheek her smile was young, and probably rare, her eyes moist. 'You're a fool, Don.'

Paul had flung open double doors to a room at the side of the hall. 'I suppose we're doing it in here.' He marched in, as I marched out on to the drive, just in time to see our legal advisers arrive in a very nice Saab 9000.

Philip Carne was smart in a blue three-piece suit, dark tie, black shoes. Very official, as befitted a will-reading. On a Sunday, too!

His account would reflect it, might even pay for the suit. Heather was carrying the briefcase. She was wearing a slim black skirt with a little black jacket and a blouse with frills all up the front. She looked suitably solemn, though too beautiful to be taken seriously as a solicitor. I stood aside, winking at her. She pouted as they walked past.

Mary had prepared the dining room, which was one of those shadowed rooms at the front, the windows heavily draped, the furnishings plain and functional. Maybe it would come to life with an evening meal, the two chandeliers sparkling, the silver-ware gleaming, the Royal Doulton polished. Now it seemed drab. Mary had left two of the eight chairs behind the table, but had distributed the other six around the room. To one end was a serving trolley bearing, as mentioned, snack sandwiches and bottles of red and white wine. Having already eaten, I poured myself a glass of wine, and chose an isolated chair to one side. The family did not sit together, but were spread out along the back wall. Mary slid in at the last moment, and when she saw that Carne and his sister were settled at the table, she quietly retired to the discreet chair she'd placed for herself in a corner.

That large and imposing briefcase held only one document: the will.

'Now!' said Philip Carne, clearing his throat. 'Mr Mann's will.'

9

He did not simply read it out. That would have clashed with his cultivated personality of racy informality. But he was careful to read every word of the details of the actual legacies.

'Last will and testament,' he said, 'of Walter Donald Mann, then . . .' raising his head and smiling thinly'. . . there's a lot of legal rubbish we have to put in to make it water-tight. After that, he listed his bequests, starting with Mary Pinson.'

He beamed at her. She looked down at her hands.

'"To Mary Vivienne Pinson, my dear and loving friend, I leave the sum of ten thousand pounds, and the continuing use of the living quarters and facilities she has become accustomed to at my home, The Beeches, to be enjoyed during her lifetime, or until such time . . ."' He looked up. 'There's a great deal of wording here, designed to cover any eventualities, such as the possible sale of the house. In that event . . .' He returned to the will. '"In the event of such loss of the facilities before-mentioned, she shall be paid the sum of twenty-five thousand pounds, such sum to be kept in trust and invested for her by the executor." That's me,' he said brightly.

There was silence. Mary was staring at him in disbelief. I caught her eye and nodded. She flicked me a smile, colour flooding her cheeks. Paul made a growling sound in his throat.

'I've never heard of anything . . . When was this will made?'

'It was signed and witnessed two days before his death.' Carne raised a hand to the flutter of voices. 'I can tell you that, apart from a suitable increase in the actual amounts, the bequest is in exactly the same form as it appeared in his former will. Can I get on? Down to the nitty-gritty?'

They were silent, but already faces were set. Carne nodded, and returned to the will.

'"To my children, Paul, Clare and Donald, I bequeath to each the sum of ten thousand pounds, such sums to be paid free of duties and encumberments . . ."'

He got no further. A chair crashed over. Paul was on his feet, shouting, Clare had her hand over her mouth, biting on dirty words. The nitty was proving to be too gritty. Donald had not moved. He sat, leaning forward, his face grey. Even in the dimness of that room I could detect sweat on his forehead. I wondered whether he was going to be sick.

'This is outrageous!' Paul was shouting, his wife tugging at his sleeve. 'I must protest . . .'

Clare lowered her hand. 'We'll see about this. We'll bloody see.' Then she beat both fists on her knees and made a high-pitched keening sound between her teeth.

Carne waited. He looked down at the table. Paul shook off his wife's hand and went forward to thump on the surface, bouncing the will about. He was shouting something into Carne's face, whilst behind him, Clare was screaming: 'The house! The house!'

Donald had not moved, but Mary had gone to him and was bending over him, whispering in his ear. He reached for her hand and held it.

In the face of Carne's impassive silence, the uproar gradually fell away. He was earning his money. Heather stared straight ahead. Perhaps this aspect of the law had not been mentioned in her training, but I could have told her that more mayhem is committed in domestic situations than all the violence on the dangerous streets.

At last Paul returned to his chair, which his wife had righted for him. But he could not prevent himself from turning to her repeatedly and venting his whispered fury on her.

'"The residue of my estate",' read Carne steadily, '"I bequeath to my niece Amelia Jane Patton." Which about covers it,' he finished, reaching hopefully for his briefcase. 'Mr Patton is with us and has produced a power of attorney signed by his wife, only two days ago.'

'Residue?' cried Clare. 'What residue, for Christ's sake? Was he mad, or something? What about the rest of it?'

'The word "residue" in this context means all that's left after the other bequests are cleared, and the death duties and so on. The rest of it as you put it, Clare. It means this property here and its contents – subject of course to Miss Pinson's bequest – and his shares in Mann Optics, plus the balance of his investment portfolio and his bank account.'

'I'm not having it,' cried Paul. 'D'you hear, I'm not having it!' Which was a bit stupid, considering he certainly wasn't. But his voice held the weary, battered defeat of a man who has lost a lot of discussions with the shop floor convenor.

But Clare was not defeated. In a shrill voice she declared she would see a solicitor, a *proper* solicitor. She said they hadn't heard the last of it, by a long chalk.

Donald was way beyond defeat. It seemed he was destroyed. I saw Mary taking him out, holding him by the arm.

I sat through it. Heather did not look at me. Paul gradually talked himself out of the room, and Clare screeched herself into floods of tears. I sat, feeling miserable, wondering whether Amelia, had she been there, would have announced there and then that she was handing it all back, out of pity, or have remained silent out of disgust.

At last I was alone with Carne and his sister. He smiled at me wanly, in apology. 'I've seen worse. More trouble is caused by thoughtless wills—'

'You think this was thoughtless?'

'Not *this* one. He thought about it very deeply.'

'So what happens now?'

'I do a lot of homework on the financial aspect, and submit it for probate. Say a couple of months . . . three. Depending on the aggro we get.'

'Aggro?' A word I hated.

'They'll consult solicitors. There'll be correspondence and phone calls. Eventually they'll be told there are no grounds on which the will can be contested. It will be proved. And that'll be that.'

'In the meantime?'

'I've explained. A certain amount of money can be made available, and I see no reason why you shouldn't move in here, you and your wife when she's fit to move. I've no doubt Mary will look after her.'

'I'm sure she could. But there's a snag.'

It doesn't take long to tidy away documents in a briefcase when there's only one. Carne was poised to leave. He paused, frowning.

'I don't know of any snags.'

'My wife isn't happy with it. She doesn't feel content to deprive Walter's immediate family, unless she can be convinced he was justified in what he did.'

He sat down again. Heather went to look out of the window. 'Ah,' he said. 'It makes things difficult.'

'Especially for me. Don't you see!' I said, impatient at his blank stare. 'You saw their reactions. It was a complete shock to them. So Walter didn't, after all, tell them he'd disinherited them.'

'I can't understand that. It would've been his very first action.'

'Yes. But if he didn't, and they knew he was intending to, then there's a very good motive for his murder.'

But what're you saying, Richard, I said to myself. Not only a locked room, but a guarded one as well.

'I see.' He beat a rapid rhythm with his fingertips on the table. He did not approve of this talk of murder. His work would be purely civil, no doubt. Heather's would eventually be criminal, her natural venue the cut and thrust of the open court. 'So . . .' His tone was severe. 'Your intention is to prove Walter was murdered, in order to make very sure your wife accepts the lot?'

'Crudely put, yes.'

It was then that Heather turned from the window. Her eyes were bleak. I could see she'd be a deadly opponent in court.

'So all that talk was empty?' she demanded. 'Your promise to

86

Chad – that means nothing? You've got to concentrate on your own . . .'

'Promise? I made no promise.'

'Your fancy words, your glib theories!'

'Will you let me get a word in!' I said loudly. She was silent, pouting, her hair untidy again. 'My wife made me promise to help my young friends, as she called you and Chad, and to concentrate on Tolchard's death. Perhaps, if I'm lucky, it might throw some light on Walter's.'

Carne said: 'I've never heard the like.' Heather looked as though she might throw her arms around me, but in her professional splendour she remembered her dignity. 'You had me worried then.'

'Me too. But you'll have to thank my wife. You can kiss her when you see her. *She* won't mind.'

I saw the devil in her eyes, and grinned. Carne said: 'Well . . . I don't know.'

'I shall have the assistance of a genuine detective-inspector,' I told him. 'So it won't be too illegal.'

He smiled.

'Just tell me something,' I asked. 'You sent a man to trace my wife. What agency did you use?'

'A firm called Burns and Rafton.'

'Of Bridgnorth?'

'Yes.'

'I rather think that Walter did, too.'

'I wouldn't be surprised. He asked me to recommend someone.'

So there we were. It was beginning to link up. I recalled the man who'd visited Amelia as dour and unresponsive, as no doubt he'd be if his partner had recently been killed.

I watched them drive away. The other cars had already left. I turned back into the house, intending to ask Mary whether I could use the phone. But of course I could. Stupid of me. I still wasn't used to it, perhaps ought not to make the effort required. All the same, I went to speak to her.

She was sitting at the table in the kitchen, not completely aware of her surroundings. She made an effort when I stood in front of her, raising her head. Clearly she didn't want to speak to me, but it was nothing personal. Her concern was for Donald, I decided.

'Where's Donald?' I asked, trying it out.

'He'll be leaving tomorrow, after the inquest.'

'D'you think I should be there?'

She shrugged. 'It's your decision, Mr Patton.'

'But you do think so?'

'It might be . . .' She waved a hand, indicating disinterest. 'Well, decent, I suppose. But you weren't here, and you weren't involved.'

'Nor was Donald, but he's staying for it.'

'It's his father.' She was severe. 'Surely he can stay here one more night.' Now her defence of him was brittle.

'Of course he'll stay here.' I was impatient. 'As long as he likes. It's his home.' Was it? I wasn't going to discuss it, either way. 'But where is he now?'

'You want to talk to him?'

'I don't know. I wondered . . . he seemed upset. Very upset. I mean, it really hit him, and there's so much I don't know about Donald.'

She got to her feet abruptly and went to look out of the window, over the gardens, as though looking for him. 'He's taken Sheba again.'

'He'll exhaust her.'

'It's Donald I'm worried about.' Then she turned. 'I know you're trying to be bright and cheerful, but I'm sorry, it's the wrong time. I can tell you all you need to know about him, but later. If you don't mind.'

I considered her carefully. She would need time to accommodate her mind to the changed situation, as I did. 'I really wanted to use the phone.'

'Oh yes, yes. Of course you do. It's in the room opposite the dining room. Can you find it?'

'I'm sure I can. And Mary – I'm glad it was all laid out in the will. It saves offering . . . you know what I mean. This way you can't refuse.'

'I suppose not. Yes, there's that.' She managed a smile, but not one of her best. I left her looking from the window and went to find the phone. There were two in Walter's room, but I'd have had to ask Mary for the key.

The sitting room across the hall, being its twin, was quite as gloomy as the dining room. Worse, perhaps, packed as it was with plump and heavy furniture with a dark velvet surface, which absorbed what light managed to get in. Two glass-fronted bookcases flanked the marble fireplace, crammed with the uniform editions intended for that purpose. They would be secured away from prying fingers searching for a good read. Heavily framed pictures were accurately positioned in the deeper shadows. There was a dank smell, as though the room had eventually won the battle against humans, who might disturb its brooding silence. It seemed a singular choice for the location of a phone, but at least the weighty silence seemed to guarantee privacy.

'It's me,' I said. 'How's things?'

'You know very well, Richard.'

'I have to ask. Politeness is all.'

'If you're feeling facetious . . . or you're slightly drunk . . .'

'One glass of wine.'

'. . . you could call back later.'

'I didn't want to sound gloomy when talking to a woman in a hospital bed.'

The preliminaries over and our relative moods explored, we each paused for breath. At last she asked: 'Was it really so very bad?'

'As I'd guessed, yes. But Amelia love, it was so strange. The family acted as though they'd heard nothing about a new will.'

She seized on the operative word. You really do have to watch yourself with my wife. 'Acted?' she asked.

'Not in that sense. If that was an act – three acts – then the National Theatre's the loser. It was genuine shock. You can see what that means.'

'I was thinking about it. Of course, you're right. The motive's certainly alive and well.'

'Even kicking.'

'So it's a pity about the dog, Sheba.'

'I haven't told you about the dog.'

'You did,' she assured me. 'By *not* saying about the dog. If she'd not been in the room with uncle Walter, you'd have said that first.'

'Hmm!' I said.

'Even before you asked how I'm feeling.'

'This *is* before I've asked you.'

'So it is.' She was very complacent. 'Why don't you do it now?'

'How are you feeling, my dear?'

'Rotten.'

'That's a lie. You never sounded chirpier. Or should I say more chirpy?'

I heard her chuckle. That chuckle of hers does peculiar things to the hair on the nape of my neck. 'There's news?' I asked, realising she was waiting.

'The house physician's been round, and says he's delighted with me.'

'Me too.'

'Are you paying for this call, Richard? You seem prepared to go on for hours.'

'I'm at the house. In effect, you're paying for it.'

'You seem determined to get me there.'

'You're here already, in spirit anyway. Not quite a perfect substitution, I admit, but I'd rather have you here in spirit than at the caravan in spirit. And how the hell would I get you through the caravan door, with all that stuff on your leg?'

That chuckle again – she was driving me mad. 'You'd never even get me into the car.'

'I could hire a van . . . no, a private ambulance. There's somebody here who'd just love looking after you—'

'Now Richard!' She cut in firmly. 'You know my feelings on this.'

'You should be here,' I told her. 'You ought to see these people, and talk to them . . .' I left it unfinished, waiting to hear the effect.

'If I only could!' she whispered.

'I miss you. I need your advice.'

'You're not coming back tonight?' she asked in a tiny voice, as always ahead of me, and realising what I was aiming for.

'It's this inquest, tomorrow at ten. Somehow it seems indecent if you're not represented, being his major legatee.'

'Residual.' But the joke no longer worked. Her voice was tiny. 'I suppose you're right, though. You'll keep in touch? Promise.'

'As though I need to.'

After a few more seconds of the conventional expressions of affection, we hung up. It doesn't really work, on the phone. Expressions, you see, that's what they're called, and that's what they have to be. Visual expressions. I scowled at the phone, now in its cradle. I could get there by eight, back here by nine in the morning, if I started early. But that would be stupid.

90

I went to ask Mary if she could find me a bed. The incomparable woman already had one ready for me, next door to Donald's.

'Convenient,' I said, beaming at her. 'I'd like a word with him.'

'Please,' she said, 'not tonight. Let me have a chat with him first. He might tell me.'

'But not me?'

She shook her head, smiling in fond resignation. 'The pride of the Manns.'

'My impression was that he's in some sort of trouble.'

'Perhaps so.' She looked beyond me vaguely. 'I'll be lucky if he tells me what it is, though.'

I smiled. 'Then I'll wait, and get it from you.'

She became immediately brisk and active, seeming to find a hundred things to do when I could see nothing. 'Well that depends,' she said over her shoulder. 'You mustn't expect too much, Mr Patton.'

In this manner silenced, I went outside to see how the scaffolding was coming along. It was finished – on double time it would be, the whole Sunday charged accordingly. There was nothing for me to look at. I went to stare at the Stag. It seemed the same, its perfection haunting me. I strolled round the gardens, threading my way down towards the river, not really aware of what surrounded me but keeping an eye open for Donald. It would not do to be seen chatting with him, in case Mary thought I was trying to steal a march on her.

I admit it, I was bored. Looking back, I realised that every time I'd been separated from Amelia, I'd had to pack the minutes with activity or I was lost and empty. So much to be done, so many aspects to be investigated, and I could think of nothing actually to tackle. I might just as well, I thought, fill the vacant hours with a trip back to the hospital.

Abruptly inspired, I turned and hurried back to the house, intent on ringing Amelia to warn her of a change of plan. I went through the kitchen without a word to Mary, yet I should have been warned by the presence of Sheba. The door to the sitting room was ajar, and I was through it before I saw him. I stopped, making no sound.

Donald was sitting at the phone table. He was in profile, and had not noticed me. With his right hand he was just replacing the handset, his left to his forehead, half in a gesture to support his head, half in a massaging movement with his fingers, as though he might be able to smooth away whatever was harrowing him. Somehow that gentle and undemonstrative soothing conveyed the depth of his despair. He was long past any vigorous outcry.

Quietly I returned to the kitchen. Mary was feeding Sheba. I said: 'He's at the phone table, Mary. Now's the time to ask him.'

I took the dog's dish from her fingers. Sheba whined in distress. Mary gave me one startled glance, and hurried towards the hall.

But I was wrong. How often my judgement is at fault! They met in the hall. I heard a mumble of voices, then Donald's, raised close to a shout.

'No, Mary! No!'

Then the slam of the front door. She had claimed he called her mother. Perhaps this was his form of rejection.

I bent and gave Sheba her dinner, so as not to witness Mary's distress.

10

In a continuation of this theme, making myself scarce, I prowled the house. Five bedrooms, six counting Walter's suite, the best facing the river. The ones at the front would be more appealing, perhaps, in artificial light. Two bathrooms. A ladder to the loft, which I didn't explore. It was a large house, by my standards, and could be a very comfortable home. I discovered a cellar, the door opening from a corner of the kitchen. I could hear Mary's vacuum cleaner busily active somewhere. In the cellar there was a lot of space, and the boiler for the central heating system. Separated from this section by a new-looking brick wall and another door, there was a sizeable wine collection in racks. I'm no wine expert, but the dust on the bottles was of a good vintage.

I discovered Mary in the hall. Was it usual to vacuum patterned marble? She noticed my shoes and looked up, switching off.

'Donald?' I asked.

The pain was still in her eyes. 'He's gone out. Probably to his brother's place.'

I couldn't imagine he'd get a healthy welcome there. I nodded.

'Failing that, he'll try Clare,' she added.

The implication was that money was involved. I said: 'Yes.' And left her to it, the atmosphere not being congenial. The living room was the obvious retreat. I was bored to the eyebrows.

Behind a screen, in a corner, I discovered a television set. I wasn't in the mood, and turned to the bookcases. The doors were unlocked. In one there was a complete set of Dickens, bound in brown, in the other was another complete set, bound in blue. Everything was in collections, with uniform binding. The Waverley novels, the Brontës, Jane Austen, Anthony Trollope. That era. An Encyclopaedia Britannica, 1923 edition. A Children's Encyclopaedia, 1957. Trying my luck with spot checks, I realised that none had been opened and read. But in a bottom corner, as though hidden with shame, was a three-volume set of The Motor Mechanic, 1942. This was black with oily finger marks. I explored at random. Treasure indeed.

The Solex and Amal carburettors in cross-section. The wiring diagram for an ignition system. A diagrammatic illustration of the operation of the synchromesh gearbox, another of the differential gear. Petrol pumps, electrical and mechanical. Heavens, how simple life had been for the motorist in those days! You could actually do your own repairs. Now you don't even dare to open the bonnet. Topping up the washer-bottle is about the limit.

The abrupt ring of the telephone in that silent room startled the wits out of me. I picked it up, my first thought: Amelia! What's gone wrong?

'Richard,' I said.

'Mr Patton?' His voice was uncertain. 'It's Chad Leyton.'

'Yes. Hello.' I welcomed the voice, unexpected as it was. He might have something to suggest that would occupy my mind.

'We've heard the news, so it's all right now.'

'Is it? What is?'

His voice had been eager. There would always be enthusiasms, briefly broken by fury if he was sufficiently obstructed. Any anger would be directed at the lack of understanding he encountered, at the futility of humanity in producing a mind that didn't flow with his own. I could imagine a tumultuous marriage ahead, always assuming he managed to persuade her. A tumultuous something, anyway, with Heather as brisk and independent as she appeared to be.

'It's all right for you to come down to the factory,' he explained with forced patience. 'Now you're the boss, sort of.'

I didn't feel like anybody's boss, though in practice I could no doubt now throw a little weight around.

'To see that staircase?' I asked. 'It can wait.'

'To see that system I've worked out.' His anxiety might have been for my limping brain, but the hint of impatience in his voice implied that he was anxious for a verdict. Perhaps it was for me to give him a go-ahead! Oh Lord, I thought, the responsibilities of management!

'I'd be interested, of course,' I said cautiously.

'Then what about this evening?'

It provided a distraction. 'But it's Sunday. The place'll be locked up.'

'Not to you it won't. Come round here, in say an hour. Okay? We've got a chicken, and Heather will be here.'

'I've already eaten one dinner . . .'

'Come at around seven. It'll give us time to talk.'

So Heather had told him I was still interested in – was committed to – an investigation of Tolchard's death. I was pleased he was keeping that in the forefront of his mind.

'Yes,' I agreed. 'We'll have to discuss things. How long have we got?'

'What? Well . . . as long as we like. Lock up after we leave. You know.'

'I meant, to the adjourned hearing.'

He was silent for a moment. It had not been a subject he'd wished to consider. He was a concentrator; he could exclude side-issues completely.

'A fortnight,' he said at last, his voice dull.

'As short as that?'

'We can talk about that, too.'

'I think we'd better.'

'Seven, then?'

I agreed. He hung up. I was disturbed. On the one hand I was expected to uncover evidence, as yet unexplored, pointing to his innocence. This from Heather and her father. On the other hand, from Chad's point of view, I was a potential arbiter of his future at the factory. His whole mind was set on his process, and a decision from management was needed, when he might shortly be in no position to go anywhere. If he was committed for trial on a murder charge, he certainly wouldn't be allowed further remand on bail. Didn't he realised that his fixation of purpose only underlined his motive for having killed Tolchard?

Perhaps I ought to try opposing him myself, I thought, adopting the role of managing director, and watching to see whether he tried to push me down that staircase.

Trying in this way to lighten my own mood, I replaced the motor manuals, and while doing so noticed that several more had been behind them. There was a workshop manual on the Stag, much battered. There was a treatise on electrical and oxy-acetylene welding, another on spraying techniques. It was clear that Walter himself had preserved his Stag.

I went to tell Mary I'd been invited out to dinner. She said I couldn't afford to put on any more weight. I agreed. She showed me which room was to be mine, and I wished I'd thrown a few things in a bag. Not even a razor. Mary recognised my dilemma and produced one.

'It's Walter's, and I've put in a new blade.'

I thanked her, hoping I wouldn't be expected to wear his pyjamas. The tube was of shaving cream. I preferred a brush and lather, but never mind. I said I'd probably be late returning, as I was going to have a look at the factory. She left me to my shave.

Feeling fresher, I walked down to her kitchen, and she had a key ready for me.

'Donald back?' I asked.

She shook her head. Her fingers played with the collar of her blouse, and she looked away. 'He's probably keeping out of your way.'

I nodded. Before I thought of a decent comment, I found the back door closing behind me. There was a distinct impression she had hidden him somewhere, and wanted him to herself.

It was necessary to remember the route I'd taken when following Heather, which meant that I was nearly there by the time I'd confirmed that a car was following me. It remained well back. Something dark. Why do so many modern hatchbacks look alike? I couldn't put a name to it.

When I operated the winkers and turned into Leyton's drive, I expected it to sweep past, so that I'd get a sighting of the driver. But it did not do so.

There was already a car in the drive, possibly Leyton's or Chad's. But I didn't get out of the Volvo in case it was another visitor, which meant I'd have to back out. I rolled down the window. I could hear voices, and by leaning sideways I could see that the visitor was Clare, and that the car was her BMW.

They were in the porch, Leyton apparently attempting to restrain her.

'And you can just take your hands off me!' she shouted.

He said something in a more subdued voice.

'Then whose fault is it?' she demanded. 'D'you think I'm a fool?'

This provoked his voice into more force. 'I'm not having you leave here in this mood. We've got to talk, Clare.'

'Talk about what? It's gone too far for talking.'

'I'm not going to be blamed—'

'Then *you* do something about it!' She was now visible, free of his hands, but unable to walk away from a good dispute. 'It's no good him coming to me. He's gone to Paul.'

'How can I—'

'He'll get nothing there.'

'Then I'm sorry,' he said, his anger at last breaking free. 'I'm sorry for him, and for you too, Clare. I can't do anything, and don't intend to try.'

She took two paces to her car, turned back. 'You've done more than enough, if you ask me.'

Then Leyton saw me at last. He hesitated, as though to scuttle indoors. Clare, not at all concerned about being heard, saw me too, walked towards me, and bent her head to the open window.

'Get this sodding car out of my way.' To Clare, all cars were apparently perverted.

If she'd been a man I'd have got out and questioned her manners. Instead, I politely backed out. So much for equality. With a roar of engine and a snatch of tyres, she swerved round me and was away. Quietly, I again drove in and parked by the front door.

Leyton was waiting for me, a small, weak smile held in place with an effort. 'Sorry about that. Clare's always a bit difficult . . .' He waved me inside.

I smiled back, less meekly. 'It's that damned will.' But it hadn't sounded like that to me. I was merely offering him an escape route.

He plugged down it, a hand to my shoulder urging me into

their living room. 'She's trying to get me to take a seat on the board.'

'Your ten shares entitle you to that, surely.'

'And with her thirteen and Paul's we might form a . . . a . . . whatsit.'

'Cartel?'

'Something like that. To oppose you.'

'It's assumed, then, that there'll be something to oppose?' I took the seat he indicated obediently, wondering how far he'd go. 'You'd still need Donald's votes behind you. His original thirteen. Is *that* what it was all about?'

He didn't answer, and had his back to me. It's a convenient device, the filling of glasses. Turning with them, he said: 'Sherry? Donald's always refused any contact with the company.'

'But he could authorise any one of you to vote his shares. Or at least, I assume he could.'

Leyton was uneasy, simply because I was pursuing it. He was caught in his own evasions. 'He wouldn't do that.' He sat opposite me. 'Chad's gone to fetch Heather. He won't be long.'

'I've got the impression Donald's in need of money,' I said gently, then, at his blank stare. 'We were talking about Donald. He might be persuaded to sell his thirteen shares.'

'I doubt it. It's not worth discussing, anyway.'

I smiled over my glass. 'Of course not. Put 'em all together and you'd only have forty-nine. This cartel of yours.'

'Yes. You'd still have the whip-hand. There's the car now.' He was half on his feet, eager to get away.

'You left the door open. Remember?'

'So I did. So I did.'

Nevertheless he found it necessary to go out into the hall. My smile was dead before he reached the door. What had impressed me was that his expression had been more of distaste than concern as we'd quietly fenced. I felt that he had no wish to oppose me, and hated the necessity. I wasn't sure whether Clare had forced it on him, or myself.

On my feet, I welcomed Heather and Chad. He'd clearly forgiven me for reminding him about his forthcoming second appearance before the magistrates, and had a broad smile for me. Heather was very serious as her eyes met mine. To her, the hearing was paramount. She was the realist. She knew the case against him. Chad, the romantic, had a naïve faith in the hairy old precept that the innocent could not be found guilty. It would perhaps lessen the shock if he was prepared for the fact that they can. Heather found herself unable to do this to him. On the surface it was necessary for her to display a cheerful confidence, when a display of her genuine fear might, in the long run, have been more kind to him.

'I'll have to look at the chicken,' said Chad. 'I bet dad's never given it a thought.'

Smiling ruefully, Leyton admitted he had not. He didn't mention that Clare had been there and driven it from his mind.

Heather, briskly aware that a fortnight is a very short period, got straight down to the essentials. 'Chad wants to show you his special process . . .' She filled two glasses with sherry, and now whisked away to the kitchen with one of them, and was back in time to complete it. '. . . and I want to show you the iron staircase, so I'm coming along.'

She said this with determination, as though there'd been an argument about it in the car.

'We'll certainly need you,' I said. 'I hadn't realised there was so little time. I'm coming into this too late.'

'Anything!' she said eagerly. 'Any little point we can use.'

'Suppose you tell me what you've got so far. For the defence. While we're waiting.'

I meant, while Chad was out of the room. She got it at once. 'I'm teaching him to cook.'

'There'll be a barrister. He'll have to be given *some* defence to offer.'

Yes, there was already a barrister. I wondered who was paying him. Had Leyton realised on his ten shares in the company? No, he'd said they were for Heather and Chad. But this would *be* for Heather and Chad. Or maybe Walter, besides raising the bail, had also offered to cover the legal costs! That sounded more likely. In which case, Amelia was paying. In which case, it would be helpful if I could produce something the defence would be able to use, thus reducing the barrister's fees. Small hope of that! I'd have to produce something that would prevent him from putting one foot inside the courtroom. I'd have to produce proof.

Heather had the defence at her fingertips. It sounded as though a barrister would be superfluous – just hand her the brief.

'We shall try to minimise motive,' she said firmly.

'The fact that Tolchard had asked him to resign?'

'Not the *fact*. The prosecution can prove that it happened. We shall show that Chad had reason to believe that Walter Mann and not Tolchard had the overall say in the matter.'

'But you told me he didn't. It was in Tolchard's contract.'

'Chad couldn't be expected to know that.'

'Yet he had you, Heather. He'd surely have discussed it with you. And you would have found out for him the exact legal position.'

She stared at me with large, innocent eyes. 'But I shall not be called as a witness.'

'What Chad thought or didn't think will never be admitted in evidence. And you'd have to keep *him* off the stand, or he'd be asked. Can he lie with impressive confidence?'

She bit her lip and shook her head. 'You're not helping, are you!'

'Devil's advocate, my dear. What else?'

'We shall show that Chad had a valid reason for having the round rulers in his hand. It was used as a signal to me.'

'You'll say he'd used it before?'

'Several times.'

'There's a limit to the numbers that can be indicated with two rulers. One. Two, perhaps, in Roman numerals, and ten in Roman. And as he'd hardly stand there indicating he'd be with you in one or even two minutes, it just had to be ten, every time. So why wouldn't he simply stick up a thumb and come running?'

'You're just being damned awkward.'

'Realistic. Come on, Heather, you're a realist. Can't you *see* it? The prosecution certainly will.'

Her eyes darkened. She nodded, looked down, lifted her head again. 'Well, it's what he did, and several times.'

'Which you'd have to swear to, so how can you claim you wouldn't be called as a witness?'

'You're just twisting words around.'

'I'm just a simple retired copper, who's spent hours in courts. D'you think any competent counsel wouldn't do it better? What else have you got?'

She looked at Leyton, who shook his head in despair. Her eyes came back to me, her head raised in defiance. I almost cheered.

'We shall rely on the question of timing. Ken, here, will say that Chad came running from the window . . .'

'Where he'd been doing his signalling?'

'You *know* that! From there, yes. And Tolchard had screamed only seconds before.'

'Ah yes! You heard this scream, you said?' I asked him.

He was grey. He whispered: 'Yes.'

'When they've got you on the stand, you'll need to say it with more conviction than that.'

'Yes,' he croaked in agitation.

I turned to Heather. 'Chad heard this scream?'

'He says he didn't.'

'Well then.'

'What the hell does *that* mean?' she demanded, keeping her voice down with great restraint. 'Well then!'

'The prosecution will say he daren't admit hearing a scream, because he'd be unable to justify where he must have been when it happened. Look at it . . . no, *think* about it. The prosecution will argue that he was at the head of those stairs. They'll probably say he was waiting there, in the shadows, for Tolchard to come along. No . . . let me *say* it! They'll say Tolchard screamed on his way down the stairs, but that you, Heather, had already signalled from outside. So Chad had to go to the side window. They'll say he ran there, and just had time to signal by the time you, Ken . . .' I glanced at him. '. . . reached the head of the stairs. You hurried, did you?'

Heather tried to speak, but I held up my hand. 'Did you?'

'Yes.'

'Why? Was there some urgency?'

'The scream,' he said positively, forcing his voice to operate, 'was so terrible.'

I turned back to Heather. 'Yet Chad didn't hear this terrible scream?'

'He says not.'

'But if he had heard it – where would you say he'd have been, at that time?'

'At the window.'

'Which is as close to the head of those stairs as Ken was? Closer, perhaps. Yet he didn't hear the scream.'

Her teeth were very white. She clenched them in restraint, her lips drawn back. It was not intended as a smile.

'Chad was concentrating on what he was doing. On me.'

'I can well believe you'd drive a man off his head, my dear. But not deaf.'

'Oh, you're hopeless,' she cried. 'You're no help at all. I wish I'd never asked you . . .' Then she bit her lip, forcing herself to silence.

I took time lighting my pipe, then blew the smoke towards the ceiling. I had no great faith in this scream, though clearly they thought that in some way it established Chad's alibi. The silence built up until Heather tried another attack.

'Chad was . . . he was two, perhaps even three minutes doing his signalling. He just couldn't—'

'Signalling an X, for ten? A whole series of X's? What for? Were the rest kisses? Now come on, Heather, you could never say that in court.'

'So what,' she demanded, 'are you trying to do? If all you want is some excuse to back out, when you've promised . . .'

I sighed. 'I'm not backing out. I'm trying to get a clear picture. Heather – can't you see? – Chad couldn't have killed Tolchard. If he'd wanted to kill him, he wouldn't have chosen such a daft time to do it, with you outside and his father just along the corridor. All I'm groping round for is something we can throw at the prosecution. So I need all the facts. All of them. All right? So now you know where we stand.'

And then, because she at last realised I was indeed on her side, she put a hand over her eyes, and couldn't hold back a sound remarkably like a sob.

Leyton said: 'Now look what you've done.'

'She needs to understand she can trust me,' I said, but he didn't know what I was talking about.

'I'll have to check on Chad,' she mumbled, and she dashed away. But it was upstairs she went, racing for the bathroom.

'May I beg another glass of your excellent sherry?' I asked, before Leyton got himself even more deeply involved with his lying.

11

Now that I was able to concentrate on him, I realised that Leyton seemed two years older than when I'd seen him last. He was holding on by his fingertips, heavier and heavier problems falling on his shoulders by the second. He was a man who would break suddenly. There was a watershed to his resistance and he'd very nearly staggered to it.

This often happens where the closest loved ones can shrug off their personal worries by concentrating on something else, any distress and fear being shouldered aside, only to be picked up and carried for them. Panic by proxy. Maintaining any pretence towards social amenities was almost beyond Leyton. What he wanted to do was retire to a corner and construct a cocoon of misery for himself, wherein the burden might change form and emerge bright and clean.

I sought for idle small talk to lighten the mood, but it bounced off him.

'You'll be coming along to the factory, of course?'

He nodded. There'd been a second's delay for it to register.

'Though there'd be nothing for you on a Sunday evening?' I suggested.

'Pardon.'

'No work. In the office. Right on top of it, are we?'

He stirred. A thin stream of pride washed through him. 'Nothing I can't handle in the morning. Shop-loading tomorrow. I leave that to the computers.'

What didn't he leave to the computers? The way he'd previously spoken, I could guess that his most haunting problem was finance. Payments and receipts, and wages. Oh, I could see him, hunched over his desk, checking and confirming.

'Computers are very useful tools,' he said, leaning forward to re-fill his glass, relaxing slightly as he launched into a familiar theme. 'You can blame 'em for anything that goes wrong. Computer error.' His mouth twisted wryly. 'Don't tell anybody, but there's no such thing. Any error, and it's because the computer's been given the wrong information. They don't make mistakes. How wonderful it would be for people, Mr Patton, if they didn't make mistakes.'

'And how boring life would be.'

'You think computers get bored? Now *there's* an idea! I can try that one for a change. "The computer's got bored." Oh, lovely!' He gave a short burst of laughter, but there was bitterness behind it. I saw his eyes go vague, his mind wandering away to personal problems.

'But you? Do you get bored, Kenneth?'

'With figures? Heavens, no.' He seemed to shake himself. 'But

102

I shouldn't be telling you these things.' He jutted his lip ruefully.

'You seem to have the wrong idea, somewhere. It's my wife who's inherited the fifty-one shares. Not me. She who'd be chairman or chairwoman or president or whatever. Though I doubt if it'll come to that.'

He looked startled. 'She wouldn't, surely, throw them on the open market? It's always been a private company. How terrible if some anonymous bank or investor took over! We'd finish up as a tax-loss or something horrible like that.'

I couldn't explain what was on my mind, and regretted saying it. 'Then maybe she'll let me run it after all,' I said soothingly. I found the idea appalling. 'But she'd do it better than me.'

Yet I'd expressed in open words one of his background worries. Walter had allowed him to muddle along, when the complexities of modern bookkeeping were beyond him. I knew now why he'd stayed so late at nights. He'd been checking, manually, on the computer output. I could see him preparing the wage packets. That day, the computer would fling out the figures, no doubt actually printed on the pay envelopes. His staff – probably a gang of chattering girls; another of his agonies – would make them up. It would all balance neatly, and they would leave, not caring a tuppenny cuss. Then Kenneth Leyton would unearth his manual ledgers, hidden away because he was ashamed of his doubts and fears and anxieties, and check the lot. He'd need to know every detail of every packet, so that he could argue and discuss as necessary, and not, as he'd suggested, have to fall back weakly on 'computer error', or try out 'computer boredom' for a change.

And I saw that he knew I'd realised his position. His eyes slid away. 'I wonder if they're ready for us,' he muttered.

We went to see. They were arguing over the sprouts, though clearly not about them. She was telling him forcefully that he'd have to start worrying for himself, instead of leaving it to everybody else, and he was saying he was taking everything very seriously.

'How serious d'you want it to get?' she demanded, and then they saw us and were silent.

'I, for one, am getting hungry,' Leyton complained.

We went in to eat. I found that I could easily manage a second full meal of the day. Afterwards, we drove to the factory.

We used my car, as it wouldn't be too far out of my way to bring them back, and also because in this way I had more control over what happened. They'd have to stay until I'd filtered the last drop of information from what was a murky mixture.

It was easy enough to find. Walter Mann had decided his sign should be illuminated, and by that time the sun had set. You could see it for miles. Amelia wouldn't like that, for a start. I drove over the bridge, negotiated the twists and turns of the opposite rise, and took the first left along the river. Here we were high above the water. We turned in left at the tall gate, which was wide open. It was, however, guarded by an elderly man in uniform in a little hut. As we drew up, he came out to have a word.

'Evening, Mr Leyton, Mr Chad . . . hello miss.'

Chad, who was sitting beside me, leaned over.

'This is Mr Patton, Frank.'

'Pleased to meet you, sir.'

'Perhaps we could have the keys?'

'Of course, Mr Chad. You'll want to be looking the place over, Mr Patton.' He went back to his hut for the keys.

'News gets around,' I commented.

'It's a small town,' Leyton said from the back. 'Everybody will be interested in you.'

I grimaced, but he wouldn't have seen it. Frank returned with about twenty keys on a large ring, which he handed to me. What did one say in such circumstances?

'Everything quiet, Frank?'

'As the grave. Except for the owls. Been making a hell of a racket.'

'They do. Hunting, I expect.'

I eased the car forward. The immediate prospect was a wide and deep hard-surfaced car park, the full width of the building, which was glass-fronted.

'Reception,' said Chad. 'This is the executive car park. The workers use the one over there, on the left.' This was an open expanse, beyond a mesh fence. 'If you'll turn right, we can run round the side of the building. We'll use the staff entrance.'

I did as he said. The tarmac swung left, and headed down towards the river rather steeply, levelling opposite a bank of wooden doors in the side of the main building. This section rose to a full four storeys, seeming, with its modern extensive use of glass, to be flimsy. I recalled long-past stories of machines crashing through four floors at antiquated cotton mills. Chad seemed to read my mind.

'Ours is all light machine work. Precision rather than bulk. Clean work. Will you pull in here?'

I drew in to the side against a high, wooden fence. We got out. 'Why here?' Because the drive continued on down.

'It's where I stopped my bike,' said Heather.

'Ah, I see. And Chad signalled from where?'

She pointed upwards to the third floor windows. 'That one there, the end one, second along.'

'My office is on the same floor,' Leyton put in. 'The other end of the building.'

He took me by the arm and led me a few more yards down the slope, so that I could look along the rear of the building. It was on this face, high up on the roof, that Walter Mann had erected his MANN OPTICS sign. This side faced back towards the town, the reception frontage overlooking only open country. This side, therefore, was the place to advertise your presence. I saw now that the sign was not internally lit, as I'd thought, but was caught in the flood of a set of lights mounted on the roof of a lower building. This one was long and low, backed by a belt of trees I could just see beyond the lights. Farther down would be the river.

'My office is just below the CS of the sign,' said Leyton. 'At night, I can almost work with the office lights off.'

'I can imagine. What's the lower building?'

'That's the research lab. It came later, and they had to hack out a chunk of ground to take it.'

The drive, I now saw, curved round the far side of the lab building and disappeared. There was perhaps another, smaller car park down there.

There was now no doubt as to the location of the iron stairway on which Tolchard had died. The steep covered walkway leading down from the main building clearly contained it. I wondered why it had been taken from the third floor, instead of the bottom one, which would have made it less steep and shorter, but I didn't ask.

Having acquired a general idea of the layout, I walked back to where Heather and Chad were waiting.

'We're getting nowhere,' Heather said with a hint of impatience.

'I wouldn't say that. You heard what Frank said. The owls have been noisy.'

Dead on cue, one of them screeched, down in the trees by the river.

Chad jerked his head in rejection. 'You're surely not saying that dad mistook an owl for a human scream?'

Sometimes you have to be patient. 'I wasn't saying that. But you work in that lab, down there. It's closer to the river, and you stay late.'

'You get used to them.'

'That's just what I'm saying. Earlier, we were talking about trying to convince a jury that you didn't hear a scream, when your father did. We might suggest the possibility that you could have mistaken a human scream for the owls, you being so used to them. Or even the scream of an animal the owl had taken.'

Heather shuddered. 'You're right, of course. Let's get inside, shall we?'

Down by the river, something screamed again. I didn't move. There was more to be said.

'You stood here?' I asked her.

'Yes. Almost exactly.'

'It was . . . what time?'

'Just getting dark. Late.'

'It would be . . . June?' She nodded. 'So . . . it was very late. Chad was in his lab, down there?' I pointed towards the lab building, its back to the trees. 'He heard your engine?'

'I pipped my horn.'

'Which he heard quite clearly from down there?'

She nodded, her eyes suspicious.

'And he came running.' I looked towards the covered way. 'He *ran*, up those stairs? All right. He ran. Through the lab, up the iron staircase, and along the corridor to that end window?'

She stared at me, nodded again, then reinforced it with words. 'That was where he signalled from.'

'With two round ebony rulers?'

She was now wary of saying anything. I glanced at Leyton senior. In that light he looked grey, but perhaps he'd have looked the same in any light. I grunted. Not one of their faces indicated any belief in the fact that it'd been a good idea to involve me. We were, as she had said, getting nowhere.

'Which one of these damned keys opens that door over there?' I demanded, and Chad took the ring from me.

All the enthusiasm had gone from it. We walked in through the side door and marched along the corridor facing us, to a central lobby. Through a window, I was looking across a narrow path at the underside of the covered walkway. From there we took a lift to the third floor, Heather and Chad clutching hands fiercely, in fear of imminent separation. We emerged on a landing at the head of the iron staircase.

'Why,' I asked, 'does it come all the way up to here?'

Leyton knew the answer to that. 'Walter's idea. He thought the contact with research ought to be from management level. This is where the top people have their offices.'

I grunted, and stared down it morosely. There was a handrail each side, but to me it looked a long and steep way down. Anybody falling down there could hardly hope for anything short of a broken neck. Behind me was the executive corridor. This, presumably, would be the way Tolchard would have come, intent on exercising his authority by ordering Chad to pack in and go home. But why had Tolchard been there so late? Was he deliberately waiting-out Walter, up in his fourth floor office, challenging his right to be last to leave? I marvelled that the minds controlling this complex organisation could, in personal matters, be so petty.

The cross corridor ran all the way along the length of the building. At one end was Chad's signalling window, at the other, presumably, Leyton's offices. The stairway was almost exactly in the middle.

Leyton confirmed my guess. 'My office is along there.' He said it meekly, the spirit beaten from him. Only Heather, when I glanced at her, seemed still to be clinging to any faith in me.

'Then let's have a look at it,' I said, to cheer him up.

We did so. He unlocked a door at the end on to a bare passage. 'The staff use these stairs,' he explained, pointing to a gloomy stone stairway. 'It opens on the side of the building, convenient to the main parking lot.'

There were a lot of entrances, a lot of outside doors for Walter to have checked.

'How about access to the site?' I said. 'Does everybody have to get past Frank and his mates?'

'Oh heavens, no. We're not properly fenced. You can get in

107

from the road both sides, even from the river and up through the trees. We're only a quarter of a mile from the bridge.'

Access for sundry murderers was therefore unlimited, especially before Walter had done his rounds.

'We're in here,' Leyton said, opening a door.

The main office, and what a hodge-podge it was! He'd clearly lovingly preserved the original wooden furniture that he'd accumulated from the early days in the shed. Ancient dark wood desks with high backs, roll-top desks, even one you stood up to, with a ledge to prevent the heavy ledgers from slipping off, all were still on show. There were no such ledgers in sight, only bulky wads of computer print-out.

Incongruously, on these hallowed surfaces were scattered all the modern menaces of Leyton's life, computerised typewriters, computer consoles and screens, and competing for available space were photocopiers alongside creaking wooden filing cabinets. And round ebony rulers were lying around every-where, now being used as paperweights.

'I'm through here,' Leyton said, opening a side door. Not for him a glass-walled room, where he might be observed agonising over his ledgers. Here he was cosily tucked away. He opened a high cupboard proudly. In it were ranked his old wages books and accounts, their red leather backs stamped in gold letters with their years, thirty of them. To him, that matching red leather swivel chair would have the comforting familiarity of the best of the chairs at his home.

'Not only Thursdays?' I asked.

'Pardon.'

'Somewhere I've picked up the idea that there were other late evenings.'

'Two or three a week, perhaps. Does it matter?'

I shrugged. 'I don't know.'

Heather and Chad remained silent. Quietly, their world was crumbling away as I pecked at the seeds of detail. I peered out from one of Leyton's windows. The floodlights on the roof of the research section were blinding, being centred on the tall sign, just above my head.

I turned away. There was nothing to be discovered here. Leyton had been gradually pushing himself towards a break-down in this room, whilst the man who had called himself his friend had let him get on with it, instead of putting in a computer expert as a second-in-command. Then he'd deleted Leyton from his will, simply because he'd protested at any change at all.

Once again I marvelled at the personality of Walter Mann, so obsessed with the idea that his family was trying to kill him that he would almost completely remove them from future control of his company, yet so proud of the family name that he had it illuminated in ten feet high letters for the whole town to see.

My curiosity getting the better of me, I opened one of the two windows and looked upwards. There it was, ten feet above, each letter like the side of a house, the surfaces mirrored to reflect the light. How appropriate that the lights also shone on the office of Kenneth Leyton, who'd worked his heart out to maintain an efficient financial base for MANN OPTICS, directly beneath the CS, standing for Conscientious Service.

I withdrew my head. 'Who puts on the lights?'

Chad spoke his first words for ten minutes. 'It's a photoelectric switch. One of our products. On when it gets dark enough, off when it gets light. It works with a—'

'Let's go and look at this lab of yours,' I interrupted quickly.

'All right.' The zest had gone from his voice.

We walked back along the corridor to the head of the iron staircase. Here, Leyton touched my arm. 'D'you mind if I don't?'

'Sit in the car, then,' I agreed. 'It's not locked.'

We watched him into the lift, the doors closing on his set face. Then the other two turned and faced me, waiting. I shrugged. They were expecting too much.

'Just stay here a minute,' I said, then I began a backwards and careful trip down the iron staircase, examining it minutely. They wanted an experienced detective, so I gave them one, though I expected nothing from it.

'What're you looking for?' Chad called down.

I lifted my head. 'We've got to consider the possibility that Aleric Tolchard simply slipped and fell. So I'm looking for something that'd make a blow to the back of his neck, something like what he'd get from a round ebony ruler.'

'Oh,' he said. 'I see.'

I looked back up at him. 'Unless it *was* a round ruler.'

He made an angry gesture. 'How could it have been?'

'Then suggest something else. The edges of these stairs are too sharp, and it couldn't have been the handrail.'

'I can't suggest anything else,' he admitted miserably.

'Then both of you come on down, and you can show me this wonderful lab of yours.'

He brightened. They clattered down to me, and he produced his personal key to the door at the bottom. Turning it seemed to close a circuit in his personality. He led the way through with the confidence of a man walking into his own world.

As it was, I supposed. After all, with Tolchard dead, and as yet not replaced, Chad was now the boss.

12

The factory dealt in photographic equipment. They experimented constantly in all factors concerning light as it affected photography. Light as refracted and reflected, as infra-red and ultra-violet, as distributed through the visible spectrum, as expended in a ten-thousandth part of a second flash. And light is clean. The research lab, its equipment and benches, were polished. Dust was an enemy. He led me through this briskly, to his personal lab, which was to one side of the end door.

Almost before he'd closed the door behind us, he launched into it. 'The idea of stereoscopic photography,' he said, 'is so that you can see your photos in three dimensions . . . in depth. You take two pictures, one for each eye, and you look at them the same, one for each eye. Then you see it exactly as it was at the time, in three-D. Stands out and hits you. Taking the pictures isn't too difficult, because you can use a special camera. It's the viewing that raises snags. Each eye has to see its own picture, and nothing of the other one. There're lots of ways of doing it, but they all require apparatus or special hand-viewing things like binoculars.'

'Keep it simple,' I said, looking round.

The room was square. I call it a room, because there was no obvious scientific equipment visible, no bench, only a couple of side tables against one wall, a projection screen against another, and opposite to it the projector itself, a special one with two lenses. In the fourth wall there was a window, with heavy drapes for use when the projector was in operation.

110

Catching my attention on it, he said quickly: 'I can show you how we do it with the projector.'

'You said something about viewing in your hand.'

He seemed disappointed. He'd wanted to show off his abilities and demonstrate his enthusiasms. 'If you like. You'll need to put these glasses on, though.'

He handed me a pair of simple, lightweight glasses with apparently plain lenses. I turned them over in my fingers. 'I thought we were talking about just picking it up and looking at it.'

He pursed his lips, shaking his head. 'Can't be done, unless you're good at crossing your eyes. I can explain on paper . . .' He gestured. I glanced towards his drafting table, which was modern equipment, with mechanical squares.

I shook my head. 'I wouldn't understand it. Let's see the whatever-it-is.'

He glanced at Heather, and grimaced, then back at me. 'Right. All right, then.'

He picked up from his desk a card six inches by three. It had a black background, and on it were mounted two colour prints, each two inches square, side by side. They were apparently pictures of the same woodland scene, which was all confused greens.

'Put your specs on,' he said, 'and look at it, preferably as close as you can focus it.'

I did so. Now I could see only one picture, and what had been a mixed-up mass of trees now separated itself out. I saw them standing behind each other, into the distance, and felt I could have walked into it along the path between them.

'Close either eye,' he told me, 'and you'll see only one. Open both, and you still see only one, but each eye's seeing the one appropriate to that eye, and your brain's putting them together.'

I handed it back to him, along with the glasses.

'How's it done?'

'Each photo is coated with a polarising surface, in opposing planes. The glasses have got lenses polarised in opposing planes, so that the wrong picture is blanked out for each eye. The trick's in the coating. That's what I've been working on, mostly in my own time, for over a year.'

The change in him was remarkable. Not simply the enthusiasm, but the fact that it was underlined by a maturity I hadn't before noticed. He was a scientist, talking about his own specialised field.

111

'And you believe this would be a commercial proposition?'

'We'd have to set up our own photo-printing lab and the apparatus for applying the polarised coatings, and mounting the prints accurately. And we'd have to produce our own cameras. Oh,' he hurried on, seeing my scepticism, 'they wouldn't need to be complicated. Simple lenses, probably Tessar design – we're equipped to grind our own – with no larger aperture than f5.6, and simple shutters—'

'Heh, hold on. Don't get too technical.'

'Something like it's been tried, quite recently. I'll warn you now. But that was renticular, the coating using refraction. They had to use a rather pricey camera. Ours would be cheaper, and the prints wouldn't be too expensive to produce . . .'

'All right. All right.'

'I think Mr Mann would have gone for it. Tolchard was pushing his own idea, but the optics would've been far too complex.'

'Wait a minute!' I eyed him steadily. He'd talked himself into the correct responsive mood for what I had in mind. 'You don't have to convince *me*. We don't know how things are going to turn out, around here, but in any event Mann Optics aren't going to do anything without you. Right? And we could well be losing you in a fortnight's time. Don't forget that.'

'You won't let me, will you! Damn it, I *try* to forget.'

'Then, before it slips away again, and while I've got you two on your own, you can tell me something. You see, I'm getting a bit tired of lies. I thought, maybe, you'd stretch things a bit and come out with the truth for a change. Kind of by accident, because you've been careful to—'

'What the hell're you on about?'

'Those blasted ebony rulers, that's one thing.'

'And what about them?'

I took a deep breath, walked over to his drafting table, and slid the squares over its surface, then I turned back to him, my anger bubbling away. I was now in a position from which I could watch both their faces.

'It's the sheer cheek of it that gets me,' I said, my voice reasonably in control. 'You told me you used round ebony rulers *here* . . .' I gestured wildly. 'You spoke about parallel lines. D'you think I'm stupid? Because I said I didn't understand your photo-graphic technicalities – did you think I'm blind? You've got *this*.' I slapped the drafting table. 'This does your parallel lines. Do I see

112

an ebony ruler? Is there one in here hiding away somewhere? No! And you had the utter gall to bring me here and *assume* I wouldn't realise.'

They were staring at me as though I'd gone mad. As I was, nearly, though I was controlling the bit of my mind that did the thinking.

'You asked for my help, which means I'm supposed to be on your side. Yet you told me lies. Ebony rulers! Lies. Signals at the window! Lies. Not one blind word of truth . . .'

'It *was*,' Heather protested heatedly.

'What?' I demanded. 'What was this grain of truth that might have crept in?'

'Chad . . . signalled.'

'With two round rulers he took from here?'

Chad's jaw was moving. No words were formed.

'Were they?' I threw at him.

'Let me explain—' Heather tried to say.

'No. Let *him* say.'

But Chad stared for another moment, then turned away.

'He signalled,' said Heather. 'With two rulers. Ebony rulers.' Her eyes were fierce, holding mine.

'Twaddle!' I said. 'He could very easily signal "ten" with his damned fingers.'

She took a deep breath. Chad heard the intake, turned, and said: 'No!'

'Yes, Chad,' she told him quietly. She lifted her chin at me. 'X for a kiss,' she said.

'It was me said that. It gave you the idea for another lie.'

'It's true,' Chad claimed.

I looked from one face to the other with wonder, not at their romanticism, but at the fact that they seemed not to understand my point. Or chose not to.

'It's not *what* you signalled,' I told them heavily. 'It's what you did it *with*.'

They were silent.

'So all right.' I shrugged. 'Maybe the company can buy the patents, or acquire them legally, and carry on this process of yours, even with you in Stafford Prison, Chad.'

I turned to the door. 'Heh!' he said. I turned back.

But they were still reluctant. I've found it easier to prise the truth from tough city louts. 'Well?'

113

Heather dropped her eyes. 'He kept them here. The rulers. Just to signal with.'

It was hopeless. I turned away. The design for the camera was developing on the drafting table. Two lenses, side by side, I saw. I decided I must not give in.

'What I ought to do,' I said heavily, 'is walk out of here, take you both back home, and drive away. And leave you to stew in it. All I'm getting is one set of lies after another.'

'You're not—' began Heather.

I swung round, pointing at the window. 'Outside that window there is probably a parking area, which anybody can get at from where I've left the car. Right?'

Chad nodded miserably.

'Aloud,' I said. 'Pretend we're taping this.'

'Yes,' he said quietly.

'And there's a door in the main lab leading out to it. I saw it. I expect you have a key?'

'Yes.'

'So that you, Heather, could easily have ridden down here and tapped on this window, and peered in. And if Chad was here . . .'

Chad pounced in. 'Now hold on—'

I cut him short with a gesture, turning to Heather.

'Couldn't you?'

She was still in a mood to resist, her face pale but purposeful. 'I could. I suppose.'

'Suppose? It would be natural. You'd done it before.' No response. I allowed a snap to reach my voice. 'Hadn't you?'

'Yes.'

'And when you'd done that, Chad would have used his way to let you in?'

'He'd done that.' Her mouth seemed stiff, and she slurred the words.

'So it would have been more reasonable, on that specific evening when Tolchard died, to do exactly that?'

'If you say so.'

'I'm asking you, Heather. Wouldn't it have been more reasonable? It's for you to say, not me.'

'Now hold on!' Chad repeated harshly, moving a pace towards me.

114

'Shut up!' I didn't look directly at him, but could detect that he'd stopped dead. 'We'll come to you . . .'

He turned away angrily, his hand brushing his head in a gesture close to despair.

'Wouldn't it, Heather?' I persisted, but now quietly.

'Yes.' She looked down, and whispered: 'Why are you doing this?'

'Because I can't help you unless I get the truth. Can't you understand that! I don't *want* to be involved. If you're not prepared to tell me the truth, then it lets me off the hook, which'll be fine by me. Is that clear? Nod once for yes.'

She stared at me, her lips a ghastly colour. 'It's dark out there. A bit scarey.'

'Since when did a young woman, going to meet her young man, worry about the dark?'

She bit her lip. I heard Chad's foot move, but I waved him to silence. Heather nodded once.

'So we're getting somewhere. On that evening, it would therefore have been reasonable for you to ride down here. So why didn't you?'

'I did,' she said softly.

'You came here? You didn't stop where you told me you did?' No reaction. 'You were deliberately lying.'

She said something indistinctly. 'Pardon? I didn't catch that,' I said. She raised her head.

'It was a Thursday.'

I looked round, hoping no one else was hearing this nonsense. But Chad had put a hand to Heather's arm and drawn her close to him, his other arm round her waist.

'We'll have to tell him.' His voice was stronger, more firm.

'Now Chad . . .'

'I can't go on with this any longer,' said Chad. He turned his defeated eyes to me. 'We were simply trying to cover up for my father. On Thursdays, he makes up the pay packets.'

Suddenly and blindingly I knew exactly what had happened. But I had to hear it said.

'Meaning what?'

He shrugged. I could just detect a thin, tired smile. Already some of the stress had run from his face. 'It's a fine thing to have to tell you. He's never got used to computers. Doesn't trust 'em. He stays late on Thursday, to check every pay packet. He still,' he

115

admitted with a strange, proud smile, 'keeps his old ledgers going.'

'But?' I urged, secretly pleased because I'd guessed correctly.

'But even so, it's getting a bit beyond him. And there I was, talking about the factory taking on more processes and new business! More staff. More complications. Me not thinking what it would mean to him . . .'

I glanced towards Heather, who took it up. Defeated, stubborn, she jutted her lower lip, and in true lawyer's style made what she could of it. 'Chad would often stay late, but always on Thursdays. He could see his father's window. There's a skylight, and if Ken's lights were on late . . . oh hell, he'd go up to help him out.'

'Not that I was much good at it,' said Chad modestly, pathetically making a dry joke out of it.

'And you?' I asked Heather.

'On Thursdays,' she said, 'I'd ride round to the bottom drive, out there, and if he wasn't in here I'd know where he was, and I'd ride back there and pip the horn. So you see, it wasn't really a lie.'

I didn't take her up on that, but asked Chad: 'You'd hear it, and know?'

'I could hear, up in dad's office. If we were nearly through I'd go along the corridor and signal her. At the end window.'

'With your two damned rulers?'

'Yes.'

'Which you hadn't been using down here to draw your cameras and what-have-you?'

He rubbed his hair into a tangle and made an embarrassed gesture towards his drafting table. It said it all.

'So you brought me into this office, calmly assuming I'm too stupid to realise? By God, I ought to kick your—'

'I forgot. Sorry about that.'

'But you *did* take a couple of round rulers along with you?'

'From dad's office, yes. He's got no end of them. He's a bit old-fashioned.'

'I saw for myself. Antiquated's more the mark.' You can tell I was disturbed, or I wouldn't have said that.

Chad drew himself up. 'He's talking about putting in his resignation.'

'For God's sake!' I said, hearing my voice rising. 'What d'you think's going on? I don't want any damned resignations. We're talking about a man's death here, and you've been making up stories.'

They stood side by side, her fingers groping for his. I sighed.

'Now let me reconstruct,' I said wearily. 'That evening, you, Chad, had gone up to your father's office to help him out. You would leave the lights on in here, to make it look as though you were still at your own work. Heather arrived, you heard her signal, and you went along to the end of the corridor.' I pointed in the general direction. 'And signalled with your two stupid rulers. All right so far?'

Their heads nodded. I went on:

'Which entailed only a walk along a straight corridor from one end of the building to the other? Right. Your father heard a scream, or heard an owl and thought it was a scream, and followed you quickly, and discovered Tolchard dead at the foot of the stairs. Meanwhile, you, Chad, had heard nothing, or had heard a scream and put it down to the owls. Your father shouted, and you ran back to him. Is that basically correct?'

They mumbled that it was.

'But don't you understand . . . if you *had* come from down here in the research section, you could hardly have missed seeing Tolchard, if he'd been lying at the foot of the stairs at that time. But you didn't come from here. You walked along the corridor at the *top* of the stairs, so you could easily have missed seeing him at the bottom. I suppose you'd been up with your father . . . how long?'

'For over an hour, it'd be.'

'So . . . any time in that hour Tolchard might have died. There need not have been a human scream. You idiot – you pair of unadulterated idiots – why did you have to hide all this?'

'Would anybody have believed the truth?' Chad asked fiercely.

'*I'm* believing it. Certainly it's better than what I heard before.'

'And we had to think about dad . . .'

'If the truth came out,' Heather said firmly, 'in open court, he'd have been the laughing-stock of the whole town.'

'And now Chad stands a good chance of being sent for trial.'

'Don't I know it!'

'So what did you intend to do about it?' I asked her, interested.

'We'll tell the truth,' she said proudly, as though it hadn't been forced from them. 'What you've heard. If it comes to it.'

'It *is* bloody-well coming to it. Do you – all three of you – intend

117

to get up in court, heads high and noble, and try to impress the magistrates with your honesty and rectitude by admitting you told lies before? I suppose you'll explain that you told the last lot of lies to cover up the fact that every Thursday Chad and his father stayed late to check that the computer hadn't nodded off from boredom!' But they hadn't shared Leyton's little joke.

'We can but try . . .'

'And can you see 'em?' I demanded. 'This bench . . . listening to this pitiful codswallop . . . glancing at each other and wondering what this new lot of lies has been made up for!'

Chad groaned. 'That's what I'm afraid of.'

'It's all right, Chad,' said Heather.

'And you!' I said to her. 'You're a solicitor. Going to be one. And you've made yourself a party to this—'

'D'you think I'd let him down!' Heather flared, not specifying which him.

'So now you've got to go to your brother,' I told her. 'He's the solicitor preparing the brief. You'll have to tell him you lied to *him*. That you all did. That he's got to admit this to your barrister, who'll probably refuse the brief now. And you, Heather . . . I suppose you've already given evidence on this in the magistrate's court?'

The harsh overhead lights stripped the flesh from her cheeks. She nodded numbly.

'Then you, proposing to qualify as an officer of the court, will have committed perjury. Godalmighty, woman, don't you know what you've done?'

'I was willing to take the risk,' she said quietly.

'You had no right to take risks with your own life, and with the lives of others.' She put her hands to her face and lowered her head. 'And tears aren't going to help. Not now, not at the adjourned hearing. It would look as though you're beaten, caught out in another load of lies. Tolchard . . . are you listening, both of you . . . Tolchard could well have slipped and fallen by accident. It would have been a theory worth using, to cast doubt. But now . . . come out with a story such as I've been hearing, and what'll they think? I'll tell you. They'll think it's a new lot of lies, thought up to cover something a damned sight more serious than staying late at the office. They'll assume it's to cover murder.'

I allowed this to penetrate, watching their faces for enlightenment. Uselessly. Chad's only defence was a stubborn dignity.

'It's a pity,' I said, 'that you had to admit to carrying a ruler at all.'

'But I didn't know, then, that they reckoned on a ruler as the weapon.'

'Of course you didn't,' I soothed him. Something, at last, had a ring of naïve truth. 'Let's get back to the car, shall we?'

He tilted his head. 'You're not mad at us?'

'Thirty years in the police force tends to make a man cynical. I don't expect anything, so I'm not disappointed. And you get to spot lies.'

I smiled to soften it. Yet if we now had the truth, why did he squeeze her fingers when she opened her mouth to add something? And why did they glance meaningfully at each other?

'Can I explain my design for the camera?' Chad asked meekly.

'Not now, I think.'

'The shutter design's rather neat.'

'Your father'll be waiting.'

We left the research section, Chad switching off and locking up as we went. At the head of the iron staircase, at first unnoticed because of the deep shadows, somebody was waiting. Not Leyton. I reached the landing. The only light was from the overspill of the floodlights filtering through the windows.

It was Paul.

'I heard you were here,' he said flatly, in the tone of a man who has rehearsed it, and then felt his nerve faltering as he stood at centre stage.

'Yes, we've—' I was smiling, if he could've seen it. He cut me short, advancing into slightly better light. To the attack.

'I think you might have waited before taking over. Damn it, the will was only read this morning.'

'It wasn't like that.'

'The correct thing,' he said formally, 'would have been to ask me to show you round. Not some young . . . It was thoughtless of you, Chad.'

'You've got it all wrong, Paul,' Chad protested, but I touched his arm and said quietly: 'Why don't you two wait in the car?'

They glanced at each other, then went to the lift. When the doors closed, I turned back to Paul.

He had the air of a man who was angry, but not to the point of letting go. There was no righteousness to back it up; he was tentative. But he'd have been justified in using a dignified

119

disapproval. He was afraid, though, even in expressing this. I could see it there in the set of his shouders, the tilt of his head, the recoil mechanism being poised. Like a faltering champion being urged from behind to the attack, he was too aware that I had the authority.

'We shall have to get together,' I said placidly. 'You and I. There's so much to be ironed out. But not now, please.'

Seizing on what he thought to be a weakness, he plunged in. 'You've got no right to come creeping round here. No seat on the board, no appointed post. It's . . . it's completely unethical.'

At the end of this speech his voice had been faltering.

'Everybody,' I said lightly, trying to make it sound like a joke, 'seems to go wandering round in the middle of the night.'

'I do not intend to bandy words with you,' he told me. 'Now please leave.'

Considering I'd obviously been about to do that, he had nothing to lose. I eased it along.

'It's not your precious factory I'm interested in, you know. It's Aleric Tolchard's death. You haven't forgotten that, I hope. It happened just about on this spot.'

'How could I have forgotten—'

'You weren't, by any chance, wandering around on that evening? As now.'

He stared at me. I shrugged. 'If not, you were just about the only member of the management who wasn't,' I told him.

'Of course I wasn't. What do you mean to imply?'

I put my finger on the lift button, calling up the means of escape. 'Nothing really. It's just that you're taking such an interest, when I was having a look at the scene of Tolchard's death.' The lift door opened. 'Good night, Paul. I'll see you at the inquest.'

The door shut off his startled face.

Heather and Kenneth Leyton were waiting silently in the car, Chad just by the office door, waiting to lock up. Nothing was said. I got in the car, expecting at least something from Leyton, if only an apology for his own lies. But from him, nothing.

I backed up to the car park and reversed round. We paused at the gate to hand back the keys, then I drove them back to Leyton's. At last they spoke, but only to say goodnight. Then I drove away.

Headlights followed me at a discreet distance.

13

It was very late when I returned to The Beeches and parked my car in front of the garages. The key Mary had given me was to her rear door, so I made my way round there, and found I didn't need it. The kitchen lights were on.

'Mary,' I said, trying not to be too severe about it, 'you're up late.'

'I like to lock up safe and sound.'

Perhaps she'd caught it from Walter, but this was not the reason she'd waited up. I didn't press her.

'You'll be hungry,' she told me.

I denied this.

'A cup of tea, then?'

To this I agreed, because she clearly wanted to talk. I sat at the table.

'Is Donald back?' I asked, turning my head to watch her because I couldn't bear all that banging behind me.

'Long ago. He's in his room.'

'Asleep, I suppose.'

'By now, he's sure to be.'

'I'll have to speak to him. In the morning, d'you think?'

'He'll be going to the inquest.'

'Me too.'

We batted this conversational ball back and forth, testing the strength of the opposition, playing ourselves in. She took the seat opposite to me, as she'd done before, cradling her mug – this time it was mugs – as she'd done with her cup and saucer.

'I had a good long talk with him,' she told me.

'To save me the trouble? It's very good of you.'

'He wouldn't have said anything to you, anyway.'

'I'd have beaten it out of him.'

She smiled thinly. 'He's never been able to keep anything from me.'

'Of course not. Did he tell you all about his money troubles?'

She inclined her head, and put the mug to her lips.

121

'Which you are now going to elucidate?' I pressed.

'Elucidate!' she said, smacking her lips round it. 'I like that. Yes, I'm going to tell you.'

'Somehow, I guessed that.'

'You'll need to know more about the family. Oh, I know, I've told you some of it, but not the important bits. Paul, now. The eldest, and he expected to be the boss of the others. What chance did he get with Clare spoiled rotten, and Walter always on Clare's side? Poor Paul, he adored his father and wanted to be around him, always. He'd sit outside in the garage, watching Walter taking a car to pieces . . . that was always Walter's thing, you know, motor engineering. It was really what he wanted to do, but somehow it drifted into other things. Lawn mowers, he wanted to make lawn mowers. Have you ever heard of such a thing!'

'Sounds a good idea. After all, grass keeps growing.'

'But he started this photographic thing, and it all grew from there. He got the stamping machines cheap.'

'You were telling me about Paul,' I reminded her gently.

'Oh yes. Watching his father. Now *that* was what Paul would have been good at, working with his hands. Give him a bit of machinery, and he'd take it to pieces and put it back again. That grandfather clock in the hall – he made it keep time. Paul was always a fanatic about time. A clock has to be *right*, or it's no use, he used to say. But by the time he was old enough to help his father in the business, it'd grown. There was no place for Paul's hands, and Walter thought of him as management material. Paul was a Mann, so he had to be in charge of something. And poor Paul's never had much in the way of brains. So – where to put him? Not finance. Ken Leyton was already in control of that. Control of the . . . oh, I can't remember the word.'

'Production control?'

'That's it. That would've been way over his head. All he's ever managed to control is poor Evelyn. I suppose that's why he married her. And buying and selling . . . the same. It had to be running the machines, which at least he understood, and the workers, who he didn't understand at all. And Paul . . . he just can't control the workers. Either shouts or appeals. No . . . common sense, I suppose.'

'But he seems to manage.'

She smiled at the unintended pun. 'But only just. Everything has to be on paper, laid out so that he can understand it. And now they've got computers . . . ai . . . yee! The problems!'

'I can sympathise.' We would get to Donald, I was certain. 'And Clare?' Hopefully, by way of Clare.

'You wouldn't expect *her* to get involved with a factory. Not Clare! She'd always had what she wanted – and it had to be the best available – without any effort on her part. So she didn't expect to start making any. When she was twenty-one she got her thirteen shares, and maybe some money came along from them. I don't know. But Walter was too busy by then to give her the interest she'd been used to from him. It was as though she'd crossed a line that cut them off from each other. Quite suddenly, on her twenty-first birthday, it came about. I could see how much it hurt her. Any little set-back always used to hit Clare badly. It resulted in a kind of independence. She decided she could make her own way with her own assets. Did you realise that she was a very beautiful young woman?'

'I can imagine that.' But it must have been a cold, matt beauty. It absorbed light, but would not be able to reflect it. 'I reckon she'd have her pick.'

'And did she enjoy herself with the picking!' She giggled, and patted her lips reprovingly. 'She scattered broken hearts in all directions.'

'Perhaps not broken. Bruised, but beating stronger from the experience.'

'You *do* understand.'

'I knew such a woman, when I was young.'

'But along came the perfect choice,' she said. 'She wanted the best, and all of a sudden, there was Aleric Tolchard. A splendid brain – he had a doctorate, whatever that is. And charm! He'd charm the cream off the milk. She brought him here – of course – and I knew at once. So handsome, so clean, and such a beautiful body.'

I raised my eyebrows over the rim of the mug. Misinterpreting, she went to provide me with a re-fill.

'Dark,' she said. 'Always tanned. He didn't stand a chance. They were married six months after Aleric took charge of research.' She stared beyond me, her eyes glazed. Weddings have that effect on women. I waited for it to wear off.

'And while all this was going on?' I said at last.

'You mean Donald?' She sighed. 'Donald went to college, the

123

only one who did. He took a double first in engineering. I was very proud of him. He's the one with the brains. And you can imagine, with all that attention to Clare, he'd been a bit left out. He thought that was why he'd been packed off to college, to get him out of the way. A quiet one, was Donald. He studied like mad, just to show everybody. And d'you think Walter noticed? Not him. He just said: "So you're back. Perhaps we can fit you in somewhere." But Donald had no intention of being fitted in. He'd grown his own sort of independence. And he thought he'd got to do better than the other two. So . . . what d'you think he did?'

'Nothing,' I guessed. 'He sat around and thought about it.'

'How wrong can anybody be!' she complained. 'No, he tried to set up in business for himself. But what good's an engineering degree for that? All theory, and nothing practical. Oh . . . it'd be all right at first. He managed to raise money. Borrowed it.'

'From his father?'

'As though Walter would encourage him in such foolishness.'

'But he got it, this money? And started.'

'And finished, and started again. And finished . . . I lost touch with it all. He'd be doing fine, with an old garage and two machines, making nuts and bolts or something. What *is* a normalised bolt, Mr Patton? That was one thing. But it failed when he took on more men. It confused him. He had to do the job himself, you see, not watch other people doing it.'

'Like Paul, working with his hands?'

'Yes. Except that Paul . . .' She put up a finger, having thought of an example. 'Where Paul could repair a clock, Donald could design and make one. He did one with a little ball running down a spiral glass tube.'

'I'd like to see that.'

'It got broken.'

'Oh? Pity.'

'He showed it to his father. Walter had no patience with such things, and knocked it off the table. Not on purpose, I'm sure, but it was about that time Donald left home.' She looked uncomfortable. 'All I know since then is what he wrote, and from odd visits here.'

'When his father wasn't around?'

'By coincidence. Yes.'

'Of course.'

124

'He might have slept under his workbenches, for all I know. He wouldn't let me help him.'

'Independent.' As all of them had been, in their different interpretations of it.

'I know there were several tries at making things go. Pressings for the Yale lock people, that was one I remember. But he was a fool with money. It came in, and he paid it out. The tax people had him in court once.'

'They don't understand people who're not careful with money.'

'And I suppose it just got worse. Borrowing money to pay debts, then more money to pay the interest on the last lot.'

I had my pipe going by then, and sat back, content to take all night on it. 'But I understand he had thirteen shares in the company to fall back on.'

She compressed her lips. 'He seems to have fallen back on them long ago.'

'He sold them?'

'Apparently.'

'Then *that* should have kept him going . . .' Thirteen shares in a company reputedly with capital assets of half a million . . . that should have brought him at least fifty thousand. I had a thought. 'Surely not outside the family?'

'He wouldn't have dared to do that.'

I supposed not. Donald could reject his father to a certain point, but no further. 'To Paul? To Clare? Did he tell you?'

'He told me.' She nodded solemnly. 'To Aleric Tolchard.'

Who was a clean and superb example of manhood, and would have been able to recognise a man in a desperate situation. No, it would not have been fifty thousand, that was certain. But surely . . .

'And Tolchard voted them?' I knew this could not have been so, knew it as I said it. 'No, that wouldn't do. Did you say, Mary – I'm sure somebody did – that Clare never voted *her* shares? She wouldn't trouble to.'

'I think she gave Aleric a what's-its-name.'

'A proxy? Yes.'

I sat back and had another think. With Clare's 13, and the 13 he'd bought from Donald, Tolchard would have controlled a quarter of the shares. Add 17 that Clare should have inherited on Walter's death, and he'd have controlled 43. All he would need to do then was hound Leyton out of the company, and Leyton clearly couldn't have lasted much longer, and he might just have acquired Leyton's 10. No, I thought. Simpler than that. On Walter's death, 17 shares would have come to Donald, who'd already shown a willingness to sell cheap. Aleric Tolchard, I decided, had had his eyes on the whole caboosh. The factory could well have become his. But in the meantime he'd not have displayed his hand, so would have kept quiet about having bought Donald's 13 shares.

If Tolchard hadn't died first. If Tolchard had lived long enough, I wondered whether Walter would have survived for many more months, in any event. There might well have been a secure base in Walter's belief that his life was in danger.

'So now?' I asked. 'Donald's in trouble again, is he?'

'He wouldn't tell me exactly what. Nothing in detail. You know. He'd borrowed more money. There's nothing coming in, and not getting the seventeen shares he expected has really put the kybosh on it. He was on the phone for half an hour.'

'I'll have to see him.'

'To do what, Mr Patton? To offer him a loan to cover a loan? He wouldn't accept it. Not in the family.'

'I'm not in the family.' And not in a position to make loans, either. We were talking in thousands, and I thought in tens. 'I'd have to ask Philip Carne about it.'

'Donald wouldn't want that,' she said quickly.

'Then what *does* he want?' I asked, with an edge of impatience.

'To sort it out himself, I suppose. He's so very independent.'

'Oh sure, I'm hearing a lot about independence. But who *can* be? Nobody can exist without some dependence on outside support. I thought buying a caravan would make me independent. But it didn't. It's only changed the things I have to depend on. *He's* been depending on loans. Somebody's been prepared to offer him credit.'

'But he'd have to give some sort of security, surely. So in that way, he's still independent.' She nodded. Clearly, Donald had said the same thing.

I pushed the empty mug around with the end of my finger. 'This mug's independent, but I can push it around with a finger-tip. It's got no purpose unless it depends on somebody picking it up and filling it . . .'

'I'll pour you another.'

'No, damn it. It was an example. The mug's independent, and its security depends on one small thing, its handle. It offers itself as a receptacle, so long as you take hold of its handle, which is its security.'

I picked it up by its handle to demonstrate.

'I've got its security now, and in return it offers me mug after mug of nourishment. But I might want more from it. I might get impatient.' I poised it above the floor. 'And let it drop.'

'Don't you dare!'

'It was an illustration.'

'Then I'm sure I don't know what it means,' she told me severely.

I wasn't going to explain it. Loans without security are dangerous, and I didn't know what security Donald might have. You can get dropped from a great height.

'Just be sure you tell him I've got to speak to him.' I banged the mug back on the table. I had half a mind to go up and drag him out of bed there and then.

She was frowning at me. 'I'm sure I don't understand you, sometimes. Why are you so fierce?'

'There's no point in being built like me, unless you can frighten people.'

'You don't frighten me.'

'Then we know where we stand. Now don't forget, Mary. First thing in the morning. I've got to see him.'

She nodded. 'You're going up now?'

'If you'll show me where.'

'I've already done that.'

'So you have.' It indicated how tired I was. I grinned at her. 'I was forgetting.'

'You're as bad as Walter.'

'And what did *he* forget? To lock his door?'

'Never that. I meant, for example, to water the plants in the conservatory.'

'But Mary . . .' I put a hand round her shoulders as she got to her feet. 'You told me he didn't leave that room for over two months. So . . . how could he have watered the plants?'

She smiled up at me. 'He forgot to remind me to do it.'

Good old Walter, I thought, as I plodded up the wooden staircase, he'd been a typical managing director, using everybody he came in touch with. It would never have occurred to him that by pandering to his own morbid fears and locking himself away, he would be putting a large burden on Mary Pinson. In the same way, it had not occurred to him that he should have insisted on marrying her. It would have saved him having to remember her in his will, in what was surely a quite paltry way, when she should, as his widow, have had it all.

Thus pondering, I went to bed. It was almost two o'clock.

I knew you'd ask about normalised bolts, so I had a word with Chad in the morning. He told me that when they stamp them out of red-hot steel to put the head on the bolt, it alters the granular structure, so that the head could crack off under load. So they heat treat them back to normal. Normalised bolts.

Every bit of useless information helps, but in practice this turned out to be a clue. The death of Tolchard altered the structure, and it had to be normalised.

Think about it. I wish I had.

14

It was at the inquest that I had the chance to ask Chad about the bolts. I think he was there to lend support to Heather, who was supporting her brother by carrying his briefcase. Philip Carne was representing the family.

They were there, ranked at the front. Paul, Clare and Donald. In that order. I did not see them whisper to each other, not once. They sat, facing ahead. I'd have liked a word with Donald, but it wasn't the time.

When I'd come down to breakfast, Mary had said she'd spoken to Donald about my wanting to see him, but all it had done was drive him out quicker.

So there he was, and I still hadn't had my word. I was on the rear bench, Detective-Inspector Melrose beside me. I could understand that he'd be interested in the inquest, his suspicious death in Wales being so closely linked with that of Walter Mann. But I'd have expected him to sit with the small group of local police. Instead, he'd chosen to hodge up to me, nudge me in the ribs, and treat me like a friend he hadn't seen for ages. He had, of course. Whose headlights had been constantly following me, if not his?

He told me he was staying at The Dun Cow in town. He asked what I intended to do that afternoon.

'A trip back to Wales, to see my wife,' I told him, to save him the trouble of tailing me.

He had an easier method of doing that. 'Give me a lift?' he asked.

I laughed, unfortunately mistiming it, because the coroner was just taking his seat. Melrose would slip the mileage into his expenses statement. I nodded silently as the proceedings were opened.

We were enquiring into the sudden death of Walter Mann. The coroner had chosen to sit with a jury. The witnesses were few. First, the doctor who had been called to the scene and certified death, then the pathologist who had carried out the post mortem examination.

Walter's death bore all the indications of a fall from a height, such as a third-storey window. Nothing had been found in the stomach contents to suggest that Walter had imbibed drugs or any substance causing giddiness or a sudden malfunction of the brain. Thank you, doctor. Can we have Police Sergeant Bean in the witness box, please?

It was Sergeant Bean who had been called to the house. He gave details of the location of the conservatory, with the open window above it, and the dog locked in the room. Walter Mann had been found face down amongst a shower of glass, with a large hole on the conservatory roof immediately above him.

Mary Pinson was the main witness. She came to the stand. Her voice was quiet but clear. She was not allowed to ramble on without assistance, but was required to answer questions put to her by the coroner. Walter's mental condition that day was explored. His morbid fears and his locking himself away for the past two months were brought to the attention of the jury, but without any specific mention of the reason for Walter's behaviour. This was not relevant to the fall, and the coroner saw no necessity to embarrass the family. Mary was asked whether Walter had seemed in any way suicidal that day. She said he had not. Mention was made of the library book, which seemed to support this.

The coroner summed up. Discreetly, reference was made to the locked room and the dog. The word was not mentioned, but it was clear that murder was being ruled out, without any suggestion that, had it not been ruled out, the three members of the family sitting before him would have been the obvious suspects.

It was all conducted with smooth efficiency. Philip Carne need not have been there; the family did not need his representation. The coroner had done his homework.

The verdict was: accidental death.

It was as I'd expected. In fact I need not have gone there apart from the matter of respect. But one thing did arise from it. When we had all shuffled to our feet and had turned to make our way out, I realised that a man sitting three rows ahead of me was the enquiry agent who had sat at Amelia's bedside and left the card, with a request to contact Philip Carne. The Burns of Burns and Rafton.

Enquiry agents work for money. They have no personal interest in their individual cases, and his interest, even if minor, would have ceased to exist once he'd walked out of that hospital ward. So why had he attended the inquest?

This question seemed to demand an answer. I pushed past Melrose, surprising him, and causing so much fuss that it drew Burns's attention to me. Recognition was instant. He, too, began shoving and edging to get out. He was thinner than me, and less polite. He reached the door first.

When I got out to the corridor he was turning right, into the street. I hurried. In the direction he was taking was the nearest car park, on an open patch of ground. I broke into a run. As well as his other attributes, he was younger and more active than me. I was panting when I reached the car park entrance, just in time to see a car door slamming shut, and a Metro swinging out towards me.

I could have stood there and he wouldn't have been able to get past me. But I saw the grim determination on his face and heard the harsh acceleration. There was a possibility that he was prepared to drive over me. So I stood aside.

At the last second he changed his mind. The car skidded to a halt and his window slid down. His face, distorted by an emotion I couldn't identify, stared up at me.

'Accident!' he spat in disgust.

Then he was away, and this time it was Melrose who had to stand aside.

'What was that all about?' he asked, strolling up.

I was wondering exactly the same thing. There'd been no apparent reason why Burns would not want to speak to me. How's your wife? That sort of thing.

'I don't know,' I admitted. 'He's the enquiry agent who traced my wife to the hospital.'

'Oh?' His eyebrows lifted, but he made no comment.

It was then that I remembered I'd wanted to catch Donald before he left. Now it was too late. We walked rapidly back, but the building was empty, and Donald was probably on his way back to The Beeches.

'Were you thinking of eating before we make a start?' Melrose asked.

'I was. Now I'm not sure. I should really try to corner Donald, somehow.'

'Lunch is on me, and The Dun Cow's only along the street here.'

In this way, wrong decisions are provoked. I looked at him for a moment. He looked back at me, smiling with his head tilted. The lunches would also go down on his expenses sheet.

'Might as well,' I said. 'I want to get as long as possible at the hospital.'

We drove out of Boreton at a little after one o'clock. I negotiated the wriggles the other side of the river, and once on open roads started moving fast. I wondered how Melrose, who'd probably left his hatchback in the hotel car park, proposed to get back to it. But I didn't ask.

It's useful to have a companion on a long journey. Stops you dozing off. He appreciated that he could not expect any answers to his idle chat at moments when I was negotiating tight corners fast, or overtaking faster, as I was using all my concentration. In fact, during these times he fell strangely silent himself. It was only gradually that he turned the empty talk into serious conversation, and began to discuss the case. His case: the death of Nancy Rafton, and how it related, possibly, to the death of Walter Mann.

Delicately, he picked my brains. I retained sufficient of my mind to steer clear of any mention of Heather and Chad and Leyton, as related to Tolchard's death. He did not seem to realise that all three deaths could be connected. Or if he did, he was keeping it to himself.

131

We were well into Wales before he mentioned the inquest.

'Interesting verdict,' he said.

'It was what I expected.'

'I mean, it just about puts a stopper on my interest in the Boreton side of it.'

Then why had he left his car there? 'I'll be sorry to see an end to our association,' I told him, eyeing the back end of a trailer wagon and an approaching car. He was silent as I made the decision, and we'd scraped through.

'I mean,' he explained a little later, 'how can I justify going on, when I'll have to convince my chief super that there's still something in it? The whole point was that Nancy Rafton's death might have been intended for your wife, if the motive for it could be related to Walter Mann's murder. Now it's an accident verdict, not murder.'

'Hmph!' I said.

'You don't go along with that?' he asked with interest.

I glanced sideways at him. He seemed mildly amused. 'Since when were the police forced to go along with a coroner's verdict?' I asked.

'But you're not in the police, now?'

'We were talking about *you* dropping it. Not me.'

'You're still plugging for murder, then? What about the locked door? What about the dog?'

As I had no answer to these questions I was silent for a mile or so. Say a full minute. Mountain roads were ahead, and I had to ease off.

'There's the window, you see,' I explained. 'It was open.'

'So?'

'I'm convinced Walter would've shut it as soon as Mary Pinson left. I can see no reason why he'd open it again.'

'Any more than he would the door.'

'Even if he'd open the door to an unexpected visitor. That in itself would have been exceptional. But to open the window, with a visitor there – I just can't imagine a situation that'd bring that about. No social and friendly reason. That open window suggests violence to me.'

We swept down a road flanked by a low stone wall, sharp left over a hump-backed bridge, and touched down just in time to negotiate a sharp right-hander. After a minute he asked: 'You're forgetting the dog? She wouldn't have stood for violence.'

132

'I've got ideas about that dog.'

'Such as?'

'Locking her away in the bathroom.'

'Before this bout of violence you mentioned?'

'Of course.'

'Would Walter allow that, seeing that she was there as a kind of protector?'

'It's all I've got.'

I rushed a traffic signal in Lampeter. He pursued the subject stubbornly.

'The only way Walter Mann would allow anybody to lock away his dog . . .'

'Or do it himself.'

'Or do it himself,' he agreed, 'would be if he'd opened the door to a stranger, or a friend.'

'Or somebody he thought of as a friend. Or somebody he knew was scared of dogs.'

'All right,' he agreed placidly. 'You can ease off now, you know. We're almost there.'

I did, but only in order to concentrate on what he was saying. There was a point he intended to make.

'But if,' he went on, 'it was a friend or somebody he knew – say Mary Pinson or Kenneth Leyton – why did he die just at that time?'

'Are you asking?'

'Wondering. You see . . . he'd locked himself away for the past two months. If he let in somebody he had no reason to be afraid of, he would probably have done the same at any time during those two months.'

'An interesting thought.'

'So why wait? It was known Walter was intending to alter his will, and that he was trying to trace your wife. It would have been so much more simple to kill him before he located her, and before he changed his will. Why wait? It only made the whole operation more complicated.'

The hospital was coming up. I'd noticed he thought of it as a 'whole operation'. I changed down. 'I see your point.'

'I'm glad of that. So you'll see the odds are that Walter Mann wasn't killed. He died from an accident. It just happened at that time.'

I swung round into the parking area and cut the engine.

Three hours and seventeen minutes. Best yet. I reached for my pipe.

'You're trying to make a point,' I decided.

'Are you still insisting he was killed?'

I nodded, the pipe bobbing in my teeth. 'There's the open window, you see.'

'That's my point. *Why* are you persisting in this attitude? You've got an inquest verdict. Nobody would be surprised if you dropped it, and accepted that verdict. But you persist. I can see it could have been a useful blind, covering your real intentions—'

'What the hell's this?'

He sighed. 'And still you don't budge! Consider the sequence. The woman, Nancy Rafton, came to Wales to trace your wife, on Walter's instructions. She succeeded – otherwise, why would she have chosen plot 13 to park in? Now . . . we have no evidence that she hadn't spoken to your wife, or to you.'

'She had not.'

'But she could have done. You would then have known that a will was being altered in your wife's favour. I've seen no evidence that you're already well-endowed with money.'

'We're not.'

'So such a will would have been of interest to you. Then Nancy Rafton died. It would occur to you that her death had been aimed at your wife. During the week following that, you were supposed to be searching for rented accommodation . . .'

He stopped and waited. If necessary I could probably substantiate that. I said: 'Go on.' Very quietly.

'But perhaps, instead of doing that, you travelled to Boreton and back once or twice. The way you drive, you wouldn't have been missed! Perhaps you discovered that Walter Mann had already changed his will, but that there was a distinct chance he would change it back—'

'So I killed him?'

'I have to consider that possibility.'

'But you've just been trying to prove it couldn't have been murder.'

'But *you* say it could have been done, perhaps because you know how it *was* done. No! Wait! I haven't finished.'

'As far as I'm concerned, you have.' I unlatched the car door.

He touched my arm. 'If you had gone to Boreton, you'd have seen what a prize was coming your wife's way, and you'd have discovered, by that time, that there was every chance your wife would reject it.'

'How d'you know that?'

'Your wife is excited about it. She talks. Women do.'

I objected to the generalisation. Men talk too. *He* was talking, and I didn't like what I was hearing.

'She could have been indiscreet,' I admitted cautiously.

'Distinctly so. Because, if she died now, then you would get it all. I've had to consider the necessity of putting a guard on her.'

'You what!' Then I realised. 'So that's why you've been to Boreton. Easier to do it by keeping an eye on me, is that it?'

'Exactly.'

Was he smiling? I couldn't tell. But it had to be a leg-pull, surely.

'I'm going in to see her now. What're you going to do? Sit the other side of the bed?'

'I'm going to visit *my* wife, and then my chief super. But don't get too cocky, Mr Patton. I've got a WPC in there, dressed in nurse's uniform.'

'I don't believe it.'

'Then try spotting which one.'

He got out of the Volvo. I wondered how he intended to get from there, but he walked straight to a dark car, behind the wheel of which a young woman was sitting. He'd had it all laid on. All worked out.

My respect for Melrose's brain rose a few notches. My trust in him sagged. I went in to see Amelia.

I had a lot to tell her, and not enough time to do it in. I'd certainly advanced the position regarding Tolchard's death, but had produced no evidence connecting it with Walter Mann's. Amelia, however, seemed more interested in Heather and Chad.

'You were too hard on those two young people, Richard.'

'When people tell me lies, when I'm supposed to be helping them, then I get rough.'

She pouted at me. 'I remember.'

'And somehow . . . d'you know . . . I feel there's something not quite right about the rigmarole they told me.'

'In what way?' she asked.

'If I knew, I'd know,' I said profoundly.

She sighed, and poured herself a glass of orange squash. 'I went for an X-ray this afternoon.'

'Everything going as it should?'

'Oh yes. It's my arm, though. I don't think they're happy about that. Certainly, I'm not.'

I frowned. Away at Boreton I'd been too immersed in the grim realities surrounding the Mann family. I felt that I'd been neglecting my duties by not worrying enough about Amelia's arm. That could have been the reason it wasn't coming along as it should.

'But you were right about the dog,' I said, to cheer her up.

'Wasn't I!' She reached out a forefinger and pushed the end of my nose. 'So it can't have been murder.'

'Locked in the bathroom—'

'Nonsense. She'd have had to be let out. Then what? Richard, your mind's going stale.' She eyed me severely. 'Or have you been spending too much time worrying about me?'

'That must be it.'

I received further instructions. I was to discover exactly what trouble Donald was in, then see Philip Carne about getting him out of it.

'Yes, ma'am,' I said. 'That was what I had in mind.'

It was time for me to leave. I kissed her and we dragged our fingers apart. I paused. 'Oh . . . that nurse over there – she doesn't seem to be doing anything.'

'D'you fancy her? I think she only supervises. You can tell by the colour of the hat band. She's been talking to me quite a lot.'

'Has she?'

'She tells me she wants to be a policewoman.'

I left, winking at the nurse. She seemed startled.

There seemed time to call in at the caravan site, to ask about Cindy. It was late evening, and the family had just returned from a day's trip in the car. The little girl was walking Cindy again. They both knew it was only a game. Cindy recognised me, but her welcome was restrained. The little girl watched us with anxiety. Her father caught my eye, shrugged, and pouted.

I drove away. Melrose was standing at the site entrance. He waved. I felt like waving back and driving on, but I stopped and reached over to unlock the door.

'Guessed you'd come here,' he said, reaching for the seat belt.

'Aren't you lucky!'

I drove off. Up in the mountains I needed full headlights. He was silent. To test whether he'd dozed off, I said:

'I've discussed it with my wife, and we've decided I'm not trying to kill her.'

'That takes a load off my mind. It just shows how dangerous theories can be.'

And perhaps that was intended as a warning.

15

I dropped him outside The Dun Cow in Boreton. It was well after midnight, as we'd stopped on the way for a meal, and I was tired right through to the bones. Three hundred fast miles in a day, cross-country, was more than I could take, especially when the intervals had been filled with intense mental activity. My brain refused to switch off. Even now, slowly weaving my way through the dark country roads, it was tossing around ideas, offering them for inspection before I rejected them. My eyes wouldn't stay in focus, and my ears, humming from the thud and whine of tyres and the roar of the engine, were playing tricks with me.

It could have been the fanbelts, I decided as I turned into the drive at The Beeches . . . slipping belts whining.

The car nosed around the final bend to the garages, and my bed beckoned alluringly. The dipped headlights shone on an indistinct bundle of locked humanity, and when I cut the engine the whining, instead of ceasing, became agonisingly clear. It was human, but it contained such a quality of animal suffering that it could have been any primitive creature howling from the past.

My knees stiff from so much driving, I staggered forward.

'Mary! Mary, is that you?'

I crouched beside her. She raised her stricken face, abruptly silent, lower lip quivering and now unable to speak.

She had been trying to support Donald's head on her knee, whilst attempting to control the blood from his face with a wet towel. I couldn't tell how long she'd been at it, but the towel was soaked with blood.

At first I didn't think he could be alive. He was curled around a ball of agony, holding his body together. His face was torn and barely recognisable. They'd concentrated on the head. I'd seen something like it before, twice. Boots. I knew that the arms would

137

probably be broken, as the instinct is to wrap them round your head. The ribs, too, would have received treatment. It's the only way to persuade the subject to remove his arms from his head. Then you can start on the head. It usually required two sets of boots, in case one of the operatives was so unfortunate as to sprain an ankle.

I bent low. How to find the artery amongst all that ruptured flesh? As my head came close, an eyelid fluttered. I looked up.

'The phone, Mary. Ambulance.'

She was staring at me blankly.

'The phone!' I snapped.

She forced herself to her feet and stumbled away, feeling with her hands along the wall.

I didn't know how long ago it had been. No vehicle had passed me going the other way since I'd left Boreton. Trying to hold his head steady, I slipped one arm, and then the other, out of my jacket, fumbled it into an awkward pillow, and worked it beneath his head.

Then Mary was back. I glanced up. 'They're coming.' She knelt on the hard surface and took his hand.

'How long ago?' I asked quietly.

She shook her head, teeth clenched to suppress the chattering. There'd been no awareness of time. I tried again. She would go, I knew, with the ambulance. I'd not be able to prevent that. So there was little time.

'They came?' I asked. 'Two men?'

She nodded.

'You were . . . where?'

'Kitchen,' she sobbed. 'Donald . . . cup of cocoa . . . his usual.' Now her voice was more steady, but no stronger than a whisper. 'They f-forced their way in. I tried to stop them. Dragging. Tried to stop them, but they hit me. I don't remember.'

They'd knocked her out. 'You found yourself alone, and you came looking for him?'

'Yes. Yes. He was here.'

'Did they say anything?'

She shook her head.

'Nothing?'

'Only one word. Funny. It meant nothing.' She drew a shuddering breath. 'Luke. Or Lucas.'

I could hear the ambulance siren. I said: 'It won't be long, now.'

138

'Yes.' She tried to stand, straightened herself, and ridiculously patted her hair, which was already covered with blood. She moved to the corner of the house, to indicate where we were. I got to my feet and stood watching.

It was a long while before they were sure they dared to move him. I followed the stretcher to the ambulance and asked where they were taking him. Mary had had time to recover, and had thrown a cardigan round her shoulders. The ambulance man asked no questions, simply reached down a hand and hauled her up.

'I'll be in touch,' I said. I wasn't sure she heard. They were fixing a drip. Something clear.

I went back and switched off the Volvo's headlights, then, in the sudden blank darkness, fumbled my way round the house until I saw the light from the kitchen window. I sat at the table, then got up to put the kettle on to make a mug of coffee. While it was coming to the boil I went back outside and fumbled in the dark until I found my jacket. With it back in the light, I could see I wasn't going to be wearing it again before it was cleaned. Perhaps not even then.

I had a quiet smoke over a mug of strong, black coffee with plenty of sugar in it, then I went up to Donald's room. The thrum in my head was easing.

Go into the next room, and you'd find very little evidence of my presence. It was the same in his. The difference was that mine was just what I'd happened to bring with me. In Donald's, it was probably the sum total of his possessions.

There was the bottom half of a pair of pyjamas neatly folded on his pillow. Mary's work, that. They were pristine clean. Mary again. On the bedside table, a comb. In the drawer of it, nothing. In the wardrobe, nothing. He had it all in a kitbag. I turned this out on the bed. A spare pair of shoes, two pairs of socks, which Mary would have loved to get her hands on, or perhaps not. Two cotton sweatshirts. A pair of tatty jeans. A few pieces of underwear. A shaving kit. And nothing else. No wallet. He wasn't the sort of man to carry a wallet. Everything would be tucked away in pockets, and unfortunately most of his pockets had gone with him to the hospital.

I tried the jeans. They had two of those tight front pockets put in them, so as not to spoil the line. As I wasn't wearing them, I could just get my fingers in. One was empty, apart from a

139

flattened portion of cigarette that didn't smell like tobacco. In the other there was a cut-out portion of newspaper wrapped round a visiting card, printed in embossed gold.

I unwrapped the cutting. The card read:

AMOS P. LUCAS
PERSONAL FINANCE

There was an address in Birmingham.

I turned it over. On the back, in pencil, was printed:

$$30+6= 36-2= 34+6.8= 40.8-1= 39.8+8= 47.8$$

This had been scribbled through, but I could still just make it out. I slipped it into my back pocket, and opened the cutting. It read:

CARAVAN TRAGEDY

Mystery surrounds the sudden explosion of a caravan on the site at Pentried Farm yesterday. A woman was killed instantly. Eyewitnesses state that the explosion occurred the moment she entered her caravan. Mrs Ivy Staines of Shrewsbury told our reporter that she knew there would be a tragedy on this plot, as it is numbered 13. She made an impassioned plea for its number to be changed to 12A.

The police are investigating the cause of the blast, and are concentrating on the theory that gas was involved.

There the cutting ended. Across it was printed in red ballpoint: WESTERN EVENING STAR 30 AUGUST.

I knew, then, why the family, even though informed of the changed will by Walter, had nevertheless been shocked to the core when the will was read. They had believed that Amelia was dead.

As I stood there in that cold room – it had not seemed so cold when I entered – I realised that there could no longer be any possible doubt that the death of Nancy Rafton had been intended for Amelia. Walter had discovered our whereabouts, and so had someone else. Action had been taken, but had gone astray. The murderer had not realised this, and had bought copies of the following evening's local newspaper, sufficient copies to cover the interested parties, to each of whom a copy had been sent. That would be the logical action. But did that eliminate Donald? Not necessarily. Although it wouldn't be necessary to send one to yourself, it would still be a good policy to retain one . . . oh ye gods, I thought, of course it would. Essential, in fact, as an insurance policy.

The room seemed even more cold. I went down to the kitchen. There was room to pace.

The murderer would have to retain a copy for himself/herself, in case one of the others said: have you received one of these? It would be necessary to be able to answer yes, and produce it. In that way, a surface polish of innocence would be preserved. No one would know who, in fact, had done it.

Done what? I asked myself. Done what, Richard, damn it? Killed Walter, that's what. Killed Nancy Rafton, and then Walter. Never mind the locked door and the dog. Killed Walter. Because, the moment that cutting was circulated, with its terse, but incorrect message that Amelia was dead, it had become open season on Walter Mann. Let him change his will, but get him before he discovered for himself that Amelia was apparently dead, because he might then leave everything to Sheba's friends, the dogs' home. Kill him before he could do anything rash, and his family would again be the beneficiaries.

They had each known, those who were intimately interested, that this had to be done, and done it was. But they would not know, those of the innocent heart, which one of them had rounded it off by removing Walter. They would eye each other askance, and wonder, and never be certain to whom they owed their warmest thanks. Until the reading of the will! And there I'd been, at first a worrying mystery, but then, shockingly, the bearer of tidings that Amelia was *not* dead. Then . . . what price the warm thanks? The fury and the despair and the frustration would be levelled at the stupid bugger who'd set out to kill Amelia, and killed someone else, thus provoking the death of Walter at exactly the wrong time.

Yet still they would not know which one to blame.

Almost, I could feel sorry for them. But the chill had seeped right through to my bones, and all I could feel was that I wanted them to suffer, as Donald was now suffering. Yet he could well be the one. This thought held me. Donald's suffering gave me no

141

pleasure. On the contrary. I had spent thirty years trying to prevent half the population from inflicting suffering on the other half, or failing that, handing them over to the courts to punish. I had never wished to inflict pain.

It was a shock to discover that now I did. I was uncomfortable with it, like trying to wear someone else's suit. It was part of the syndrome I'd already shied from: the loss of my confidence and self-esteem. Now I was surrendering it, in a cold anger I could not dispel with immediate violence.

Angry now with myself, alone and brooding and with Amelia 150 miles away, I stumped out to the Volvo, completely forgetting to put off the house lights and lock up, and drove with fierce determination to the hospital. I had to show my concern, display it, as Mary had not displayed her grief. But Mary had felt her grief, and no display had been necessary. I felt nothing but an emptiness. By the time I parked the car my contempt for myself was assuming grand proportions. My display was shoddy.

I found Mary in the waiting room of Casualty, along with a great number of other waiters. It had been a fruitful night. I sat beside her.

'Any news?'

She shook her head. There was a livid bruise on the left side of her forehead, and in the morning that eye would be black. I wondered whether anyone had taken a look at it. Ladies of her age are susceptible to violence. I told her I'd go and ask for news, and went looking for the senior staff nurse, but before I could find her a policeman intercepted me. I should have remembered that hospitals are required to report such cases.

'Would you be Mr Patton, sir?'

I nodded, and he took me into a reasonably quiet corner. After I'd given full details of what I knew, but omitting any mention of where I thought the two heavies might be found, he snapped his notebook shut and offered what he knew himself.

Donald had a broken rib and a right arm fractured in three places. There was a possibility that he'd lose the sight of one eye, and an ear had nearly been torn free. There was no fracture of the skull, fortunately, but all the same he would be kept under observation. He was still unconscious, and was expected to remain so for at least twelve hours.

The policeman went away, but nevertheless I went to the office and spoke to the senior nurse there. I'm not up on the colours, so I didn't know her rank. I asked whether anyone had looked at Mary Pinson.

'The lady beneath the poster on meningitis?'

'That's her.'

'We're keeping an eye on her.'

'To see she doesn't doze off?'

'Something like that.'

'Can I take her home?'

Her quiet, dark eyes considered me. 'It would be better if you didn't. Just let her sit there quietly.'

'I'll come again in the morning.'

She touched my arm as I turned away. 'He's not going to die, you know.'

I smiled and nodded my thanks and went back to Mary, rehearsing an edited version in my head of Donald's injuries. I wasn't sure she took it all in.

'I'll take you home,' I said.

'No.' Her pursed lips were stubborn.

'All right. Then I'll come back later.' It was no good saying: the morning. It was all one to her.

She tried to smile, and I left her. Believing that staying was her own idea, she would at least not be worried on her own account.

I was nearly at the door when I remembered something. It was a bit of a shock. Sheba! Where had Sheba been? I went back to Mary.

'Where was Sheba, Mary?' I asked. Where *is* she? I wondered. Not – please not – lying under a hedge with her ribs caved in!

She smiled at my anxiety. 'Oh . . . Clare's got her. She came this afternoon and said she'd at least take the dog.'

'She had no right.'

'I didn't feel like arguing.'

'Of course not. Now . . . get something to eat, Mary.' Something else I'd forgotten! 'Can I get you some coffee?'

She shook her head, and reached out to touch my hand. 'You get back, and get some sleep.'

At last I got away. Out in the car park I found Melrose leaning against my car.

'It gets around,' I said.

'They keep me informed. Is it bad?'

'Didn't they tell you? Only as bad as two pairs of boots could make it.'

143

He thought about that for a moment. 'Any ideas?'

I answered indirectly. 'Tomorrow, I could find use for a tough young constable, preferably off-duty and unmarried.'

'It's like that, is it? I can't say I approve.'

'To watch my back.'

'It's not my patch,' he said. 'I don't know the field. Only one chap I might recommend. Me.'

I stepped back and considered him, lounging casually against my paintwork. 'Somebody with more weight.'

'I'm a mover. Pick me up at The Dun Cow?' he asked. 'It's all muscle, what you can see.'

'Around ten?'

'Fine.'

I drove back to The Beeches to get what sleep I could fit in, which turned out to be four hours, as I was woken by the phone. Even so far away downstairs, its ring penetrated my subconscious, which translated it into an alarm clock. I knew I had no chance of reaching it before it cut off, and I was correct. It was just after eight-thirty. Ruffling my hair, disturbed by uncertainty as to who might be ringing me so early, thus suggesting an emergency, I went into the kitchen and brewed tea, preparatory to a wash and clean-up and a shave.

It caught me again with shaving cream on my face, but this time I got to it.

'Richard Patton,' I gasped.

'This is Paul Mann, Mr Patton.'

'Did you call me earlier?'

'Yes. I wanted to ask—'

'For God's sake, at half past eight?'

'We start at that time at the factory, you know.' He said it with a hint of severity.

I was relieved, and noted he'd pounced on his phone the moment he'd reached his desk.

'I was up very late. Sorry.'

There was acid in his voice. 'Celebrating, no doubt.'

'No cause to celebrate, I can assure you. Haven't you heard about Donald?'

There was a pause while he decided on his attitude. In the end, his voice was cautious, but with an overtone of distant alarm. 'What about him?'

I told him about Donald. All the details. He was breathing

144

heavily as I spoke. When I'd finished, he said: 'The damned fool.'

'In what way has he been foolish?'

'I knew it would come to something serious. Money, of course.' He spoke with distaste.

'He came to you, did he?'

'I'm tired of giving him hand-outs. He never had any idea of how to run a business. Now it's come to this.'

'Yes.'

He paused a decent five seconds. 'I thought we ought to get together, Mr Patton. I'd like to show you the production lines . . .' And so on, and so on. I listened impatiently, the drying cream beginning to flake off my chin.

He was going all formal on me, having faced the facts as they were and realised he was going to have to live with them. He resented the fact that Chad had got in before him in the buttering-up act, but was now prepared to concede a point or two and admit to my existence.

In the end, I cut in impatiently. 'We'll certainly have to do that, Paul. Can I give you a ring? I'm rather busy today.'

'Oh yes. Fine. Great. I'll be waiting.'

Then, because he hadn't asked, I told him where Donald was, including the phone number, in case he might arouse an interest in his brother's welfare. He thanked me, and rang off.

While I had the phone in my hand I rang the hospital myself. There was an improvement. They don't admit that, unless it's distinct. I said I'd be along.

After a quick breakfast I drove fast for the hospital, where Mary was miraculously still awake, and considerably more optimistic. Donald had recovered consciousness and she'd been to see him, and he'd recognised her and spoken a few words. Mary was now prepared to return home.

There, I sat her at her table and banged on the kettle, rattled the teapot, crashed down the mug, sugar bowl and milk jug, all as she would like it, and said:

'Can I leave you to brew it?'

'You're going out?'

'Urgent business, Mary. I'll expect to find you in bed, when I get back.'

'You will not, you know.'

I grinned at her, and went to find Melrose at The Dun Cow. I was only half an hour late.

145

16

'D'you know Birmingham?' he asked, as we drove into the outskirts.

'No. Do you?'

'I'm a native of Birmingham. When you told me the address . . .'

Which I'd done as we'd driven out of Boreton. 'Yes?'

'I very nearly asked to get out. To phone for reinforcements,' he explained.

'As bad as that, is it?'

'Shall we say, if you leave this car parked outside, you'll be lucky if it isn't stripped when we come out.'

'So what d'you suggest?'

'We leave it at the nearest nick, and walk. Possibly half a mile.'

'Right. We'll do that.'

This we did, and without the car I felt naked. It was that sort of district. There was nothing visible that indicated we weren't safe on those naked streets, but I had an uneasy feeling of being observed, though the streets were strangely empty. Our feet rang hollowly. *His* feet rang – I was wearing soft heels. I realised he was walking in heavy shoes, heels and toes tipped with steel. He had drawn on string-backed driving gloves, and beside me he was striding with a spring to his gait that I hadn't previously noted. He had the poised tension of expectancy, and it was visible. Perhaps this was the idea, broadcasting his awareness. Perhaps it was he who was making me uneasy, infesting the district with aggression as we moved through it.

'Doesn't look as though there'd be money around here,' I said.

'You don't see rats till you disturb them.'

The streets consisted of rows of crumbling terraces, their mullioned bay windows rotting, their doors askew and often ajar, their glass now more often hardboard or planks, roughly nailed in place. We were looking for number 257.

It appeared to be like the others. The door was open into a tiled, narrow hall, reasonably clear of gusted litter, with stairs to one side, uncarpeted. The address on the card had been: third floor. We mounted, me in front because this was my scene. Now Melrose was managing to step quietly. On the third floor we had a choice of four doors, but only one carried a replica of the visiting card, thumb-tacked to the peeling surface. I pushed it open.

There was a genuine receptionist, her desk almost masking the ancient rusted iron fireplace. She was sharp and polished, like stainless steel. She smiled, her teeth honed to a cutting edge.

'Good morning.'

Beyond the eyeshadow and mascara her eyes were wary, in spite of the welcome, which had been automatic. Visitors did not normally arrive in pairs.

I nodded to the door beyond her. 'Is he in?'

'Yes, but he's . . .' Her fingers slid towards the phone.

Melrose's hand appeared under my elbow and his fingers clamped on her wrist. 'Is there a ladies?'

'The gents is along . . .'

'For you, ducks. Go there. Lock yourself in. Do yourself a favour.'

Without apparent effort he drew her round the desk. 'Scat!' he said, and slapped her bottom. She scuttled from the room.

For a second I paused at the inner door. There were voices. I held up my fingers. Three of them. Melrose nodded. I opened the door and we went in.

This inner office was more impressive. An attempt had been made towards a veneer of class. Lucas's desk was of polished rosewood. It supported three phones, two probably dummies. In front of him was a nested set of in-trays, one on top of the other. Requests for his financial assistance were clearly overwhelming him. His steel filing cabinets gave an impression of containing secret records of hundreds of gentry he'd satisfied in the past. The small safe against the wall behind him was so placed as to be well in sight. It could conceivably contain cash money. His smile told me he was only too eager to part with some of it. There could've been nothing sweeter than that welcoming smile, nothing so sour as it twisted, as he realised that something was wrong.

I held the visiting card a foot from his nose. 'Is that you?'

He moistened his lips.

'Is that you?'

He made a movement with his right hand, his weak grey eyes holding mine.

I'd given no indication of having spotted his assistants. As we'd walked in, one had been lounging against a side wall, the other standing to one side of the desk. But I'd observed them, and noted their placings and their general demeanour. I'd expected older, heavier men. These were the new breed, the young and deprived, earning a crust. They couldn't have been more than twenty, old enough for the muscles to have developed, but too young to have built up experience. Their toughness was superficial. It was the handing-it-out toughness, not the taking it. The gesture from Lucas awoke the one by the desk. He'd not, until then, dared to move a muscle.

To him, I was an older man. The sneer on his lips indicated that. Perhaps he didn't put everything into that first swing, not the speed nor the accuracy. He'd aimed for my belly. I swung sideways, and removed the sneer with a quick right to the mouth. Watch it, Richard, I told myself. The knuckles. He'd decided I was being insolent, and moved in to finish it. I saw him swivel on the left foot and poise his right. It was an obvious move, and there was an effective response. You swing round the rising foot, get both hands beneath it, tread on the static foot, and heave upwards. His mouth opened. It should have dislocated his hip. His cry was a quivering whimper, when it should have been a scream.

It has always been my aim, in such encounters, simply to incapacitate the opponent quickly, without inflicting too much pain. But now I recalled, not the severe injuries to Donald, but the bruise on the side of Mary's forehead. I *wanted* to hurt him. I wanted him to stay hurt. Bitter rage took over.

Perhaps this was as well. I'd been too easy with him already, and my efforts had not, after all, dislocated his hip. I threw him away from me against the filing cabinets, and he bounced back, stumbling a little, but with his fists flying. I caught a bright reflection of light. He was wearing brass knuckles. I parried one blow, my left forearm going numb, then I buried my right in his guts, kneed him in the face, and hammered his kidneys. He paused, shaking his head, his face grey, then he advanced again. I backed, appeared to slip, and was on my back on the floor. He did exactly as instinct dictated. He came close enough and drew back his right foot for a kick at my ribs. It was what I wanted. I hooked my right foot behind his left heel, rolling on to my right hip, and kicked him as hard as I could on the left knee. I heard it crack. He howled, and began to fall on to his face. I twisted so that he would miss me, flung myself on his back, and with both hands grabbed his head and banged his face on the floor. Until he was silent, then a little longer.

I got to my feet. Too old for it, too old. I ached, and my knees were shaking. I looked round to see how Melrose was doing.

Not for Melrose the dirty in-fighting I'd used. Melrose was a cold, precise machine, chopping his man to pieces, toying with him, dancing and sliding round him, and hurting, hurting, hurting. The blows flew in. The lout was reeling, but Melrose kept him short of unconsciousness, would not allow him to escape by lying down. Now his opponent had no awareness of what was going on. He was flailing uselessly with his arms. Coolly and professionally, Melrose cut him to ribbons.

'That's enough,' I said, my breath a little short.

Melrose heard. He planted himself, then swung in a right beneath the heart. I heard it, heard the air gasp out of the youth, then he fell flat on his face and was still.

I turned my attention to Mr Lucas, who had thrust himself as far back as possible in his seat, his jowls sagging and his bald head matted with sweat. I picked up the card from his desk.

'Is this you?' I asked.

He whispered: 'Yes.'

'Good. We're getting somewhere.'

I turned the card round and showed him Donald's pencilled figures on the back. 'And these?'

He looked up at me with appeal.

'I'll give you a clue,' I said. 'Donald Mann. Did you make him a loan?'

He moistened his lips, his tongue thick and fleshy. 'Yes.'

'So the opening thirty is the loan?'

'Yes.'

'And the added figure of six is the interest?' They'd been Donald's own calculations.

He stared at me in desperation. The thug at my feet groaned. Melrose stepped forward. I didn't see what he did, but there was no further sound.

'Was it?' I insisted.

'Yes.'

'Monthly?' I put out a finger and touched his nose, Amelia's gesture, but now carrying a vastly different implication.

'Monthly,' he croaked.

'That works out at twenty per cent a month,' I told him, as though he didn't know. 'Over two hundred a year. Compound interest, that would be. Say three hundred a year. Am I right?'

'Give,' he said, 'or take a little.'

I looked round at Melrose, who raised his shoulders. It seemed to encourage Lucas.

'Fair!' he cried in a high voice. 'Very fair, on an unsecured loan.'

'Unsecured!' I stirred the unconscious thug with my toe. 'These two were your security. And I suppose that was thousands?'

He nodded, gaining confidence. 'I advanced him thirty thousand.'

'On a promissory note?'

'It has to be in writing,' he said, trying for dignity.

'Let me see it.' I leaned closer. 'Produce it.'

He reached sideways to a drawer.

'No,' I said. 'Not in the drawer. Your safe.'

There was hatred in his eyes as he turned away and crouched to his safe. I reached over and yanked open his drawer. There was an ancient, but probably lethal, automatic pistol in there. I tossed it to Melrose, who examined it with interest. It was something we hadn't expected.

Scrambling back to his chair, Lucas handed me a sheet of paper.

It was typed. So she could type! I skimmed through it quickly, then turned to Melrose, who was idly sighting the pistol at the centre of Lucas's forehead.

'The security was Donald's seventeen shares,' I told him. 'The ones he would have got when his father died.' I turned back to Lucas. 'But he didn't get them, did he?'

He showed his teeth. 'Unfortunate.'

'You'd have had those shares off him, if he had?' I demanded.

'Yes.'

'Did *he* realise that?'

He actually sniggered, a hissing wet sound that nearly earned him my fist in his mouth. He sobered. 'I don't think Mr Mann really understood.'

'What *did* he think? I'm getting tired, Mr Lucas. Tell me.'

'He thought he'd sell them in the family, and pay me off. That was ridiculous, of course.'

'And how much has he paid, out of his thirty thousand?'

'With interest deducted—'

'How much has he paid? You can forget your interest.'

'He's paid eleven thousand.'

'Then maybe you'll get the other nineteen. Maybe.' I turned away, then remembered. 'One more question. Did Donald suggest to you that his father might not live much longer?'

He planted his palms on the surface of the table. 'I was willing to wait as long as it took. The interest satisfied me.'

At last I made a move to leave. Melrose casually fired the pistol, putting a bullet into the surface of the desk.

'It actually works,' he said in surprise.

I folded the promissory note and put it inside my anorak pocket, zipping it in safely. My last sight of Lucas was his grey face staring sightlessly after me. Outside on the landing, Melrose was banging on doors and shouting: 'You can come out now, love.'

But she would have been well away by that time.

We walked back to pick up my car, Melrose to hand in the pistol. They had something at last on Lucas, and I guessed there'd be a squad car round there in minutes.

On the drive back to Boreton, Melrose was silent. He'd taken off his string-backed gloves and was flexing his fingers.

'Thanks for your help,' I said. 'I'd never have managed alone.'

'It's been a pleasure.'

'Why the shoes?' I asked. 'The steel tips. You didn't use your feet.'

'They notice such things. It bothers them and distracts them.'

'I'll have to remember that.'

He was silent for a long while, then at last he suggested: 'You could forget that nineteen thousand. He'd never dare to sue.'

'You don't know my wife. She's got this strange idea about being fair and right.'

'To scum like that?'

'Even to me.'

He grunted. 'I'd like to meet her.'

I glanced sideways at him and grinned. 'You keep your distance, friend.' He was too blasted good-looking for my liking. 'Anyway, she doesn't go for young and immature men.'

151

'Stop this car, and I'll make you take that back.'

'Not while you're wearing those shoes, mate.'

We laughed. The interchange had been inane, a reaction from the morning's work.

I dropped him at The Dun Cow, and he simply waved and walked away. I drove on, to The Beeches. I felt fit to drop.

Mary was dozing in her windsor chair in front of the Aga, but was wide awake at once.

'I told you to go to bed,' I said severely.

'Not till you got back.'

'Yes. Well, I'm here. Off with you.'

She made no move. 'I bet you haven't eaten.'

'For heaven's sake, I can do myself bacon and eggs. Get some rest, then you can go back to the hospital. Can you drive yourself?'

'Of course I can.'

'Then, when you see Donald, and if he can understand, give him this.' I handed her the promissory note.

'What is it?' She blinked at it. 'I need my specs.'

'It's a legal document relating to the loan Donald took on, and couldn't pay back. He'll know.'

She eyed me suspiciously. 'That's where you've been?'

'I took a friend, and we had words with the two gents who were here last night.'

'You're just a ruffian,' she told me. 'I knew it the first moment I saw you.'

'''Fraid so.' I took my lower lip between my teeth and she punched me on the shoulder.

She turned at the door. 'I've put clean towels in the bathroom and there's plenty of hot water.'

'Thank you, Mary. I'll just phone my wife first.'

'Then tell her from me you've been fighting. Men! Like little kids, all of you.' And, head up, she went.

Heavily, my muscles stiffening up, I trailed into the living room and sat at the phone table. As I reached for it, it rang. I picked it up.

'You were going to get back to me,' said Paul plaintively.

'For Christ's sake!' I burst out, and I slammed it down again.

17

I phoned Amelia and apologised for not calling her before. I asked about her arm, and she said there'd been some infection, but a change of antibiotics had been used and it was already improving. I brought her up to date with the news, omitting mention of the visit to Birmingham. I did not tell her that Clare had taken Sheba, because I'd guessed at her reason for this, and Amelia wouldn't have liked to hear it.

But we were constrained, and not reaching through to each other. I put it down to my exhaustion, and tried harder.

'You're sure you're all right?' I asked.

'Improving all the time.'

'There's something wrong,' I decided.

Her voice became tiny, but crystal clear. She was hugging the phone close. 'I'm being watched, Richard.'

'What?'

'Officially watched.'

'That nurse—'

'Don't be ridiculous,' she said. 'That was the staff nurse. No, there's a policeman parked on a bench in the corridor. I get glimpses. And it's not always the same one.' I was silent. 'Richard?'

My brain was fighting to assimilate it. Melrose hadn't been kidding, he really did suspect me. I didn't know how to handle it, what to say.

'Are you still here, Richard?'

I cleared my throat. 'Oh . . . that!' Did it sound so false the other end? 'I heard some stupid theory – you know – about Nancy Rafton's death.'

'What theory?' I'd paused too long. Her voice was sharp.

'That it might have been intended for you. Nonsense, of course. I didn't pay much attention.'

'But the policeman's *here*. I can see him this second.'

'Playing safe.'

'I don't want to be played safe with, Richard. I want to *be* safe.

Surely this can't have anything to do with the other . . . with what you're doing there.'

'I shouldn't think so, my love.'

'Then finish it quickly, Richard. Please. I can't lie here . . .' Then she controlled her voice. 'I want *you* to guard me,' she said in a tiny voice. 'Hurry, please, Richard.'

What could I say? How reassure her? 'It won't be long now. I know how Walter was killed. I think I know who did it. Clear it up in no time, now.'

'Promise?'

'Promise,' I said.

The last bit after that was private, and a bit garbled anyway, because I was cursing myself for a fool. I couldn't see any end to it, and I'd lied. But a promise is a promise.

I had my bath and my bacon and eggs, decided that the anorak would have to do, though it had lived in the boot of the car for months, and went to see Clare. Unfortunately, I had to ring Paul to ask for the address, which upset him because he reckoned he had the first call on my invaluable company, so I had to promise him I'd call in at the factory later. Another promise! By a bit of luck, Clare's place was only half a mile beyond the factory.

They had probably bought the bungalow when they were married. It was one of a sprawling complex, perched on the steep slope on the west side of the river, half each side of the road. They mounted into the wooded slopes, the trees having been preserved and the houses carefully sited. Even though the slope ensured that all, except those at the top, would be overlooked, efforts had been made to ensure privacy. It had been a costly project. The status of the residents reflected this fact. You could tell it from one glance at the cars.

Clare, perhaps because she'd grown up beside a river, had chosen one of the lowest of the estate. It was nestled down by the water, reached by winding and intersecting roads, secluded, select, and substantial.

When built, the trend had been towards an absence of garages. Car-ports were the thing. This had the advantage of allowing you to put away your cars and still have them on view. As Clare's was at the end of the cul-de-sac, there was no one to notice the Audi Quattro and the BMW 320 that occupied the ports as I drove in. The Quattro would have been Tolchard's, I guessed. He was a four-wheel drive character, who'd involve all four in taking him to his management slot, though he was only half a mile from the factory.

I got out and had a look round. Immaculate lawn, rose beds, immaculate trees, an artificial pond. The rush of the river was soothing. I stood in the cantilevered porch, large enough to park another car, and pressed the button. Delicate chimes announced my presence.

Clare had abandoned mourning as being too restrictive. She was dressed in slim, tailored slacks in a blue, silky material, a cream blouse, and with a tiny bolero jacket over it. Her make-up was expert and discreet. She stared at me with wide and startled eyes, and said: 'Well . . . hello . . .'

'I've come for my dog,' I said without preamble, making no effort to sound sociable.

'Oh . . . hoity-toity! You'd better come in.'

'If you'd just bring her out.'

'Oh come in, and stop being coy.' She stood back, and I saw that the hand that had been holding the door had a cigarette trapped in the fingers. 'I'm not going to eat you.'

I closed the door behind me. She was moving away from me with a feline grace that was almost predatory, though she did not make the mistake of moving her hips too much.

'I was just getting myself a drink,' she tossed back over her shoulder, her hair moving enticingly. She had it loose that day, had probably only recently shampooed it.

I followed her into the room she would probably call a lounge. As at The Beeches, this room was at the rear to take full advantage of the view over the river. It had an almost complete wall of sliding, double-glazed metal windows overlooking a terrace patterned in hexagonal, multi-coloured paving slabs. The fitted carpet was plain mid-green, the pattern raised, the Swedish furniture loosely arrayed with a lighter green upholstery. Three walls were plain, the fourth of natural stone, in it set a fireplace now housing an electric fire on legs, thus implementing the impression that it was a live one. There were even fire irons and a scuttle at one side, logs visible but never used. Sheba was spread in front of this on a thick oval rug, apparently unaware that the flickering from the fire was cold, and no more than artificial.

'There she is,' said Clare, tossing a negligent gesture with her hand in the direction of the fireplace. 'Quite happy, as you can see. What'll you have?'

155

The drinks cabinet had sliding glass doors, and a tray on its surface with a soda-water syphon and glasses. Two glasses.

'Nothing, thank you,' I said. 'I'm not much of a drinker. You knew I'd come, didn't you?'

'A man like you . . .' She turned from the drinks, her eyes bright with mockery. 'You were probably weaned on scotch. Why else d'you think I brought Sheba here?'

Now there was amusement in her eyes, and a challenge. It gave her pleasure to reveal her hand, without actually displaying it.

I didn't feel like playing her game. 'I realised that, of course.' It wasn't necessary, with all that glass, to approach the windows in order to admire the view. Nevertheless I strolled over, fishing out my pipe. 'Sheba was never your dog.'

'Please tell me what you'll drink. I can't stand here for ever.'

She equated masculinity with strong drink. I smiled at her, holding my eyes on hers, and gently shook my head. She made an impatient sound, and looked away.

'Then you don't mind if I do?'

I shrugged, though she wouldn't have seen it. 'It's your home.'

'You're a guest here.'

'Not a guest. A visitor. I'll just take Sheba . . . Where did you put the lead?'

She turned fast on one heel and glared at me, took four paces to a three-seater settee, and threw herself on to it, but managed not to spill one drop from her glass.

'For God's sake!' she said. 'What have I got to do? Down on my knees? Stay a while. I'm going crazy here, all by myself. It comes to something when I've got to kidnap a blasted dog to get a man into the house.'

There seemed no necessity for me to turn from the view. Her tone told me everything. Three months had been too long. She was, she was blatantly telling me, a healthy woman with healthy appetites, and the house was empty, even encouragingly isolated. That, anyway, was the hand she revealed. I was not yet sure what hand she meant to play.

'You need only have picked up the phone,' I said, lighting up, bouncing the smoke from the glass.

'And you'd have come?'

'No.' Puff-puff. 'I'm married.'

'Oh dear. Poor you.'

It was degenerating into an adolescent game of word-play. I

156

turned from the window. Her last words had been sharp and dismissive. I went and sat beside her. She smiled. Perhaps her martini could have been more dry. I smiled back, and produced the newspaper clipping Donald had been carrying.

'Did you get one of these?'

'No, I did not.' Even more dry.

'Through the post,' I amplified.

'What is it?'

'You got 'em backwards. You should have asked that first.'

'Let me see.'

'You'd better put that drink down.'

She did so, on a small, glass-topped table, forcefully.

'Let me see, damn you.'

In case she might have wished to destroy it, I held it up in front of her eyes. She squinted at it. Vanity had prevented her from wearing her close-up spectacles.

'I can't read it,' she said pettishly. 'Read it for me.'

She was playing for time, wondering where we were going from there. I did so, reading it slowly to oblige her, in that if not in the other. I looked past it to her eyes.

She was not quick-witted. Even now she had not decided on her attitude, and a hand went angrily to her hair, whipping it back.

'What does it mean?'

'It relates to the death of a woman in a caravan in plot thirteen of a site in Wales.'

'Am I supposed to be distressed?'

'I wondered if you'd read it before. Perhaps you received one by post?'

'I think you'd better take Sheba and go.'

'You didn't give me the lead.'

I don't think she caught the double meaning. The lead she'd given me was now forgotten.

'Where did you get it?' she demanded.

'You haven't answered my question.'

'What question? What?'

'I've already asked it twice. Did you receive one of these in the post?'

'I *told* you I didn't.'

'But that was before you gave it any thought. You'd have done better to say that you had. I got it from Donald, by the way.'

157

She rose to her feet with such vigorous anger that the table shook, but she grabbed up her drink before it toppled. 'I think you must be mad.' She saw that I was watching her with a smile, and gulped at her drink. 'How from Donald? Why would he give you that?'

'I didn't say he had. I took it from the pocket of his jeans.'

'Took it?'

'He being in hospital.'

'Donald's in hospital?'

'Haven't you heard? Paul should have phoned you. Donald's in hospital because he was beaten up over a debt. The people involved like to terrify their customers into paying. He was beaten up because of the inheritance that he didn't get from your father.'

'Which none of us got,' she snapped.

'And which he was counting on, even though your father had no doubt told him he'd been disinherited. Virtually.'

'He didn't . . .' She stopped.

'Didn't tell Donald, you were going to say? But how would you know that? From the simple fact that your father didn't tell *you*?'

She had to have time to work that out. With her face white now, she stared at me for a moment, then whirled away to her drinks cabinet, clattering the glass, making a performance of it to demonstrate her anger at me. She turned back. I lifted my head.

'Father didn't tell *me*,' she said with dignity.

'And yet you knew about his intention to change his will?'

'I'm not going to listen to this, in my own home . . .'

I got to my feet. 'Two minutes, and I'll go.' I raised my eyebrows. She said nothing, so I went on. 'You knew of your father's *intention*, of course. He would have broadcasted it. But somebody, who knew his intention, attempted to kill my wife by blowing up the caravan on plot thirteen. That same somebody circulated copies of this newspaper cutting to the interested parties, to indicate that there was no longer any necessity to worry about the new will. Because my wife was dead. But it would not be necessary to send a copy to one's self, I'd suggest.'

'What are you saying?' She was frowning as though it was beyond understanding.

'That it follows . . . the one who *didn't* get a copy was the one who sent them.' I looked round. 'Never mind the lead. Sheba, coming home, girl?'

158

Sheba awoke instantly and gambolled over to me. I heard a drawer bang open, and turned. She was waving a bit of paper.

'I got one, damn you.' The pallor had gone. Anger had flushed her cheeks.

I took it from her, folded it with the other, and put them both away safely. 'And now – can I leave?'

'You put me at a disadvantage, and then you walk out!' She tried to follow the disgust with a smile, but it was ghastly. 'What does it mean? I don't understand.'

'There was general disbelief when the will was read. There was an equally general disbelief that my wife was still alive. It was thought she'd died before your father. As simple as that.'

'I knew nothing about it.'

'But you understood very well what the cutting meant?'

'It was a complete mystery to me.'

'Then why did you keep it?'

There was no way out for her. I saw she realised that, and I wondered whether she'd fall back on tears. She did not. Her reaction startled me. She suddenly threw back her head and laughed.

'Oh you poor, dear man. Here I am, leading you astray, and you being all naïve and moral! Of *course* I knew he'd made a new will. Of *course* I believed your wife was dead. What would you expect, that I'd weep for her? I don't know her. She was no more to me than those other anonymous deaths we hear about on the news.'

'To me she is.'

'But of course. Silly man. Sit down, you great idiot. You fill the room, standing there.'

I sat, because I didn't understand this new angle she was trying out. Her abrupt candour had disarmed me.

'But you'd be used to that,' I observed. 'Wasn't your husband a big man?'

'Big, yes, in size. And in energy. And in forcefulness, like you. But not in . . . what's the word? . . . sort of domination.'

Me? Dominating?

'No,' she decided, her eyes measuring me. 'Personality, that's it. Understanding and sympathy . . .'

Where did she get all this twaddle? 'We can't all be the same.' I tried to sound modest.

'But of course not. What would be the point?' She gave me the full benefit of a suggestive look, and threw back her head as though to say: that's put it in a nutshell. Then she said: 'I'll go and make some tea, seeing you're not a spirits man. Al could take it, and it never seemed to touch him.'

And yet, this commendation was expressed with contempt. At the same time, Aleric had been degraded to Al. Somehow, I felt sorry for him. She, too, could take her liquor, but it certainly touched her, judging by the look she tossed me as she swept out.

It was thinking time for both of us. I still couldn't see what she was trying to get across. I waited. There were distant sounds. She eventually returned with a silver tray, a silver tea service gracing it, and egg-shell china for me to worry about, me with my bulk and my domination. She had found time to do a little adjustment to her hair. Drops in her eyes? Would she go that far? But certainly they sparkled. And I? Had I found time to run a comb through my hair? I can't remember.

She set down the tray. 'That's him over there.' She nodded towards the shelf above the fire, to which Sheba, confused as I was, had returned. The head and shoulders photograph of Aleric Tolchard had caught a certain arrogance, a confident angle to his head, the strength of the chin and the determination in his eyes.

'Sugar?' she asked.

'I'll help myself.'

I returned to my seat. She chose to sit opposite to me now, though you can't do anything interesting with slacks. The tea was Earl Grey.

'Your wife,' she asked, 'is she getting better?'

This was more than she'd asked about Donald. 'There was some worry about infection in her arm, but the antibiotics are winning.'

'Poor woman. Such a pity.'

I wondered which was the pity, the pain or the recovery. Her teeth, her smile round them, challenged me to guess.

'She's quite a fighter,' I assured her. Warned her.

'I can't wait to meet her. She'll be arriving soon, I hope. To take over. To the house . . .' Here, she faltered. The house had always been her main objective.

I said it might be a few weeks yet.

'Anything could happen,' she observed, 'in a few weeks.'

'I wouldn't think so.'

'It would be such a pity if it did. To inherit all of it, and not even see it!'

'We mustn't be morbid,' I told her, my voice beautifully in control.

'But *you've* seen it.' The smile again. It was switching on and off like fairy lights, presumably to hypnotise me. 'You wouldn't want to lose it now.'

'But I wouldn't, would I.'

'Of course not. Silly me. You'd get it all.'

I raised my eyebrows. She cocked her head in question at my question. We played it like two dummies, remotely controlled.

'If she died,' she explained.

'Ah yes.' I allowed myself to sound relieved, at last comprehending. 'As your husband died. That, too, was very sudden.'

'Too? But she's alive.'

'Nancy Rafton isn't. The woman mentioned in the cutting,' I explained. 'Though her name's not given.'

For a moment she glanced aside, but not quite quickly enough. Then she busied herself with the cups again.

'He had an exercise room, you know,' she said, apparently changing the subject. 'I could show it to you. Do you exercise, Mr Patton? Must I continue to call you mister?'

'Richard, and I don't.' Apart from the occasional punch-up.

'It's all in there, Al's stuff, his weights and his rowing machine and his skipping rope. God, what a way to spend your time! Out every morning before breakfast in his joggers. Four miles. Coming in hardly out of breath, straight into the shower, a quarter of an hour under his sun-ray lamp. A fanatic, that's what he was.'

'It must be very wearing.'

'Wearing! I was fed right up to here with it.' She gestured to her throat, which, just at that moment, she was displaying at its very purest curve. 'Two evenings a week, it was off to his squash club in Birmingham. Bang, smack, slash, take that you little bastard! Oh, he could hammer all hell out of a tiny ball. My husband was a man, Richard. A real, genuine hunk of powerful machinery.'

Which puts me in my place, I thought. 'But fit. Very fit.'

'One hundred bleeding per cent fit,' she declared, spacing each word. 'He was macho. Mucho macho. Make no mistake about that.'

What the hell was she getting at?

She moderated her tone to a hushed tenderness. 'But do you

161

hear the pitter-patter of tiny feet, Richard? Any childish laughter?' She couldn't hold it, though. 'Not on your damned life, you don't. Aleric Hubert Tolchard was impotent, Richard. He was no more use than a jelly baby.'

What did I say to that? She hadn't brought me there to tell me she'd been deprived for three months, she was telling me it had lasted ten years. Ten years of waiting for the right man to come along? One with prospects, if only he hadn't already got a wife! What was the crazy woman saying? That she'd welcome me if I got rid of Amelia?

But she was full of surprises. Abruptly she transferred her anger, and was on her feet, her eyes furious, her mouth distorted with anger.

'So now you know what I think of big, clumsy oafs who think they can bully me, Mr Richard Patton.' She drew a hand from behind her back and threw something at me. 'There's your blasted lead, and there's your dog. Take her with you.'

I untangled it from round my neck and was on my feet, had taken one step towards her, and with a snarl Sheba was flying at me. Her weight, her teeth in my anorak sleeve, fortunately padded, took me back on to the settee. The worst thing you can do in these circumstances is fight. I let her work at the padding, speaking to her in a calm voice – as well as I could manage that – over and over. And gradually she stopped, released me, and stood staring at me in confusion.

Behind it all, Clare was laughing, too close to hysteria for comfort.

With a fair show of dignity, Sheba and I walked out of that house. As I drove away – Sheba beside me and panting her frantic love in my left ear-hole – I wondered whether *that* was what Clare had wanted to show me. That Sheba would support her. That Sheba could be so confused as not to recognise the aggressor. But surely Clare would not have wanted to demonstrate that *she* could have thrust her father from that window, Sheba or no Sheba.

I was parking in the side car park of the factory before I got it. Clare had been telling me that ten years was too long, and that she'd had a secret lover for a large part of them. Then, if I found out elsewhere, I would not assume it had anything to do with Tolchard's death. As though I would! Clare was too cold and brittle to allow a little affair to lead to murder.

There was also another small matter she'd made quite clear. If I had any ideas about getting rid of my existing wife, I needn't go to Clare for solace. Hadn't she told me plainly that she didn't like my type? She'd go for the very opposite.

Mind you – with enough money behind me – you never could guess what might happen, could you!

18

I had driven past the main entrance, the forecourt seeming to be full, and pulled into the larger parking area provided for the worker bees. The surface was poor, but firm enough at that time. There was a convenient short-cut, trampled through the diamond mesh fence and opposite to the side entrance. This was one of those custom-and-practice facilities, implicitly approved by the management, in proof of which I discovered the time clocks just beyond the side door. Clocking-off time seemed to be 4.30. It was now half-past three. Paul would be getting anxious.

I walked round the corner of the main block, and on to the forecourt. It saved stopping for a chat with Frank, who couldn't see me from his hut. Though it probably wouldn't be him, at that time.

The reception lobby was open-plan, no more than a large expanse of carpeted floor, with a lone receptionist isolated at her desk in a corner. Remote from her, three vinyl-covered easy chairs squatted round a low table. The walls were lined with display cases, the table loaded with photographic magazines.

I gave my name. Her pertly pretty face came alive. She said Mr Paul was expecting me, and whispered into her phone. I waited, prowling round the display cases. You'd be surprised at the number of different accessories photographers seem to need.

He came down for me himself, a welcoming hand thrust ahead. This was a changed Paul. He'd come to terms with the situation, and decided to swim with the tide rather than get swamped.

In the lift he told me what he'd hoped to show me, though there was now little left of the day. He said this with rueful admonition. He took me first to his office ('I'm not much in here – have to be where the action is'), then showed me Walter's ('We mustn't leave it empty too long'), and we put our heads into the boardroom ('My, but there've been some battles in here'). I expressed interest, but he did not exude the enthusiasm of Chad, not even the near-exhausted attitude of Leyton, but more that of a man defeated by boredom and a constant attack from forces he didn't understand.

We went through all three shop floors. Here, I could have developed an interest, in machines operating and processes being carried out, and intricate assembly being done by nimble fingers. I love watching people work. From time to time he would stop at the elbow of one of the operatives, who were for the most part women, and say: 'No, dear, try a gentle pressure on that lever. Let it feed itself.' Or to another: 'Not more than two seconds of contact, there's a good girl. You'll burn it out.' I noticed that he loved that part of it, and I was aware that the foremen and forewomen seemed to find something to do in the distance when he was near.

Sit him at a machine and he'd have been happy all day. As a works manager, I guessed, he was uncomfortable, and therefore not a success.

We returned to his office, just in time for a pot of tea before the building emptied. Everywhere I went I was confronted by tea.

'Perhaps you'd like to see the production schedules,' he said.

I shook my head, realising that I'd barely said a word since I'd arrived.

'Or the order books? We've tied up a very handsome order from Germany.'

'I wouldn't understand them, Paul.'

'Orders for enlargers. We make our own projection lenses, you know. I didn't have time to show you the polishing shop. Also our own colour filters. For the colour enlarging. No?' He smiled bleakly. 'There's no hurry. Perhaps we'll have more time to discuss things this evening.'

'Evening?'

'I've been instructed to bring you home. Evelyn is preparing something special . . .'

'Mary Pinson will be expecting me,' I tried desperately.

With a thin smile he played his ace. 'I phoned Mary, and told her you'll be back later.'

'It was very good of you.'

'Evelyn especially wanted the chance . . .' He let it die, watching my expression with anxiety.

What the devil was worrying him? Something had to be said, and he had trouble getting it out. As bad as his sister! Smiling, I asked how Donald was. At least, he'd enquired. They were now certain there'd been no brain damage – his reflexes were operating. He'd had to have his jaw wired, and his ear would never look pretty. He had not lost the sight of one eye.

'Damned fool,' said Paul. 'Borrowing money like that.'

'All businesses live on credit,' I observed.

'Well yes, but he never got a business going, did he?'

It seemed that he himself would never get going. The factory, which had not seemed noisy, now assailed me with its silence. To move things along, I produced my two cuttings from the newspaper.

'Have you ever seen one like those?'

He looked up, his eyes brightening. 'Oh yes.' And obligingly he fetched out his wallet and increased my collection to three. He was so bland about it that I wondered how stupid he might be.

'You know what it means?' I asked.

'It's obvious, surely. Everybody knew that father was intending to change his will. That ridiculous nonsense about feeling threatened! Well . . . I ask you! The only thing to do when people get those ideas is to ignore them. The ideas, not the people.' He flexed his lips in a thin smile. 'He'd have come round, given time. I wasn't worried. Not even when he announced he'd traced his niece, and was going to alter his will in her favour.'

'My wife.'

'Yes. Of course.' He seemed surprised that I hadn't realised that.

'You said "announced". How was that done?'

'The same way everything's been done lately – by phone. He seemed to think he could run the factory by remote control.'

'Which of course he couldn't?'

'It's placed a heavy burden on my shoulders.'

'I'm sure it has. So you knew, at once, that the cutting was intended to inform you that my wife was dead?'

'Isn't that obvious?'

'You received this news with . . .' I couldn't think *how* he'd have received it. '. . . with equanimity?'

'It took the worry out of it, that's for sure.'

165

'With relief, then?'

'Exactly.' He beamed.

He wasn't stupid by any means. He'd understood precisely what the cutting meant, with all its implications. Paul was simply a completely self-involved man.

'But surely,' I said, 'it must have been clear to you that the cutting had been sent to you by one of the other interested parties?'

'You're way off beam there, Mr Patton.'

'Am I?'

He had his fingers linked, the result lying on the desk surface like a wad of pink dough. He was watching me with the patience due to an idiot, who didn't comprehend the simplicity of it. But who *were* the interested parties? About whom did he think I was speaking? Clare, Donald and himself. Peripherally, Kenneth Leyton, but he could in no way have gained by Walter's death. With Amelia dead, he would have inherited nothing. With her alive, he was excluded from the will, and by his own wish.

For Paul, I spelled it out. 'You, Clare and Donald, they're the interested parties. Surely it must have occurred to you that one of you three must have sent these cuttings to the other two. To take the worry out of it, as you say.'

He rubbed his hand across his mouth, and leaned forward. 'All I was disputing was that you're seeing the wrong implications from it. I knew Clare had sent it . . . them, it now appears. Now . . . we can't have you going around with poorly thought-out ideas.'

I got to my feet and went to look out of his side window. The empty car park, apart from a Volvo. Poorly thought-out!

'But it *follows*,' I told him, turning back. 'Whoever sent you that things must have blown up the caravan. Surely that's simple enough. Now you're accusing Clare.'

'Mr Patton . . . please.' He sighed for my stupidity. 'Don't you think I've given it thought? Whoever attempted to kill your wife – if that's how it was – had to know where she was located, or expected to be. Right?'

'I agree.'

'Father engaged enquiry agents for that.'

'She was killed. You can't say she . . .'

He was shaking his head, tut-tutting. I was receiving a lesson in pure logic. I went to sit down again and began filling my pipe.

166

'Who knew *first*, and most accurately, where you and your wife were expected to be?' He raised bushy eyebrows, a professor prompting a backward pupil. I said nothing, giving him his head.

'That same firm of enquiry agents,' he produced with quiet pride.

He had to be insane! 'But I just said, that agent died. You must surely realise that.'

'A mistake.'

'Undoubtedly.'

'But one that could pay off . . . for the remaining partner. Don't you think?'

And blast him, insane or not, it was beginning to fit neatly. I shook my head. I didn't want this. 'And Clare?' He seemed reluctant to explain this. 'How does Clare come into this?'

'Clare was known to them, that's how. It's natural she'd be the one to be approached.'

'In what way known?'

'Didn't you know? I'd have thought it was all round the town. She'd had Aleric investigated. Damn it, she wanted to see the back of him. I think she was hoping he'd been seeing somebody . . . I mean, why else his two evenings a week in Birmingham?' He laughed, a shishing sound through his teeth. 'Dear Clare, what could she expect? God knows how many men *she's* had since they were married. Thought she was entitled, I suppose. Spoilt rotten, Clare was. You can tell.'

I could. I could also have told him that, according to Clare, Aleric would not have been hunting for women in Birmingham. Men perhaps. Impotency is not necessarily bilingual, or whatever the word is.

'So Clare would be approached,' I conceded cautiously. 'Presumably there'd be some money in it – for the remaining partner?'

'Don't you *see*? I thought you policemen were good at this sort of thing. If father thought your dear wife was alive, and made a new will, then it wouldn't change things, because she wouldn't be.'

'Eh? But she was . . . is . . . alive.'

'But my dear friend . . .' I'd become his friend. 'Nobody would know that. How could they? You'd be buzzing around in your little caravan, and it'd be *assumed* she'd died in the explosion. That sort of knowledge could be worth something.'

167

I very nearly walked out on him. Did he really think that Philip Carne, faced with the death of a beneficiary who'd been alive the week before, would let it go at that? He'd demand a death certificate. And there I'd been, admiring Paul's logic!

'I think,' I said politely, 'that you're over-simplifying.'

'But all the same . . .' He waited for me to accept something, even one tatty corner of his logic.

'Clare?' I asked.

He stared at me. He waited for me to say it.

'She might have sent you that cutting?'

'You could say that.'

He seemed content to leave it at that, and slapped his palms on the desk surface, preparatory to rising. There was an air of relief about him. He'd managed to achieve what he'd intended.

They were a clever lot, the Manns. Clare with her ferile deviousness, Donald with his naïve brilliance, and Paul with his self-seeking cunning. Paul had very nearly succeeded. All he'd been doing was trying to point me at Clare. I knew that now, and could even admire the way he'd wrapped it up. He was doing this, not because he believed in her involvement, but simply to make trouble for her. He hated his sister. Possibly he even blamed her for the position he now found himself in. If she hadn't come on the scene, and absorbed his father's attention, he might well have been able to demonstrate his basic potential, which certainly wasn't management.

He hated her, and assumed I'd be able to involve her in some way. What he didn't know was that Clare, had she wanted a divorce, already had grounds. Her marriage hadn't broken down, as the law demanded for a divorce. It hadn't even started. She could have annulled the marriage on the grounds of non-consummation.

He was saying: 'Evelyn will be expecting us.'

'Yes.'

'I'll lead and you follow. Better stay close when we get into town.'

Closely linked, then, we fought our way through the going-home traffic that clogged the centre of the town – ten minutes to get over the bridge – and eventually turned out of it into quieter streets, finally driving into the arc of a driveway and stopping in front of a very respectable town house, which could well have been Regency.

It turned out to be a terrible evening. Not that Evelyn didn't try. Her meal was excellent. Paul would expect that of her. The conversation flowed. There was no laughter. Two children, a boy and a girl of ten and eight with eager eyes and puckish faces, would have played hell if I hadn't been there, but were severely restrained by Paul's cold eye. Afterwards, they disappeared into a television room, and Evelyn excused herself. Paul and I retired to his study, a cosy place, heavy with furniture and brooding with masculine pomposity, where we sank into soft chairs with a decanter between us, and he droned on endlessly about the operation of the factory. If I'd listened carefully, I could have taken over the place in the morning. But I didn't.

The decision I had to make was whether to phone Amelia that evening, and risk this second call in one day indicating that I had a fear for her safety, or not to phone, and risk her assuming I had no concern for her safety. There was no in-between. His persistent voice robbed me of initiative, and inertia took over. Besides, I was very tired. I might have dozed. His voice ceasing brought me back to attention. He was looking at his watch.

It was ten o'clock. I said I was sorry, I'd kept him up late. He said surely I wasn't leaving, and we played around with that theme for a few moments, before he went to unearth Evelyn, and I could at last get away.

Mary was waiting for me, a brighter, more active Mary, now that Donald was on the mend. I said I'd been stuck at Paul's. She told me Evelyn had phoned to tell her that. They'd had a friendly chat, and Evelyn had been worried about Donald.

'You told her he was improving?'

'Yes, of course. But she's always had a soft spot for Donald. What she's worried about is what happens afterwards, when he's on his feet.'

I scratched my chin. 'I rather thought he'd be found a position in the factory.'

She shook her head. 'He'd refuse.'

'I don't think so. I'd beat him up myself if he refused.'

She touched my arm. 'I knew you'd think of something.'

I went to bed, leaving her to lock up.

Wednesday morning. I awoke thinking: Clare, Clare! When I should have been thinking: Amelia, Amelia.

After breakfast, I phoned her. Amelia, not Clare.

Improvement was being maintained. 'I'll be out of here in a week,' she told me with determination.

'They wouldn't let you.'

'I can't just lie here . . .'

'Is he still there, your policeman?'

'A different one. He's rather good-looking, really.'

'I'll have a word with him, on the way in.'

'Don't you dare, Richard!'

'To see if he's noticed you've got your eye on him.'

It lightened the mood. 'You're coming today, then?'

'Got to pick up a change of clothes from the caravan.'

'I hate you.'

'I thought I might find time to pop in to see you for a second.'

A pause. 'That's your nonchalant voice, Richard. You sound pleased with yourself. Does that mean it's finished?'

'Well . . . no. It's not. But there's progress.' What progress, you fool?

'This afternoon?'

'I want to call in at Bridgnorth on the way, but I'll be with you.' Bridgnorth being closer to Wales than Boreton.

'None of your speeding, now.'

'Of course not, my dear.'

We hung up.

You can see why I had to stop off at Bridgnorth. There might not have been one atom of sense in Paul's ideas, but Burns could well have been the one to circulate the newspaper cuttings. Burns had been eager to avoid me. He owed me an explanation for that, at least.

So I drove to Bridgnorth, not really optimistic about my chances of seeing him. I mean, enquiry agents make their money going out and enquiring, not sitting in the office. But on the way my thoughts were not on him. Hammering away in the background was the name: Clare.

It could well have been her. She was sufficiently cold and vicious to have pushed her father through an open window. Believing Amelia to be dead, she would have had a motive. By heavens, yes, she *would* have had motive. For the house alone, she would be capable of murder. And when you considered her advancing share holdings . . .

Her own 13 shares, the 13 her husband had bought from Donald, plus the 17 she might expect from her father – already

170

she would hold 43. Add to this the possibility that Donald might be persuaded to sell her his expected 17 shares (as I knew he'd hoped to do), then she would be riding high with a controlling holding of 60 shares.

I'd not considered her position in that light before. Of course, those luscious plans had disappeared, Amelia not having died. But abruptly and horribly I saw that Clare's manoeuvring the previous day had not been a mere toying with sex-play words. She had genuinely intended to put across the idea that our mutual future could be enlightened if Amelia were to be killed. By me? By her? It wouldn't even have mattered to her, as long as it was done. And as soon as possible.

I found that I was, after all, driving fast.

Bridgnorth is very like Boreton, in that it exists on both sides of the river. But most of it is on one side, in two halves. Low Town and High Town. They're separated by a great sandstone mass, towering above the river. Pedestrians can use a cliff-side lift, but it doesn't take cars, so I had to wind up the steep right-hander from Low Town to High Town, park by a miracle nose in on the main street, and hunt out Burns and Rafton on foot.

They occupied the first two floors of a narrow house squeezed between a pork pie shop and a jeweller's. A card in the window stated: Burns and Rafton. Discreet Enquiries. The door opened at a push. The one on the right from the hall had a sign: Office. Please Enter. I did.

He was there. No receptionist. Just Burns. He grunted at the sight of me.

'Wondered how long it would be, Mr Patton.'

19

He seemed no more cheerful than when I'd seen him last. Business appeared to be slack.

'Just wanted a word,' I said, taking a seat he hadn't offered.

'Well?'

'Have you done work for a Mrs Clare Tolchard?'

It surprised him. 'Well now!' He sat back and thought about it. 'What if I have?'

'I wondered if you'd care to discuss it.'

'You know I can't do that. Where would my professional reputation go?'

He was still considering what I'd said. I was presenting something he hadn't expected.

'Suppose,' I said, 'I ask questions, and you simply nod or shake your head?'

'You can do that. I might decide to do neither.'

'Right.' I took out my pipe and fondled it. He frowned. I put it back. 'You made enquiries for her, relating to a possible divorce?'

He nodded. He took a pack of cigarettes from his pocket, and turned one round in his fingers. Trying to give them up, I guessed.

'You were asked to follow him on his trips to Birmingham?'

He nodded.

'You followed him there . . .'

He shook his head.

'You didn't? Then what? For God's sake, you can't cover everything with a nod or a shake.'

'He went to Kidderminster.'

'All right. To play squash there?'

He shook his head.

'A woman?'

He shook his head.

'So you didn't get your evidence?'

He nodded, then shook his head.

'What does *that* mean?'

'It wasn't a woman, but it would've got her a divorce, I reckon.'

'Then what . . .' I stared at him. 'A man?'

He nodded.

'Don't start that again, now you've opened your mouth. He had a man friend? Oh, lovely. How long ago?'

'Three years. Sure to be.'

'But she's done nothing . . .'

'I wouldn't know.'

'You'd have been called as a witness.'

'I meant she didn't go for a divorce. What she *did* about it is what I don't know.'

She'd felt free to find her own man, that's what. I shook my head. 'It doesn't matter. The point is, you knew her.' No change

172

in expression. 'Well enough, perhaps, to send her one or two copies of a newspaper cutting, for distribution, in the hope of some reward . . .'

Now I got a reaction. He leaned forward. His large, hard hand slapped down on his desk surface. 'What the hell're you talking about?'

I answered by producing one of my three copies, and handed it to him. He was so long sitting there, staring down at it, that he could have read through it three times. When he looked up his face was haggard.

'I didn't send this.'

I spoke softly. 'The thought occurred to me . . .'

'D'you know what this is about?' he demanded harshly.

'The death of your partner. I'm sorry—'

'The death of my wife, Patton. Nancy was my wife.'

I couldn't say anything.

'When I went to the hospital to speak to you and your wife, I'd gone to Aberaeron to arrange for her to be brought home.'

If he'd broken down and wept it would have been less distressing. But his eyes were dry. His jaw was set, the hard hands now hard fists. When he spoke again, I felt that each word was torn free separately.

'Do you imagine I didn't know what had happened? Nancy went to trace your wife. You were known to have a touring caravan, so she took ours. She located you, or where you'd probably be returning. She drove back here, leaving the caravan, to tell me how the situation stood. Then she drove back.'

If he'd been saying this in court, not one word would have been challenged. Each was etched in acid truth.

'She died,' he said. 'Later, I had a call from Philip Carne. Could I locate Amelia Jane Patton? Of course I could. My wife had already found her.'

'But it was Walter Mann she'd been working for?'

'She'd found her for him. We'd already reported that. I went round to see Mr Mann.'

'Then, later, *he* was dead?'

'And didn't it take a great detective to connect the two!' His cynicism was ice cold.

I took a deep breath. He seemed to have run out of bitter words. He lit the cigarette, and I took out my pipe again.

'But between the two deaths,' I said gently, 'there was a short period. During that time, copies of that newspaper cutting were circulated to the family.'

He nodded. This time it was a signal for me to continue.

'And by that time, realising what it was all about, you'd have decided that someone in the family was responsible for your wife's death?'

This time his lips moved. It could have been a sarcastic smile.

'So I'm suggesting that to strike back at them, whichever of them might have done it, you sent one copy each of that cutting to all three. To build up hope, and then to have it snatched from under their noses when the will was read.'

He sneered at such an idea.

'You mean you didn't?'

'I said not.'

'You're telling me you did nothing?'

He shook his head.

'Then what?'

He gave a thin smile, opened a drawer in his desk, and took out a sheet of paper. With no comment, he tossed it at me.

I caught it in mid-air. It was an A4 sheet of notepaper. On it had been gummed a newspaper cutting, above which was printed: WESTERN EVENING STAR 1 SEPTEMBER. The cutting read:

Identification has now been made of the woman killed in last Friday's caravan tragedy. She was Nancy Rafton, of Bridgnorth in Shropshire. Mystery still surrounds her death, and the police have not ruled out foul play.

Also seriously injured in the blast was Mrs Amelia Patton, of no fixed address. She was taken to hospital with extensive injuries. An interview with Detective Inspector Melrose will be found on page 7.

'I sent that,' he said. 'A copy of it. To where it would do the most good.'

I guessed, but all the same I asked. 'Where?' He meant the most harm.

'To Walter Mann. He'd know what it meant. I thought it would stir up something.'

'Oh, it did. It did. And can you tell me when you sent it?'

'I delivered it by hand. Through his front door letter-box. On Saturday.'

'*The* Saturday?'

He nodded.

'Then you killed him.'

'No. No. They did.' He made an attempt at a grin. His lips certainly drew back, and brown teeth showed. But it gave him no pleasure. I thought he was slightly insane, and wasn't certain I could blame him for that.

'May I have a copy of this?'

'That *is* a copy.'

I looked again. Photocopies are getting so good these days. It was a copy. I folded it away and stood with one hand on the chair back. 'I didn't hear anything about this at the inquest.'

'I wasn't asked.'

I left him to his thoughts, found my car, and drove like hell away from there. West. To Amelia.

But after a couple of miles I drew into a lay-by, filled my pipe, and got out for a walk round the car a few times, puffing madly. I had to examine what I had before I presented it to my wife. She had a tendency to see right through my ideas, and point out a vital snag here and there. But I could discover none. I now knew how it had been possible to kill Walter Mann, and from that the rest followed, Tolchard's death and Nancy Rafton's.

I drove on, stopped for lunch, drove on again. There didn't, now, seem to be any great rush.

Her leg was no longer in traction. The dressing on her arm was less obtrusive, giving an impression of improvement. She was in good spirits.

'They had me sitting in a chair this morning, Richard. If it wasn't for the arm, I could try a walking frame.'

'Splendid.'

'Now tell me why you're looking so pleased with yourself.'

Silently, I produced the copy of the cutting, as supplied by Burns, offered it to her, and watched her read it.

'I know people like to see their name in the paper,' she said, 'but if I have to be involved in an explosion . . .'

'The woman who died was Burns's wife. He sent a copy of that to your uncle Walter. Now . . . what would Walter think? What would he do?'

'I know what I'd do. I'd be furious.'

I nodded agreement. 'He'd realise in a second that somebody had tried to kill you. Because of the will. But what would he *do*?'

She smiled like an angel, knowing how much I enjoyed expounding my theories. 'You tell me, Richard.'

'He'd got a phone there. He'd ring round and get each of the people involved to come and see him, and demand to know if *they'd* done it. One by one . . .'

She was shaking her head, lips pursed. 'Mr Leyton first.'

'Oh?'

'He would be the obvious one to have known where we'd been traced. Uncle Walter would see that at once. He'd phone *him*, and ask him who he'd told.'

Told you, didn't I? Amelia sees everything so clearly. She was correct, of course. Leyton was the obvious one to be phoned first. Leyton could have been indiscreet. After all, he had told me he'd opposed any change in Walter's will. He could well have thought it was his duty to warn the three children.

'Right,' I agreed, smiling. 'So he phoned Leyton. Leyton told him who, and he'd ask that person to come round and see him.'

'Just that one?' she asked sweetly. 'Why not all three? Together.'

'Donald wouldn't have been available.'

'Do you know that? You don't know where Donald was that day. All three, I'd suggest. Richard, wouldn't you think so?'

'All right. Three together, or two, or even one.' I took a deep breath. 'I wasn't trying to draw a picture, I was simply offering you a reason why he'd open his door to somebody he'd refused to admit for two months. He'd feel he was safe, because he'd already changed his will.' I shrugged, just a little put out.

She laughed. 'Your face! Richard, I'm only trying to prevent you from making a fool of yourself. But there's still the problem of Sheba. What about her?'

'Two things. Walter might have shut her away, anticipating that his anger and distress would upset her, and also I've got proof that Sheba doesn't necessarily react as you'd expect.'

Here I'd led myself where I'd not intended to venture, but there was no avoiding it. I explained how I'd had an interview with Clare, omitting the bits about her attempt to suggest that the situation could be improved if Amelia were to die. I simply put it that I'd infuriated her.

'I can understand that,' she said. 'You do that often.'

'And she threw the dog's lead at me. I stood up . . . and Sheba went at *me*.'

176

She laughed. 'I get your point.'

'So . . . one of the three went there on invitation, and knocked Walter unconscious—'

'Sheba or no Sheba?'

The seat was becoming uncomfortable. I moved restlessly. 'However you like to put it, it was done. By somebody. I now have an explanation of how they got in: they were invited. And that there's at least a vague suggestion that Sheba wasn't necessarily an obstruction, and I can show how the door could have been left in a locked condition afterwards, by replacing the key round Walter's neck.'

She brought her hands together. A clap would have been painful. 'You *are* doing well.'

But I could see the enthusiasm wasn't there. 'I'm not so sure.'

'Then you ought to be.'

'It's all theory, with not an atom of proof to support it.'

'Pooh!' she said. 'Put it all together, and you'll get your proof.' She eyed me consideringly. 'You know who, don't you?'

'Only a guess, and as I say, no proof.'

'You're not a policeman now.'

'Yes. Well. If it happened like that, and Walter was killed because of that cutting, then it follows that whoever did it also killed Nancy Rafton. And Boreton's a hundred and fifty miles from here. I doubt Paul could have gone missing long enough, because the explosion was on a Friday. Donald possibly, but I doubt he could have afforded to get here. That only leaves Clare.'

'Do you think she would have been capable . . .'

'Yes. Capable of anything.'

She raised her eyebrows at my tone. 'But there's still Mr Tolchard's death. You haven't said anything about that.'

'All I've got is negative. You see, Clare could have annulled her marriage, but she didn't.'

'Don't you mean dissolved?'

'Not really. Her marriage hadn't even been consummated.'

'Legal words, Richard. You mean he couldn't . . .'

'So she said.'

'You discussed her sex life?' She was appalled.

'She did. I just sat there like a clown.'

'Poor man,' she said feelingly. She didn't mean me, she meant Tolchard.

I wasn't going to express an opinion on that. 'The point I want

177

to make is that if she'd ended their marriage, she couldn't have got her hands on the thirteen shares he'd bought from Donald. With Tolchard dead, she did. And it's easy to get into that factory. There was a clear hour between the time Chad went to his father's office and the discovery of Tolchard's body.' I shrugged.

'So what do you intend to do about it?' she demanded.

'Nothing myself. I'll take that cutting to Melrose, and he can sort it out from there.'

'You were going to try to help Chad.'

'This will do it. Prove two of the killings, and the other follows.'

She was playing with the lace on the bedjacket I'd bought her for her birthday. 'I wish I could be sure of that, Richard.'

'Once I've told Melrose how somebody could've been invited in, and how the locked door was wangled, he'll clear it up in no time.'

'And then he can take his guards away?'

I had to get going, and catch Melrose before he went to bed. On my feet now, I grinned at her. 'I saw him on the way in. He's certainly good looking.'

'That's a different one. I've identified three now.'

'I'll see about it, love.'

I left slowly, exhibiting reluctance, waving at the swing door, but once outside I put on speed. The policeman was strolling the corridor. I didn't speak to him.

I did the return journey in three hours and four minutes, though that was to The Dun Cow, not all the way to The Beeches. It was twenty minutes to closing time, and I found Melrose in the saloon.

He was leaning casually against the bar, a pint glass clasped in that lethal right hand, chatting to a couple of large men who could have been off-duty policemen. I ordered a lager, loud enough for him to hear and recognise my voice, then I looked round for parking space and took my glass over to a corner, where a small table was located in the angle of two bench seats. After a couple of minutes he pushed his way through and joined me.

He had a fresh pint, and raised it. 'Good health to you.'

I plunged straight in. 'Would you mind telling me why you've put a guard on my wife?'

He stared at me, the glass rim poised in front of his open mouth, then he took a large swallow and put it down. 'The short answer to that is that I haven't.'

'I saw him there. One of your men.'

'Describe him.'

I did that. He gave a snort of something, contempt or amusement. 'That's young Pearson. Got his eye on the staff nurse. He'd be waiting for a word with her.'

'My wife says she's seen three of them.'

He nodded. 'Yes. Davies, Pearson and Jones. They've all got their eye on her. We're hoping to get her into the force.' He sucked up beer. 'That'll liven the place up a bit,' he added lugubriously.

'I don't know that I believe you. You've still got this stupid idea that I'd harm her.'

'What? You! I've met her, you know. You didn't know? Well, I have. And I've seen you in action. You're no danger to her, Mr Patton. What're you having?'

'I'm on lager, but . . .'

He was already at the bar, obtaining service with the ease of an experienced copper. I had the sheet of paper ready on the table for him when he got back. He noticed it at once; very nearly put his glass down on it. 'What's this?'

'Burns, the Bridgnorth enquiry agent, sent a copy of that to Walter Mann on the morning he died. Read it, will you.'

He picked it up and read it carefully, his right hand wandering absently round his glass, then withdrawing. He finished, and looked across at me. 'And?'

'It offers an explanation of how Walter, in his locked room, might have invited somebody inside whom he'd normally have kept out.'

He seemed unimpressed. 'Does it? Tell me how.'

I explained in detail, crisply this time because I'd rehearsed it with Amelia. I went on to explain how the key could have been taken from Walter, and replaced in the conservatory. Though his glass was raised and lowered as I spoke, his eyes never left me.

'I've seen a copy of this,' he announced calmly. 'It was in Walter Mann's trouser pocket. He had on old slacks, an open-necked shirt, with a baggy old cardigan over it, and shoes.'

'And a key on a chain round his neck?'

'That too. Hung inside his shirt.'

'Which is what I've been talking about.'

'You do keep trying, don't you! I think you've been trying too hard. You've been hopping around from one place to the other, like a mad thing. From one death to the other. You're tired, Mr Patton. You've exhausted your brain. No.' He held up his palm. 'Let me say this. Thump me later, but by heaven I'm going to lay it out for you first. Your basic thinking has been wrong, hurried. Just look at it. One: the dog, Sheba. You've simplified the whole scene there. Whatever happened, violence would have to have been involved. The dog would've done something – reacted violently. Somebody would've been marked. Who? I've seen no indications. All right. It was just a thought. But just look at your thinking on the next point.'

'My thinking has been—'

'Hurried,' he interrupted. 'Point two: you're saying Walter Mann would've phoned and ordered a specific person to visit him, because of what he suspected had happened – Nancy Rafton's death.'

'What's wrong there?' I had to interrupt, or explode.

'I'll tell you. Now . . . the person going there would – *did*, we're certain – believe that your wife was dead. Okay? They had been invited into this locked room of his. Yes, I'll say they. Assume all three, if you like. They, I say, were admitted. It would be an ideal time to do away with him, because the new will, assuming your wife was dead, would result in everything coming back to them.'

I growled in my throat, and managed to nod. I'd seen where he was heading.

'So did they rush into that room like a howling pack of hyenas and fall on him before he had time to open his mouth?'

'You're deliberately making a mockery of it.'

'I'm making sense. They'd at least wait to hear what he'd say. And all he'd need to say, Mr Patton, was two words: "She's alive." That's all. It would stop 'em in their tracks. Kill him then, and they'd lose everything. As they have. Can you really imagine he wasn't given time for that?' He emphasised the last word by banging his glass on the table.

I croaked: 'I'll get 'em in.'

'No. Let's finish this.'

I sat back. He was calmly and expertly cutting me to pieces, as he'd destroyed the lout in Lucas's office. His eyes were blazing with intelligence, and pitiless.

'Go on,' I said.

'I'm sorry,' he said, not sounding it, 'but you've never stood a chance in this. There're things you don't know. All I've just said is completely irrelevant, because Walter Mann could not have been pushed from that window, however clever you might be about that key.'

'If it's irrelevant, why plod through it?' I growled.

'To slow you down, Mr Patton. You're over-stressed. I was about to say, there's forensic evidence you don't know. It's something we didn't mention at the inquest. Too gruesome, we thought. He fell face down, you see, flat on his chest. The key, inside his shirt . . . well, it was kind of impressed into the flesh. It could not have been replaced like that. Could *not*, Mr Patton.'

The thrumming in my head I put down to too much driving. The skin across my forehead seemed hot and tight. I cleared my throat. 'You'll have your own theory, no doubt?'

He smiled sourly. 'A small idea. The way I see it, he received this cutting . . .' He slapped his hand on it. '. . . and I think his first thought wouldn't be to blame somebody else. It'd be to blame himself. He'd brought it about. I believe he committed suicide. The open window was there . . .' He shrugged. 'It fits. It's simple and uncomplex. Reject it, though, if you want to.'

'Suicide.' Even to me it didn't sound like my own voice. 'That was something also mentioned at the inquest.'

'It was only an idea, but after all, he *had* been hiding himself away for a couple of months, so he couldn't have been completely sane. I kept quiet about it. The relatives don't like to hear verdicts like that, it makes them feel guilty. And the thought did occur to me that my friend, Mr Richard Patton, wouldn't want suggestions of insanity being tossed around in a court of law.' He grinned in a ghastly way. 'They could lead to all sorts of unpleasant legal squabbles over the will.'

'I'll remember you in mine,' I said sourly. 'So . . . now?'

'Now I'm convinced that Tolchard's death was an accident.'

'But can't prove it?'

'No. I believe Walter Mann's was suicide, and that only Nancy Rafton's was murder. As I can't offer one scrap of proof on that, I've been recalled to Wales. I go home tomorrow. So it's over, Richard. Finished, for you and for me.'

There was a short period of silence, broken by the barman calling time. Very apt. There was nothing left in my glass, nothing left in my mind. I didn't look up when Melrose got to his feet and walked away.

181

I drove back to The Beeches, handling the car from instinct. Everything I'd worked out was destroyed. Unless Walter had been killed, nothing made sense. My brain was wearied with it, tossing the same old facts around, and coming back to the same point. I was at a dead end.

My headlights flicked over a motorcycle parked in the drive. I very nearly backed up and drove away again. I didn't think I could face Heather. She was waiting by the garages. There was no dodging it.

I walked up to her. She said: 'You haven't been in touch. We were wondering . . .' There was no life in her voice. Her stance was awkward, a stiffness that arose from her uncertainty.

'Would you like to come inside?'

She shook her head. 'If there's nothing to say, what's the point?'

My theory had included Tolchard's death. Without the rest, I could offer nothing. 'There's nothing to say,' I admitted.

She scuffed her boot in the gravel. 'It's going to sound terrible in court.'

'If you've decided to tell the truth.'

I caught her minimal nod. 'Yes, we've decided that.'

'You've told your brother?'

'I couldn't face him. I've got to have time.'

I had to offer her something. 'I think I know why Tolchard was hanging round that night, and it wasn't just to lock up.'

I cursed myself. There'd been a sudden, optimistic toss of her head.

'He'd guessed something about Mr Leyton's activities, and Chad helping him,' I explained. 'He was hoping to catch him out and expose his . . . his inadequacy.' Might as well face it. 'I believe he wanted to force Mr Leyton out, and hoped to buy his shares.'

'Oh,' she said.

'It's not much use, I know. But it would explain why he might have been lurking at the top of that staircase.'

'But that makes it worse!' she burst out. 'Don't you *see*?'

'Yes, I see. I thought you ought to know, though. I'm sorry, Heather, there's nothing else.'

She made an attempt. Give her that. She even managed a half smile. 'Well . . . you've tried. Thanks for that.'

But I hadn't been trying, had I? I hadn't been thinking about

182

Tolchard all day, but about Walter Mann. And look where that had got me!

I watched her walk away. I said goodnight to her back, and she flicked her hand in acknowledgement. Then I turned off the Volvo's lights and went inside.

20

I do not remember going to bed but clearly I had, because there I was in it when I awoke. I couldn't even remember getting to sleep, and had the impression I'd tossed and turned all night. Mary said nothing about my condition when I went down to breakfast. Probably I didn't exchange a word with her.

I took Sheba out for a walk. We roamed the garden and the river bank. She took me to show me the otters, who seemed to recognise her and invited her in to play. She declined. Otters have sharp teeth. The general idea of all this was to let some fresh air into my brain, but subconsciously I realised I was saying goodbye to it all.

You can appreciate my reasoning. I had promised to help Chad in respect of the death of Tolchard. I could do this in only one way, the chance of showing accidental death now being remote. And as Chad had the only decent motive so far, I'd have to prove a better one. Which I had. I'd explained it to Amelia. I might be able to prove that Clare stood to gain by her husband's death, when she could well have turned out to be a loser if he'd been contemplating divorce. This he might have done, if he'd been aware of her sexual activities. A proud man. He'd not want to be shown as inadequate. Thus, she might have killed him.

But, having done so, she'd soon realise that this action had prompted her father into paranoiac fears for his own safety. This had eventually led to Walter's new will, or the threat of it, which had warned Clare that she was about to lose more than the death of her husband had gained her. So Walter had to die before he messed things up for her.

And there was Walter claiming he'd traced his niece. There was urgent action to be taken, and it went wrong. Amelia did not die – but would Clare know that? She would believe that Amelia was dead. She *had* believed that. So now there was even more urgency to kill her father, before he discovered that the will he'd just drawn was invalid.

It was at this point, when days, hours even, were important, when Walter was still locking himself away, invulnerable, that he'd settled it all for her by killing himself! It could not be so. The whole pattern had been broken by chance, by coincidence. Another few minutes, and Clare might have been informed that Amelia was still alive, and that it was then too late to kill him.

And just then he'd killed himself?

No, I would not accept it. Yet, if I did not . . . then what? I'd be opposing police opinion, and my actions and theories would be challenged, and they would be forced to show that Walter had a reason, however remote, for having committed suicide. From that there would be queries of mental stability, challenges to the will, and, whatever Amelia's decisions as to fairness, it would all be snatched away from us.

Didn't I tell you about fate? A tricky lady.

I went back to the house and had lunch, then out to the back and to the conservatory. The scaffolding was there, but still the glaziers had not come to finish the job. I'd have to phone somebody about that. No I wouldn't; I'd have no authority. Very soon, all authority might be snatched away. I might not be able to bring Amelia here, not even be allowed to park the caravan in the drive.

Hell, I thought, get on with it Richard. 'It' being an attempt to discover how someone might get out of a locked room, and lock the door behind them, when Walter had taken the key with him.

I stood inside the conservatory, imagining it as it would have been then, without the scaffolding. Would it, for instance, have been possible to climb down by rope, and in through the hole in the roof? Walter had left a sizeable gap, but who would have dared to do it? One slip, one slightest swing, and you'd be cut to pieces. Then, how to explain the resulting wounds? No. Eliminate that.

I went outside and stood back, examining the facing wall. This side there was no convenient ivy or wistaria. The walls were bare beneath the windows. The nearest down pipe was at the corner of the house, a good ten feet away. No way down. Just no way.

Up? I considered that. The eaves above the window could not have been reached.

No one, without a key, could have left that room, with a locked door behind them.

Without a key! I prowled the drive. The only person *with* a key had been – was – Mary Pinson. Mary Pinson, who'd gained that greatest prize of all, security, from Walter's death. But she had possessed it before. You're mad, Richard, insane!

So, being insane, and desperate if you must know, I got into the Volvo and went to see Clare again.

There was a futile idea that I might be able to break her down by sheer force of personality, or entice an admission from her with my subtlety. It was unfortunate that I went there feeling like a whipped dog.

'Well!' she said. 'Look who we've got here.'

'May I come in?'

'I see no reason why.'

'A few questions . . .'

'If you're from the Mormons . . .' Then she gave a bark of dead laughter and said: 'Oh, come in, you big fool.'

She'd got me beaten before we started. Being unpredictable, she could not be manoeuvred. She led the way into her lounge, and indicated the settee.

'*Now* you'll take a drink,' she decided.

'It's just that I hate spirits.'

'There's sherry. Or white wine.'

'White wine, please.'

It seemed that we couldn't talk without a glass in our hands.

She brought my glass over and placed it on the table before me. I saw that the third finger of her left hand now bore a ring I hadn't noticed before. A ruby surrounded by small diamonds. Had she unearthed the engagement ring Aleric had given her, in sentimental memory? Hardly likely, I thought. She'd discarded the wedding ring.

I looked up. She was smiling down at me. A woman, she knew, could not have missed it. A lump of a man might. I pretended I had.

'Paul's been showing me over the factory,' I said. The wine was crisply dry, but not cool. Wasn't she going to sit down? Did she intend to hold that smile? 'The general impression,' I explained, 'is that I'll be taking some interest in it. I wonder why people assume my wife will not? Do they think a woman couldn't do it?'

'She might not want to.'

'True. But if I do – take an active part, I mean – I'd need to know about your position. You've never taken an active part, I've been told. But now . . .'

I was maintaining an admirably impersonal approach, considering that now she was dressed in a slim skirt, slit at one side, and a very chic blouse, with her hair caught back in a ribbon. She was wearing more make-up than the slacks had qualified for, and to emphasise it she popped out a bit of tongue and moistened her lips.

'Aleric always voted my paltry thirteen shares.'

'But he's no longer with us.' I'd noted he was now Aleric. 'Surely you might be persuaded to – now?'

'Such a bore.'

At last she sat, opposite me as I'd guessed, the skirt obligingly revealing an area of thigh. If I was a good boy, she might allow *me* to vote her shares.

'But not so paltry now,' I pointed out. 'With the thirteen you've inherited from your late husband, you'll have over a quarter.'

She hid behind her glass. Almost pure gin again. 'You know—'

'The ones he bought from Donald.'

'Oh yes.' Her eyes slid beyond me. 'You'll know about those.'

'I've become involved with Donald's affairs.' Then, so as not to make a point of this, I added: 'I'm sure you'd make a most admirable addition to the board.'

We were coming along fine. I might just as well have been a visiting salesman. But I was dealing with volatile emotions.

'Why would I want to be on your blasted board?'

'It wouldn't be mine. My wife's—'

'She'd give you a proxy, as I did for Aleric.'

'I'm not so sure about that.'

'Then why don't you bloody-well ask her?' she demanded, waving to a side table bearing a green phone. It clashed with the carpet.

'I don't think that's necessary,' I said soothingly. 'This is only what they call an exploratory conversation.'

'Then don't explore me, not with your words, not with your eyes, not with anything.'

She couldn't keep her mind off sex. In case I was succeeding, she gave an ineffectual jerk at her skirt.

'It would be useful, though, to know your intentions,' I said

186

smoothly, caught a spark in her eyes, and went on: 'If you're not interested in voting them, perhaps you'd be interested in selling.'

'Not to you. Not to anyone,' she flared.

'You have a very possessive feeling towards them? You surprise me.'

'They're mine.'

'Hard won, were they?'

'They didn't come as easy as . . .' She stopped, realising I'd gained a point. Her eyes were like the ice in her glass. It tinkled as her fingers moved the glass. 'You bastard!'

'It's convenient he died,' I said.

'What?' It cracked out.

'Otherwise you might have had to annul the marriage, and . . .' I put back my head and laughed. '. . . and claim custody of the shares.'

By God, how far d'you have to sink, Richard? Do you have to degrade her completely? She was looking at me with her lips a little apart, teeth just visible, and there was pain in her eyes. She glanced down at her glass, which contained too little to be worth throwing at me. Abruptly she got to her feet to replenish it. I turned my head. She was walking with legs not quite under control. It had been a low blow.

By moving sideways a little I could see her in a mirror across the room, in profile. Her face was stiff. She was fighting to control it.

When she walked back and took her seat again, she had succeeded. She spoke in a voice I hadn't heard before, lower-pitched and with a hint of appeal in it, which she couldn't quite erase.

'I don't know what you're trying to do. Shame me, I suppose. But I've got nothing to be ashamed of. I explained that, but perhaps you think that was a joke, too. You're quite correct, I could've annulled the marriage. I went to see a solicitor, and that was his advice. While there was still time, he said. But do you imagine I could have done that? Do you really believe that Aleric would have let it happen? For the thing to have got to court, and for him, the macho-supremo, to be revealed as impotent . . .'

'But surely the two go together,' I said softly.

'What does that mean? If you're going to start being funny again . . .'

I held up my hand. 'Pax. I simply meant that given the

187

impotency, he'd just *have* to prove to himself his perfection as a man.'

'Oh, you're cute. A man who can think! Fancy that. Then try thinking of me, brother.'

The surface hardness was congealing again. I already knew that beneath it – pushed under a long way, perhaps – there was probably a warm, and certainly an emotional woman. She'd had to take on a shell. How else could she have survived?

'I'm thinking,' I assured her. 'And wondering how you could continue—'

'Without a man?'

I shrugged. 'Too obvious. I doubt you'd need to go that far. Going without,' I explained. 'I meant, without leaving him. Running away . . .'

'As Donald did?'

'He was running towards, you would be running away.'

'That's why I didn't.'

'Then I'm surprised you didn't take the other way out. Killing him.'

'Ah!' She tapped her teeth with the glass. 'Clever, Mr Patton, very clever. But no, I can be more subtle than that. I could have put belladonna in his food, I suppose, but that damned physique would have shaken it off. D'you know what I did, friend?'

'You consoled yourself with other men.'

'But *that* he knew, and didn't care tuppence about. No. I took a regular lover. I let him know *that*. I let him know a name. Someone who would shock him. He'd see it as an insult. He did see it as an insult. I let him know it was permanent, that I loved this man, and that I was living with Aleric in this house as his wife by name only. As he'd been, with me, for years. And I challenged him to divorce *me*. I told him I wouldn't defend it. I told him to go ahead and do it, and his blasted secret wouldn't come out in court. I taunted him with that, daring him to risk it. But he wouldn't. I reminded him that this place is mine, in my name. That infuriated him. But he didn't dare to divorce me. If he did, I'd take away his proxy to vote my shares on the board. I told him that if he didn't divorce me, I could still take them away. He was furious. He didn't dare to reveal to everybody that he'd got Donald's. That was supposed to be for later. So he would lose his seat on the board, and all that precious influence at the factory he'd been building up. I said, go on, divorce me, or sit back and watch me with my lover. I told him I'd bring my lover here, and take him to our bed. But he didn't dare to divorce me. I *told* him all that. Over and over. And d'you know what he did?'

I shook my head. I'd noticed how many sentences in that speech had begun with 'I'. What he hadn't done was strangle her, which was surprising. She had deliberately set out to undermine his self-esteem, when it couldn't have been very strong already.

'What did he do?'

'He went into his exercise room and increased his press-ups to eighty each morning.' She gave a little tinkle of brittle laughter.

I wondered whether Tolchard had been toning-up his biceps. 'And this other man, the one you mentioned as being in love with? How did he enjoy being used as a threat?'

'You're a completely cynical bastard, aren't you!' She said it kindly, in a considering voice. 'It's just that you don't listen. I told you, I love him.'

'You said you'd told your husband that.'

'Because it's true. Do you know what it can mean, to find someone – suddenly, not expecting it – who's gentle and under-standing, and . . . and loving? Can you guess? Yes, I love him. Yes, I'm going to marry him, whatever he says, to have and to bloody hold, and just let some sod come along and try to spoil it, and *then* you'll see sparks flying, my friend. Then you'll know.'

The threat. It had to come. She saw me as a destroyer. She saw me, quite accurately, as the one who would like to pin her down as her father's killer. If I tried too hard . . . look out, Richard.

I smiled. I raised my glass to her. 'I'll be pleased to be at the wedding. Proud to kiss the bride.'

She slid smoothly to her feet, smiling at last genuinely. 'You *do* understand!' She stood over me. 'Why wait for the wedding?' She bent forward and kissed me. It went on rather too long for a bride-kiss, but who's complaining?

I eased myself to my feet because there was a lot of that settee doing nothing and waiting for something to do. I said I ought to be going. She pouted. We moved out into the hall.

'And now?' she asked softly, as she opened the front door.

'Now what?'

'What're you going to do?'

I was supposed to answer that I was going to look elsewhere. I said: 'I don't know.'

The door closed behind me. I drove away until I was out of

sight, stopped, lit my pipe, and wondered what the hell I'd gained from all that. Having decided nothing, I drove back to The Beeches, passing the factory without a single glance.

I spent a while wondering whom I might interrogate, but there was nobody left. Heather came round for no particular reason, found me unresponsive, pouted, and sat with Mary, talking women talk. I asked Mary for the key to Walter's room, and went to have another look at it. There might well have been a clue in that room. I searched his desk and the drawers, and a lot of what I found I didn't even understand. No inspiration intruded. In the bathroom – what the hell did I expect to find in a bathroom? In the bedroom – ponderous and accommodating furniture, a bed you could have camped under and a wardrobe you could hide in.

Assuming you were locked inside that suite of rooms, your victim lying beneath an open window, would you choose to wait and hide . . . or slide back the stiff bolts of the door to the corridor and get the hell away from there? You'd leave. The alternative was to hope that when the locked door was at last opened you could slip out unnoticed. But Mary had not come up here to open the locked door until she'd had the police with her. Try getting past them!

Angrily, I went back into the main room.

That stupid plastic bag was still hanging around. Fun and games with a bag on a length of string, lowering his library book and hauling it back with the morning's post in it! I kicked it across the room, then hesitated. It hadn't simply flopped around my foot. It *had* gone across the room. It had weight and substance.

Curiously, and yet with my heart beating faster, I bent and picked it up. The string was fastened to one handle and passed through the other. It fell open, revealing three envelopes and a quarterly magazine from the Stereoscopic Society.

I hadn't given that plastic bag a thought, not one flaming thought – not considered . . .

21

'Mary! Mary!' I pounced for the door, was out on to the landing and half-way down the wooden stairs when I saw her, standing startled at the foot, with Heather behind her.

I controlled my voice. 'Will you come up here for a minute?'

She mounted steadily. 'Such a kerfuffle! You frighten people to death.'

I stood aside for her to enter. It was Heather who was looking more startled. 'What is it?'

I spoke to Mary. 'Look in this bag. Is this the post you put in here that Saturday?'

She looked inside. 'Well yes. I suppose so. As far as I can tell. I remember this bigger one.' She meant the magazine. Then she withdrew her hand. She was holding a crumpled ball of paper, which I took from her and opened up.

It was a white envelope, addressed simply to Mr W. Mann. No address, no postage stamp. In the top left-hand corner was printed: Burns and Rafton – Enquiry Agents.

And Walter had had its contents in his trouser pocket!

'That clinches it,' I said, feeling a great gust of triumph sweeping its warmth through me.

'What?' Heather demanded. 'Clinches what?'

'The reason for the open window. The locked door.' I took Mary's arm and took her to the window, and pushed it up. 'He was standing here. He pulled up that bag, containing the post you'd just put in it, and you walked away. Imagine him here. He peered in to see what had come, and spotted that envelope, opened it, and read what it contained. What it contained, Mary, was a copy of a newspaper clipping, which showed him that somebody had tried to kill his niece – my wife. I'd suggest he'd be furious. He crumpled up the envelope and threw it back in the bag. Would you agree?'

'I suppose you must be right.' But Mary sounded confused, not appreciating what it meant.

'That's what the evidence indicates. So . . . then what would he do?'

'I'm sure I don't . . . you're hurting my arm . . .'

'Sorry.' I released her, turning to Heather. 'Let's have a legal mind on it, Heather. Logic. Shall we have some logic?'

'I don't know what evidence you're talking about.' She didn't have an overwhelming interest in Walter's death, but she tried to convey enough to satisfy me.

'We have this,' I told her, standing beside the open window. 'This was open when he was found. He was lying on his face inside the conservatory down there, under a large hole in the glass. He'd opened the window himself, and he'd just hauled up this bag of post, which Mary had collected from the hall. Sheba was in here with him. As she is now. Do you get the picture?'

Heather nodded. Her eyes were bright with interest now. 'So he saw that letter . . . the one you think's so important . . .'

'Which I know to have been delivered by hand.' I nodded, and she picked it up, taking it.

'So he'd naturally open it.'

'Before he shut his window?'

'Could be. It was delivered by hand. He'd be curious. Yes.'

'And in ten seconds he'd realise that someone had made an attempt to kill my wife. Then what?'

The blood had run from her face. She moistened her lips, and glanced at the open window. 'He'd . . . he'd want to know who. To find out, I suppose.'

'He'd be disturbed, you'd say? Even angry?'

'If it was me . . . yes . . . furious.'

'And?'

She shook her head. Her lips moved, but she said nothing.

'My first thought was that he'd jump to the phone,' I told her. 'He would realise who was most likely to have known where my wife was located, and who were the people most likely to have benefited from her death. I thought, at first, that he would phone, and ask these people to come and see him, one by one . . .'

'No!' she cried, more passionately than it seemed to warrant. 'No,' she repeated more quietly. 'It's not a thing . . . for a phone.'

'And yet I haven't even told you the other evidence. You're very quick, my dear.'

'What other evidence?' she asked with suspicion.

'If he'd given it calm consideration, if he'd taken the time to

192

open the rest of his post systematically, he might then have decided to make phone enquiries. But he didn't do that. He would, if he'd planned to ask people here, have had that newspaper cutting laid out on the desk, waiting.'

To illustrate, I took my copy from my pocket and slapped it down on the desk surface.

'But he didn't do either of these things,' I went on. 'And the copy of that cutting was found in his trouser pocket. What does *that* suggest, Heather?'

She had to force her lips apart. Her voice was a whisper. 'He seems to have . . . must have decided to . . . to go himself and confront . . .' She stopped, her eyes hunting so as not to look into mine.

'Confront, yes. Furious probably. Raging maybe. What I'm saying happened is that he went straight from this room, leaving Sheba behind and leaving the window open, but locking the door behind him automatically. That has to mean he didn't die from falling out of this window. He went away, and he spoke to somebody – probably had a blazing row with them – and died there.'

I heard Mary whimper, and turned. She was staring at me with big, round eyes, tears in them.

'He probably followed not far behind you, Mary. Didn't you see a following car?'

But really, she was unable to say anything. I turned. Heather had her hands clutched to her face, fingers nearly in her eyes. And, blast it, my own words had reminded me that there was something else I'd forgotten.

'His car!' I said. 'Nobody looked in his car.'

As of course they would not. He had not used it for two months, and there was no reason to suppose it had been driven that day. I brushed past them and ran down, leaving Mary to close the window. Sheba ran excitedly after me.

The Ford Granada was in the middle garage. Its doors were unlocked and the keys hung from the ignition lock. I threw all four doors open and examined the inside carefully. On fawn upholstery, blood shows up clearly. It was dry and dark now, on the rear seat and on the floor in front of it. Blood. It explained why there'd been so little evidence of blood in the conservatory. I turned my attention to the front seats, aware that Heather was watching me silently.

'He drove away in his car,' I told her. 'He was brought back in it. There'd be a fair walk ahead for somebody.'

There were no clues in the front, nothing the murderer had conveniently dropped. But there was a trace of dried blood on the ignition key. There would maybe even be a fingerprint, if that still bore any relevance. I turned to show it to Heather, but she was no longer there.

'Heather!'

I left there at a flat run, burst in and through the kitchen, out to the hall, and threw open the door into the sitting room. Heather was just replacing the phone. I went over to her and snatched it from her hand, but the line was no longer connected. I slammed it down.

'Who were you phoning, Heather?' Her white face was set. 'What did you say?' There was a tiny shake of her head, teeth clenched, jaw thrust forward.

I caught her by the arms, one hard fist on each, and shook her. 'What the hell did you say?' I shouted.

Her mouth came open with the violence of the shaking. The fear in her eyes was at the abrupt viciousness of my assault. I stopped. Her head jogged to a stop. 'What?' I asked quietly.

'Only . . . only two words,' she panted. 'He knows. That's all I said.'

'You stupid—'

'I had to give him a chance.'

'A chance to do what?' I snapped. 'Come on. We've got to hurry.'

This time I took her hand. She needed support, not physically but emotionally. I dragged her out of the front door, as the shortest route to the Volvo. She trotted sideways behind my shoulder.

'Let me go.'

I stopped by the car. 'Do you know what you've done?'

'You're not to say that!' she sobbed. 'Just to give him time.'

'To go running? Where to, damn it? Get in the car.'

'I can do it quicker on my bike.'

'I don't want you there first. Get in the car, Heather, or I'll belt you one.'

She got in. I slammed the door on her and went round quickly. She was still fastening her seat belt when I took it fast out of the drive.

194

It was all right as far as Boreton. But the time was six-fifteen by the dashboard clock. Commuters were heading home. There was a hold-up on the bridge.

'I told you I could've got through,' Heather complained bitterly.

'I want you with me. I want explanations. Not flim-flam. The truth. You knew in a flash who I was talking about, in that room. I saw that. I should've realised. If Walter dashed out so abruptly, then he had to be heading for the one person he'd trusted with his confidences, the one he'd told when Amelia was traced, and where she'd been traced to. This was a person who stood to lose either way, Walter dead or alive, now that the new will was made, but stood to gain so very much in another direction. Right? This person I'm talking about would be found by Walter in a similar three-storey room.'

We were now at a complete standstill. I had difficulty resisting the empty-minded impulse to rest my hand on the horn. Up ahead, I could just see, somebody had got a caravan leaning against a lamppost. Why didn't they keep these amateur caravanners off the road!

'It could not . . .' she whispered.

'What?'

'Have been intentional.'

'Oh Lord! And you going to be a lawyer. But you knew damn well that the other death was. Tolchard's. You and Chad, you must have known that.'

'I don't understand.' Such a tiny voice.

I put my hand on the horn. It was a measure of my impatience with her. 'You know that, very well. I've had enough of you and Chad and your wretched stories. I had to have two goes at squeezing it out, and even then it wasn't the whole truth. I suppose a solicitor's the one to know how to construct the best lies.'

'That's a rotten thing to say.' Her spirit flared.

'But you lied about Tolchard's death.'

A few seconds, and then she said it. 'Yes.'

'That cover-up you and Chad worked out, that wasn't for any paltry fussiness over wages. It was to cover up the fact that you and Chad believed Kenneth Leyton had killed Tolchard.'

'It wasn't like that,' she said, with surprising conviction.

'Why don't they *move*!' I looked at her. 'What was it like?'

'Chad and I . . .' Her voice failed. She coughed and tried again. 'Chad and I, we *thought* we were covering for . . . the fussiness. Chad walked back from that end window . . . and there was his father at the top of the iron staircase, with Mr Tolchard dead at the bottom, and Chad had no thought that his dad could've done it. Chad had been in the wages section for an hour, so it could've been an accident.'

We were moving. Not much, but moving.

'Even though his father had got one of those ebony rulers in his hand,' she added.

'Eh?' I glanced sideways, and nearly rammed a car that'd stopped dead ahead.

'Chad had come, running along the corridor, to signal to me. But he'd only brought one ruler. As you said, we didn't need rulers by that time. But his father . . . Ken, you'd need to understand . . . away from that wretched office, he was always full of fun. I didn't . . . don't know who I love most, Ken or Chad. They sort of took me into their family. Ken's been marvellous. Can't you get this thing moving?'

'Trying. Trying.' We'd stopped again. 'Tolchard,' I reminded her urgently. 'What were you saying?'

'He'd seen . . . Ken, that is . . . Ken'd seen Chad take only the one ruler, so he went after him along the corridor, taking another with him. Just like him. I wouldn't have put it past him to signal me a kiss, himself. But he spotted Tolchard there, lying down at the bottom of that staircase, and stopped. So we thought, Chad and I, that Tolchard had just slipped . . .' She hesitated. There was no heart in the telling.

'But later you knew more?'

'We'd told the police, you see. About Chad and the signal. But Chad wasn't supposed to be up in the wages office, so we covered for that.' Now it was all spilling out. 'Even when they arrested Chad, we had to keep to it. Because we'd realised . . . believed . . . that Ken had done it. And . . . and it's been horrible watching him, knowing he'd have to admit to it, but hoping . . . you know . . . just praying we were wrong. But it couldn't be said, not out loud. We had to watch poor Ken, suffering like that! But really, it had to be him. You see, we knew about Clare.'

Yes, Clare. We were moving again. I had to force the car through, but only made a few feet. Clare, who'd played for high stakes. Who'd played, anyway, happy with her lover because

196

Leyton was exactly what she would want, would need. He was type-cast for it. But then . . . her husband's death. What had that been? The two men meeting, hating each other? A careless word from Tolchard; a careless blow from Leyton. And that, as far as Clare was concerned, ruined everything, because Tolchard's death had pushed her father into threatening to change his will. I wondered which of her desires had dominated, her love for Leyton, which had probably been genuine, or her avaricious plans. Yet she'd exhibited an engagement ring. Surely she could not have expected Leyton to allow his son to go to prison, so that he could marry her!

Across the bridge the traffic was easing, part of it filtering right. I forced the car left on to the river road, which was fairly clear, and banged down the throttle. 'He would not have let it happen.'

I hadn't realised I'd spoken aloud. She misunderstood, and said: 'But it *was* happening. You don't think Ken stayed late *every* night! On the ones Mr Tolchard went to play squash . . .'

'Yes, of course.'

I swept the car into the first car park and stopped opposite the break in the fence and the side door. We both scrambled out, and I won the race for the stairs. Three flights up. She was pressing at my heels urgently. The office was open. I ran through it into his private office, stopping dead and causing Heather to press behind.

He was not there. On his desk there were no ledgers, just a sheet of paper, his fountain pen beside it. A phone, off its cradle, lay next to it. The window was wide open. I walked over to it, and looked down. Turned back.

It was a Thursday. 'Chad?' I asked. 'Downstairs? Go to him. Phone the police from there. Bring Chad back with you. Is that clear?'

Her hand was over her mouth, the suppressed scream in her eyes.

'Then do it. And Heather . . . you're not to go outside.'

With a suppressed sob, she clattered away. I heard a chair fall. Then I went to read what he'd been writing.

My darling,

You know it couldn't work out. They know now. Heather has just phoned. I want you to understand that it was an accident. Walter came here, completely out of control. He tried to kill me. It was an accident. I know you blame me, but I want you to know I was not to blame.

And so on. What began as a letter to her became a confession. The death of Tolchard was described in detail. He claimed he'd struck out in anger. He ended:

So please do not think badly, or too sadly, of me, I . . . I cannot say this on paper, my love

No more. Not even an end to that sentence. He'd decided to phone her. I put my head down to the desk surface. The line was still open. Softly, I could hear a radio playing. Music. Joyful music. Mozart.

I heard the cars arriving, put my head out of the window, and shouted. Two officers walked round to the path below and bent over the body of Ken Leyton. One of them looked up and shook his head. I turned back to the room as Melrose walked in, followed by a team of men. I gestured. There were no suitable words. Yes there were. I said: 'That line's open. Don't hang up.'

'Explain,' said Melrose crisply.

'There a confession, and in it he calls her darling. No name. I'll go there. It's only up the road.' I gave him the address. 'You wait by the phone. Yes?'

'Who's giving the orders round here?'

'Please. She knows me.'

He hesitated, then nodded. I turned to leave. Chad and Heather were in the outer office.

'I'm sorry,' I said. 'He's dead.'

For once, the words 'I'm sorry' were expressed with their true meaning.'

They clung together as I walked out of there.

The bungalow was quiet, seemingly deserted. I was about to ring, but put my hand to the door and it swung open. Had she left it for him? I walked in quietly and through to the lounge.

She was sitting in the seat I'd last seen her occupying. Her head did not turn as I entered, though she must have realised I was there behind her. The radio was a portable, still playing. I went across and switched it off. Still she did not move. Her eyes were on the phone, off its cradle as Leyton's had been. Tears brimmed in her eyes, but did not spill free. I walked to the phone and picked it up.

'Melrose?'

'Yes. I'll be along.'

I hung up, then went to sit on my usual settee. Familiarity might help, though her face was set and her eyes were blank.

I said: 'He's dead, Clare. He threw himself out of the window.'

The tears at last flowed and her lower lip quivered.

22

I realised what could have happened. He had phoned to say his goodbyes. She'd appealed and begged, but he'd simply laid down the phone his end. Had she hung on, not daring to break the connection in case he came back on? Then out to the hall to leave the door for him, in case he came to her? There had been just that chance. But when he did not, the phone had been forgotten.

But had it happened in this way?

'Dear, sweet man,' she whispered.

'Yes. I can understand why you loved him. But love can become so damned confusing.'

An awareness entered her eyes. I went on: 'There's love that starts as a passion, more sexual than anything else. But later, when understanding enters into it, the emotions become confused. All you want is that person, for ever and ever, never letting go. That's when it becomes complex, because other desires are still there, and it's difficult to decide which is the most important.'

'You're talking sentimental nonsense.' She tossed her head, but her hair seemed heavy. 'Will you get me a brandy? Please.'

I nodded, and went to do that, and saw that the police car had drifted quietly along the cul-de-sac. Melrose wasn't stupid. I took the drink back to her. She gulped at it greedily, and coughed. I waited. Not for her recovery, but for Melrose to appear behind her in the doorway.

When he did, I continued: 'It is not nonsense. I do believe you didn't know what you really wanted, this new love for Ken Leyton, or the death of your husband, or control of the factory. Or the lot.'

'You can sit there, at a time like this . . .' She bent her head to the glass.

'You probably chose him at the beginning for his contrast with Aleric, to flaunt him. But . . . getting to know him . . . yes, that much I'll have to accept or I'll go mad. I'll believe you grew to love him. You could have freed yourself of Aleric, but you've explained why you couldn't. Or rather, you've told me how you probably explained it to Ken Leyton. I wonder, did you actually try to persuade him to kill Aleric? Your oblique suggestions, your subtle persuasions.'

She gave a harsh bark of grim humour. 'Are you trying to tell me he did it for me? Oh come on, Mr Patton.'

'Not that. I'm saying he didn't do it at all.'

I did not dare to look directly at the doorway, but I had the peripheral impression that Chad and Heather were there too. I prayed that neither of them would make a sound.

I saw Clare's lips moving, but her breath merely brushed the rim of the glass.

'I believe *you* killed your husband, Clare. You would know all about those Thursday evening sessions, and naturally you'd know Aleric's habits. You knew he was at the factory that night. The lights were not on in the main part of the factory. You could wait in the shadows until he came along and reached the head of the staircase. One blow . . . what did you use, Clare?' I looked round casually. 'There's a statuette over there, and a candlestick. No? Never mind. But you'd seen Chad go up to join his father. Aleric could lie there until he was discovered . . . so you simply went away. And here's a laugh, Clare. You'll enjoy this.'

I felt rotten. She was staring at me viciously, her lips clamped tightly together. We couldn't have raised a smile between us.

'Chad and Heather,' I said, 'believed Ken Leyton had done it. Leyton thought you might have done it, but what could he say? Oh, all these interesting situations coming along! But oh dear me, what complications Aleric's death created. Your father, locking himself away . . . now that was a turn up for the book, especially when he threatened to change his will. You'd be right up to date on the news, of course. Leyton heard it, chapter by chapter, from your father, and he would pass it on to you. Fine . . . until it seemed it would all go wrong. You'd got Ken Leyton to deal with, you see, and he already had his suspicions. How long was he going to continue to love you, and be influenced by you? I mean –

200

would he really have let his son go to prison? I think not. Not even for you.'

'Christ, but you're a lying swine,' she burst out, half rising to her feet.

Smiling, I shook my head. I didn't want her to realise we were being observed, so I waited until she subsided.

'I think it's the truth, Clare. I'm trying to imagine the situation at that time. So very tricky. Your whole basic scheme was falling apart, you see.'

'Scheme? What damned scheme?'

'I can add up, Clare. They taught it at school, in my day. The shares. You already had thirteen, plus the thirteen Aleric had bought from Donald, which were now yours. Twenty-six. Plus – when you married him – ten that Leyton owned. Thirty-six. Plus seventeen if your father died. Fifty-three. Bingo. You'd be in virtual control of the factory. You'd love that.'

Her face was suddenly distorted. 'I'm not having you say that,' she screamed.

'Did I add it up wrong?'

'I loved him. I wanted . . . wanted . . . oh dear Lord . . .'

'So which came first for you, Clare?'

'Get out of my house!' she whispered.

'Presently. I was wondering whether you had difficulty per-suading Ken to go along with you.' I tilted my head. 'You're supposed to say: with what? Why, of course, the killing of my wife.'

She stared past me.

'Was it you circulated those news cuttings, Clare?'

'Go to hell.'

'It doesn't matter. What does matter is your father's death. It was so wrong, wrong. My wife was alive. It was a desperate mistake for your father to die then, before he had a chance to think about what he was doing, and change his will back to how it'd been. But of course, his death *was* a mistake, an accidental killing, because Ken Leyton didn't intend it. I suppose. But I'm wondering . . . could you forgive him that? Because, on your father's death, you'd lost it all. Even if you still married him – even if you went ahead with *that* – you'd still be well short of control.'

'I *wanted* it!' she shouted. 'I had to bully him, shout at him, till he'd agree to marrying me. He wanted to wait . . .' She stopped.

201

'Wait until his son was committed for trial – and then still wait? How long d'you think he'd have held out, Clare?'

She punched the chair cushion, furious still at Leyton's righteousness.

'But you realised that even over your father's death he tried to protect you. There had to be no connection between you and that, even by way of himself. I don't think he did what he did in self-protection. It was not his style. But he took Walter's body, in Walter's car, to The Beeches, and there he found everything laid on for him, with the window open to the room he knew would be locked. He had only to reach up with a rake handle, or something like that, and break a few panes, lay the body face down on the glass, then break a larger gap. Then he would put the car away and walk back to the factory. Really, he did that for you, Clare. Do, please, show a little gratitude.'

'Lies! All lies.'

'I think not.'

'He told me he'd written a confession . . .'

'Told you on the phone that he'd not mentioned you? He'd do that, wouldn't he, splendid, chivalrous Ken? Even go to the lengths of including a confession to Aleric's death. For you, Clare.'

I'd hoped this would break her down in tears, but she was too tough for that. 'You couldn't prove one word of it,' she cried. 'It's nothing but words.'

'Let Ken take the blame, eh? But he couldn't have been the one to kill Nancy Rafton. It was a Friday, Clare. The one day, pay-day, when he couldn't have got away. And it would've been necessary to wait another day in order to get copies of the local paper. How unfortunate that it misled you into thinking you'd succeeded.'

But the success was still hers. None spilling over for me. She gave me a short, blank stare, then threw back her head and laughed hysterically.

'You'll never prove a thing.'

I knew she was quite correct. There was nothing I could prove. I stared at her, feeling the exhaustion wash over me, knowing that I should have been able to swamp her with a tide of my own self-confidence and undermine her into a furious, tearful confession. Or trap her in a net of closely-meshed theory that she couldn't escape from. But I could do no more than stare at her and know I'd failed, when I'd have given anything to have been able to toss it at Melrose's feet as an accomplished success.

Then, unable to continue to face her, I shrugged, got to my feet, and turned away. Old, I felt old. Stiff and tired and beaten.

It was my signal to Melrose. He stepped forward. She was on her feet, whirling on him.

'What the hell!'

'She's right, Richard,' said Melrose. 'Case closed. No proof.'

'Hah!' she said. 'And who might you be?'

'Detective-Inspector Melrose, Mrs Tolchard. I came to inform you of the death of Kenneth Leyton, but I see Mr Patton got here first. Please sit down.' He smiled thinly. 'I haven't come to arrest you for the murder of Nancy Rafton, nor for the murder of your husband . . .' He waited, the same smile patiently fixed, until she'd lowered herself slowly back on to her chair. 'That's better. What I *have* come for is to arrest you for the murder of Kenneth Leyton. You are not obliged to say anything unless you wish to do so, but whatever you do say will be taken down in writing and may be given in evidence.'

There was a long silence. Chad and Heather, in the doorway with uniforms darkening the hall behind them, were absolutely still, his arm firmly round her. Clare was drawing in deep, hysterical breaths. I stared blankly at Melrose.

On a gust of emotion, Clare cried out: 'You're insane.'

'I think not. You spoke to him over the phone. The line was still open.'

She raised her chin. 'I've not contradicted that. He told me he'd made a confession.'

'Not mentioning you?'

'There was not one word—'

'So you've read it?'

'He *said* there was not one word.' She was fierce, bright, electric.

'Mrs Tolchard, the engine of your car is still warm.'

There was triumph in her eyes. 'That's not so.'

'The Quattro? Sorry, I assumed that was yours.'

'You're trying to catch me out.' Her hair swirled heavily.

'You spoke to him. You knew what he intended to do, but you had to be *certain* you weren't mentioned in any confession. You said: hold on a second, and left the line open, knowing he'd do that, waiting for you to come back to the phone. Devoted Leyton, as I understand him to have been. He would pick up the phone, listen, put it down on his desk, pick it up. But he wouldn't hang

203

up on you. How long to the factory, Mrs Tolchard? In the Quattro – two minutes? Up the stairs. Burst in on him. You fool, Ken, or something like that. Get a look at his confession, with not a word in it about you. So that was all right. But Leyton – what would he do, Richard?'

Finding it tossed back at me, I was caught unprepared. 'He'd see her there, a stronger character than himself, as his support. Yes, I think so. He'd reached for her help.'

'Exactly. Thoughts of suicide fading away. Was there possibly some way out, for both of you? And you'd see this man, Mrs Tolchard, whom you say you loved, as a broken reed, and as someone, if he lived, who might after all implicate you. He was suddenly very dangerous to you. He had to go.'

'I was not in that room!'

'No?' He opened his hand, which had been clenched at his side. 'We found this in his hand. Could it be yours?'

I recognised it. Her reaction took one hand to cover the other, but too late. The finger was naked. As was the fury on her face now.

'It's a cheap trick.'

'The window would already be open,' he went on. 'How better to persuade him through it than screaming at him that it was all finished, and throwing the ring at him? And if that didn't work, running at him and pushing him out. It's perhaps ironical that he fell on the same spot as your father, when Walter died.'

But she was still fighting, hunting for anything she could dispute. 'He did not . . . did *not*. Ken told me. Father fell from the other window.'

Melrose sagged, at last allowing himself a grimace of distaste.

She clearly saw this as a clincher, misinterpreting Melrose's expression. As it was, but in the wrong way. Gradually, the awareness flowed into her face. Her hands were halfway towards covering it when she collapsed.

Melrose signalled to his team. I sat down slowly on my usual settee.

After having considered all the details, Amelia has decided what to do. Her decision is that Paul and Donald shall each have 17 shares, leaving herself with an interest in the firm. Donald is to be persuaded to take up a position on the board, as design controller, and to work with Chad on the design for the camera. This is to be called the Mann-Leyton. Look out for it.

The house is prepared for Amelia. I am driving to fetch her tomorrow. Cindy has been a problem, as the child seemed distressed at any suggestion that they should be parted. Her parents asked to keep Cindy, even offered money. So we agreed, though not to the money.

The problem of Clare's possession of her shares, and her availability to vote them, remains. I understand she is still protesting her innocence, but evidence against her is accumulating.

I am to be Chad's best man. There's a laugh. Best. He couldn't have searched very far.

After tomorrow I shall have a Volvo, with attached caravan, for sale. If you're interested.